MIDSUMMER'S

RAJANI LaROCCA

YELLOW
JACKET

YELLOW JACKET

an imprint of Little Bee Books

New York, NY
Text copyright © 2019 by Rajani LaRocca
Illustrations copyright © 2019 by Little Bee Books
Illustrations by Rachel Suggs
All rights reserved, including the right of reproduction
in whole or in part in any form.
Yellow Jacket and colophon are trademarks of Little Bee Books.
Manufactured in Canada MQ1 0221
Originally published in hardcover in 2019 by Yellow Jacket
First Trade Paperback Edition 2021

10 9 8 7 6 5 4 3 2 1

Library of Congress Cataloging-in-Publication Data
Names: LaRocca, Rajani, author.
Title: Midsummer's mayhem / by Rajani LaRocca.
Description: First edition. | New York, NY: Yellow Jacket | Summary:
Loosely based on Shakespeare's A Midsummer Night's Dream, eleven-
year-old Mimi Mackson entangles herself and her family with mischievous
fairies when she seeks to win a baking contest. | Identifiers: LCCN
2019002900 (print) | LCCN 2019005383 (ebook) | Subjects: | CYAC:
Family life—Massachusetts—Fiction. | East Indian Americans—Fiction.
| Baking—Fiction. | Magic—Fiction. | Characters in literature—Fiction.
| Massachusetts—Fiction. | BISAC: JUVENILE FICTION / Fairy
Tales & Folklore / Adaptations. | JUVENILE FICTION / Fantasy &
Magic. | JUVENILE FICTION / Cooking & Food. | Classification:
LCC PZ7.1.L353 (ebook) | LCC PZ7.1.L353 Mid 2019 (print) | DDC
[Fic]—dc23 LC record available at https://lccn.loc.gov/2019002900
ISBN 978-1-4998-1064-6

For information about special discounts on bulk purchases,
please contact Little Bee Books at sales@littlebeebooks.com

yellowjacketreads.com

PRAISE FOR *MIDSUMMER'S MAYHEM*

★ "A delectable treat for food and literary connoisseurs alike."

—*Kirkus Reviews*, STARRED REVIEW

"What a wonderful, intriguing, and magical book. And wow, did it ever get my taste buds going! Each time I picked it up, I felt the urge to head to my kitchen. . . . What I loved most was the smartness of it. It never once doubted its young readers."

—Kathi Appelt, Newbery Honor- and National Book Award-nominated author

"*Midsummer's Mayhem* is an enchantment of a novel bursting with magic, mystery, and mouthwatering baked goods. Readers who have their own baking-show dreams will be cheering for Mimi until the very last page."

—Kate Messner, award-winning author of *Breakout*, *The Seventh Wish*, and *All the Answers*

"*Midsummer's Mayhem* is a delightful confection of a family story full of heart, magic, and a baking championship with mysteriously high stakes! LaRocca takes an almost-throwaway reference in Shakespeare's *A Midsummer Night's Dream* and reclaims it by having a multiracial Indian-American family at the center of her tale. Mimi's pluck, gentle courage, and knack for combining flavors will capture readers' hearts, imaginations, and undoubtedly, taste buds!"

—Sayantani DasGupta, author of the *New York Times*-bestselling Kiranmala and the Kingdom Beyond series

"Taking its inspiration from one of Shakespeare's most popular comedies, *Midsummer's Mayhem* is a sweet and fun story about mistaken identity, bumpy romance, and the everyday magic of baking."

—Barbara Dee, author of *Star-Crossed* and *Halfway Normal*

"Laugh-out-loud funny one moment and mouthwateringly delicious the next, *Midsummer's Mayhem* is an utter pleasure to consume from the very first page! LaRocca's debut novel entices and bewitches—I dare you not to fall under its spell."

—Tara Dairman, author of *The Great Hibernation* and the award-winning All Four Stars series

"Absolutely scrumptious! I fell in love with this book and devoured it in one day. LaRocca crafts a spell of tricky fairies, lovable mortals, and heartfelt magic. Mimi is determined, resourceful, and unfailingly kind. Perfect for aspiring bakers, younger siblings, or anyone with a passion."

—Anna Meriano, author of the Love Sugar Magic series

"Rajani LaRocca has concocted a delectable story about family, friendship, baking, and magic that readers are sure to devour! Relatable, lovable Mimi is easy to root for, and LaRocca brings the whole cast of characters to life with her deft descriptions and realistic dialogue. Readers will delight in *Midsummer's Mayhem*!"

—Erin Dionne, author of *Lights, Camera, Disaster*

"An absolute delight—LaRocca's delectable debut is whimsical, frothy, and so much fun. An inventive take on a classic comedy, *Midsummer's Mayhem* is a sweetly told tale of family, friendship, and following your passion. This is a book for the dreamers and doers alike; effervescent, full of heart, and ultimately joyful."

—Olugbemisola Rhuday-Perkovich, author of
Two Naomis and *8th Grade Superzero*

"This riff on *A Midsummer Night's Dream* is heartfelt and ridiculously fun. Mimi, sweet as sugar with a heart of gold, creates as many problems as she solves, but readers will be cheering for her and her family the whole way."

—*Booklist*

"An entertaining and epicurean retelling of *A Midsummer Night's Dream* . . . Strikes a perfect balance between the pleasant and the melancholy, as sweet and savory as one of Mimi's confections."

—*Shelf Awareness*

For Mira and Joe, who prove every day that magic is real

And for Lou, who will always be my best friend

—RL

TABLE OF CONTENTS

CHAPTER 1: THE NEW NEIGHBORS 1

CHAPTER 2: THE WHILE AWAY CAFÉ 13

CHAPTER 3: A STRANGE HOMECOMING 27

CHAPTER 4: PRACTICE DOESN'T MAKE PERFECT. . . . 39

CHAPTER 5: LEAVES OF GREEN AND GOLD 51

CHAPTER 6: HOME. 65

CHAPTER 7: INTO THE WOODS 75

CHAPTER 8: HONEYSUCKLE COOKIES 91

CHAPTER 9: WEIRD AND WEIRDER 103

CHAPTER 10: A TIME FOR THYME 117

CHAPTER 11: BACK AT THE WHILE AWAY 131

CHAPTER 12: THE SONG. 147

CHAPTER 13: THE EPIPHANY 157

CHAPTER 14: MAYHEM MANAGED 167

CHAPTER 15: THE QUEST FOR THE REMEDY 177

CHAPTER 16: THE WORST SONG EVER. 191

CHAPTER 17: ON THE SWING SET 203

CHAPTER 18: A REVIEW TO REMEMBER 211

CHAPTER 19: THE LULLABY. 219

CHAPTER 20: THE GOODBYE. 227

CHAPTER 21: PUFFY FAY .235

CHAPTER 22: THE CHEATER. 251

CHAPTER 23: FLOUR AND FLOWERS 261

CHAPTER 24: THE BETRAYAL 275

CHAPTER 25: THE BEST CUPCAKES 283

CHAPTER 26: THE PLAY 291

CHAPTER 27: QUESTIONS AND ANSWERS. 297

CHAPTER 28: THE INVITATION 309

CHAPTER 29: HEART'S WORK 321

CHAPTER 30: DREAMS AND REALITY 329

CHAPTER 1

THE NEW NEIGHBORS

The song from the woods first called to me on a bright June morning while I sat on the back porch swing rereading my favorite cookbook. I could only hear a few notes, a small taste of a half-remembered melody that meandered through the air, but I was instantly hungry to hear the whole thing and discover where it came from. I crossed the yard and stopped at the edge of the woods. As the music drifted toward me like an irresistible aroma, I held my breath and stepped into the trees.

"Hey, Mimi!" My big sister Jules's voice yanked me back to reality.

I spun around. She was dribbling a soccer ball, of course.

She leapt over the ball and ran to me. "I need your help."

I pushed my hair out of my eyes. That's the kind of hair I

have—the kind that's always in my face. "Did you hear that?" I asked, sure I could still hear lingering notes in the summer air. "I want to—"

Jules grabbed my arm and pulled me toward the porch. She pointed at the driveway next door, where a moving van and a silver car were parked. "The new neighbors are here. Let's bring them the brownies you baked this morning."

"But those are for Dad." Welcome Home brownies, since he'd been gone all week.

"Make him something else. Come on, don't let them see us yet."

"But—" A tall teenage boy with shaggy brown hair was carrying boxes into what used to be my best friend Emma's house. So *that* was why Jules wanted to go next door.

"He's cute, huh?" Jules said.

I shrugged. He looked around Jules's age, fifteen or sixteen.

"I want to make a good first impression. Bring the brownies, and whatever you do, don't tell Riya."

Our sister Riya is a year older than Jules, and five years older than me. She's like an Aleppo pepper—striking and fragrant, but with a substantial kick.

We reached the back porch and Jules pulled her dark hair out of its ponytail. "I'll be down in a minute." She sprinted inside and bounded up the stairs.

I turned to the woods and listened again. Nothing. I

missed the song already. Where had it come from? It had been a single, fluid line of melody, repetitive, insistent. It might have been a bird, but it had an elusive quality that made me wonder. And why did it sound so familiar? I couldn't care less about the new neighbors. I wanted to turn right back around and head into the woods, like I used to do with Emma. She loved quests. If only she still lived next door.

But Jules would take my brownies over there whether I liked it or not, so I figured I should at least make sure they were presented attractively. I grabbed my cookbook off the porch swing and went into the kitchen.

As I cut the brownies and put them on my favorite purple platter, I couldn't help smiling at the scent of chocolate and cinnamon. These were supposed to be for Dad, who loved chocolate (who didn't?) but would particularly appreciate the warm spices I'd put into them. I'd even added a dash of cayenne for extra zing.

"How now, spirit! Whither wander you?" My brother Henry made a beeline for the brownies. I blocked his arm before he could grab one and he recoiled dramatically. He was constantly reciting lines from the latest play he was performing in and barely spoke normal English anymore.

"None for you, Shakespeare," I said. "Not unless you come next door with us. We're taking them to the new neighbors."

Henry bowed deeply. *"Fear not, my lord, your servant shall do so*." He took a pitcher of lemonade from the fridge and poured a glass.

"What's going on?" said Riya. I hadn't heard her come into the room. But then, being light on her feet was one of the things that made Riya such a great dancer. She looked up from her phone just long enough to scrutinize me with hawklike eyes.

"Oh, nothing," I said nonchalantly. Jules would kill me if Riya found out our plan and tried to tag along with us. Every boy Jules liked seemed to become obsessed with Riya instead.

"We're saying hi to the new neighbors," said Henry. "I'm going for Mimi's fantastic brownies."

"How remarkably boring," said Riya with a smile. She turned back to her phone.

That was a close call. I let out a relieved breath and finished arranging the brownies. Bits of the song from the woods played in my mind. It tugged at me, like a secret waiting around the corner.

Jules barreled back into the room. "Ready, Mimi?" Her hair was in a ponytail as always, but it was neater than usual, and her lips glistened. She stopped short. "What's everyone doing in here?"

Riya sized up Jules. "We've been waiting for you. We all want to meet our new friends next door, don't we?"

Jules glared at me and mouthed, "Thanks!"

I was about to explain that it wasn't my fault, but Jules had already grabbed the platter and stormed out the door.

"Jules! Hold up!" I called.

Jules muttered under her breath as she launched herself down the porch steps. She found the soccer ball and started dribbling it into the yard next door.

"Well, that should impress whatever boy she's after. If there's one thing boys love, it's a girl who can kick." Riya glided down the steps and started across the grass.

I turned to Henry. "Quick, before they pull each other's hair out."

"I'll put a girdle round about the earth in forty minutes," said Henry. Whatever that meant. But he was out on the porch with me in four seconds.

As we hurried into Emma's yard, I thought I saw something move behind the swing set. No, it was just a bird. I listened again for the song, but only the whisper of wind in the trees floated back to me. The melody had been happy, and sad. It reminded me of all the time I'd spent in the woods with Emma and how we'd never have another summer together, laughing and telling stories in the woods we both loved.

The boy I'd seen earlier was walking from the side of the house to the open trunk of the silver car when he noticed us.

"Hi!" said Jules. She stopped the soccer ball and held out the plate. "Welcome to the neighborhood! Want to kick the ball around? Or have some brownies?"

"Sure." The boy's face was covered in freckles, like an everything bagel. He eyed the soccer ball, then moved his hand toward the brownies, then stopped and grinned goofily at Jules.

"Of course he wants to eat the brownies," said Riya. She snatched the platter and held it out.

The boy glanced at Riya, and, like most boys, he couldn't stop staring.

"I'm Riya Mackson." She tossed her long, wavy hair away from her face like a shampoo model. "And this is my older brother, Henry. We live next door."

Henry dipped his curly head in a salute.

"Cole Clark," said the boy.

"And this is our little sister, Anjuli."

"Jules," Jules said through her teeth as she glared down at Riya. Jules might be a year younger than Riya, but she's at least four inches taller, almost as tall as Henry.

"And our littlest sister, eleven-year-old Mira. But we all call her Mimi Mouse."

I tried to smile. I'd gotten the nickname from Dad when I was three, but it bothered me to hear her say it now, like I was still some tiny creature. I had to admit, though, that it fit. My siblings were always in the spotlight, while I scurried in the shadows.

"We brought you these," Jules said, grabbing the platter back from Riya and handing it to Cole.

"Awesome," said Cole, eyeing the brownies. *My* brownies, not that anyone was going to tell him. "Let's go eat them over there." He nodded at the patio, where there was a low stone wall to sit on.

A red-haired woman emerged from the house and waved at us as we made our way to the patio.

"These are *amazing*," said Cole. He finished one brownie and took another. "I'm already starting to feel at home."

"Glad you like them." Jules scrunched her shoulders. "Welcome to Comity, the hometown of the talented and famous."

"What does that mean?" Cole asked, reaching for a third brownie.

"We may seem like just an ordinary town outside of Boston," said Riya. "But dozens of famous people are from here—starting with the Revolutionary War hero George Babbit."

"And the philosopher David Allen Trudeau," said Henry.

"And Theresa Lee Falcott, the writer," said Jules. "And loads of others, including last year's winner of *American Diva*."

"Fascinating," said Cole. "Maybe I won't miss San Diego after all."

I rolled my eyes. They'd forgotten to mention the most

important famous person from Comity: Puffy Fay! He was the best pastry chef in the country. He'd written my favorite cookbook, and he hosted a baking competition on Food TV.

But before I could say anything, Henry asked, "Do you play an instrument? My band's looking for a bassist."

I didn't need to hear the saga of Henry's band again, so I wandered to a swing, sat, and inhaled the sharp smells of the woods. There were several acres back there, and a creek that flowed southeast to join the Sketaquid River. Emma and I loved roaming the woods all year round, but especially in the summer, when sunlight filtered through the leaves, washing everything in shades of green, and the forest was filled with the sounds of twittering birds. We had climbed trees, waded into the creek, and sat in our hangout for hours telling each other stories about secret forest creatures. Sometimes I could swear I heard the woods talking to me, coaxing me to stay longer. I hadn't had the heart to go there since Emma left. But after hearing that song, I knew I had to.

A soccer ball rolled to a stop in front of me.

"Kick it back, will you, Mimi?" Jules bounced on her toes on the patio.

I stood. "I can just carry it—" I pushed away unpleasant memories of my elementary school soccer games.

"Come on, it's not that far. Just make sure you put some oomph into it."

"Okay," I said. I took a breath, backed up a step, and kicked the ball hard.

It sailed to the patio and landed right on my platter of brownies, which fell off the stone wall and shattered as it crashed to the ground.

"Oh no!" I hurried to assess the damage. The area was strewn with shards of purple ceramic and dark chunks of brownie. I sighed and started to make a pile of the largest pieces. So much for Dad's treat.

"I'm so sorry," said Cole, stooping to help clean up the mess. "Those brownies were delicious."

"Don't worry about it," said Riya. She turned to Jules. "See what you did?"

"How is it *my* fault?" Jules asked.

"Why do you always have that ball attached to you?" Riya prodded the brownie-covered ball with her toe like it was diseased. "Can't you just give it a rest?"

"*You* give it a rest." Jules brushed off the ball and held it on her hip. "Mimi was the one who kicked it. You know how uncoordinated she is."

Cole looked back and forth between my sisters and then at Henry with a puzzled expression. Henry shrugged at him and helped me clean up as my sisters continued sniping at each other.

"Hey!" Jules cried out and rubbed her head.

Something small dropped out of the sky. *Pop!* It made a dull sound as it bounced off Riya's shiny hair. She ducked and covered her head.

"Stop it!" she bellowed.

Something pinged Cole on the skull. "Ow!"

I looked up. It was a bird. A brightly colored little bird. It glided over Henry and dropped something small that ricocheted off his forehead as he squinted into the sun. The bird finished its bombing run and flew to a big oak at the edge of the yard before returning with small objects clutched in each foot and its beak.

I braced myself, but I didn't get hit. Everyone else got pelted at least twice more.

I finally got a good look at the bird as it rested in the oak tree. It was about the size of a bluebird, but with a bright yellow breast, brilliant green wings with a small blue patch, and a black stripe on its face. I'd never seen anything like it. It stared at me with a shiny black eye before flying off into the woods.

Jules straightened up and glared at Riya. "What was that?"

"A bird," I said, but I could barely believe it myself.

"Right." Riya scowled at Jules.

"It dropped these." I plucked one of the objects from the patio. "Acorns."

"Birds don't drop acorns on people," said Henry, scratching his head. *"Lord, what fools these mortals be!"*

Cole looked at me thoughtfully. "A squirrel might," he said.

"But we'd have to be under its tree."

"Riya! Jules! Are you out here? Time to go!" It was Mom, calling from our yard.

"Over here, Mom," I called back. "In Emma's yard." I shook my head and wished it were still Emma's yard. Cole seemed nice enough, but his existence made my sisters even more impossible than usual.

Luckily, Riya had a dance rehearsal, or Jules would have gotten all weird about leaving her with Cole while she went to soccer practice. Henry said he'd stay to help the Clarks bring boxes into the house.

As Riya and Jules headed to the car, I realized I hadn't saved a single brownie for Dad. I couldn't wait to see him—he'd make me feel better, or at least help me laugh about everything. There was no time to make another batch, and I was all out of chocolate anyway, so I decided to bike into town to pick something up. I asked Mom, and she said it was fine as long as I was careful and came back before she returned with my sisters.

I glanced up at the oak as I walked home. There was no sign of the bombardier bird.

I couldn't help pausing at the edge of the woods. A breeze ruffled pine needles and maple leaves, and it felt like a warm breath on my face. I listened, hoping to hear the song again. But I didn't.

Not then.

CHAPTER 2

THE WHILE AWAY CAFÉ

I rode my bike to the end of my street and made a left on Main. The air rushing past my face refreshed me, and I felt my plan come together. If I couldn't give Dad something I'd made myself, I could at least buy him something special. Luckily, there was a new café in town that I wanted to check out.

I pushed my hair out of my eyes and tucked it into my helmet. As I biked down the quiet street, my mind drifted back to the strange little bird. How come it had hit everyone but me with the acorns?

The café was situated on the corner of Main and Birch, backing up to the river and the woods beyond. A large front window was painted with intricate calligraphy, surrounded by curling leaves and flowers: THE WHILE AWAY BAKERY AND CAFÉ, it read. And in smaller letters underneath, A SWEET

SPOT TO SPEND THE DAY. It was way more interesting than the dry cleaner that used to be there. And it wasn't the only new restaurant in town. Henry had told me about a new snack shop down the street, the Salt Shaker. Comity was becoming, as Dad would say, quite the gastronomic destination.

The café was beautiful inside, decorated in pale greens, with clusters of wooden tables, mismatched chairs, and vases bursting with fresh wildflowers. Soft, dreamy music played overhead, and the faint scent of tree pollen and grass wafted through the air. It felt like being in the woods. The place was empty; there wasn't even anyone behind the counter.

A bright pink poster near the door caught my eye:

Attention Bakers Ages 8–13!

Enter the

While Away Café

Midsummer Baking Contest!

First Round: Bring in your BEST baked goods
to earn a Golden Leaf!

Second Round: The Golden Leaf Winners will bring in
more baked goods to be judged and
will be narrowed down to THREE.

Third Round: A Live Bake-Off
on Midsummer's Eve!

Your Delectable Delights could win you
Enchanting Prizes!

A wave of warmth trickled through me like melted butter. A baking contest! In Comity!

"A heartfelt welcome to the While Away," came a nearby voice. Startled, I turned to find a curly-haired waitress right next to me.

"How may I help you have the sweetest day?" she asked.

My excitement about the contest had made me forget what I was doing. I spotted the display case at the opposite end of the room.

"Can I look at your pastries?" I asked.

The waitress curtsied, flopping her brown curls forward, and indicated the way. She wore a wild skirt made of fresh green leaves and bright pink flowers.

A variety of tempting treats filled the pastry case. There were pies, cookies, brownies, tarts, and my favorite, cupcakes. Each cake was beautifully decorated with perfectly piped frosting—swirls and rosettes, leaves and miniature flowers. I decided to get two different cupcakes and give Dad a choice when he got home.

"I'd like one of the chocolate cupcakes, please, and that purple one with all the flowers."

"Oh, yes. And will you have a drink, my dear?" Her accent was slightly odd, but I liked it.

"Just the cupcakes, thanks."

She put them on a plate and led me to the back of the store.

"Come sit you down then, at this table here."

I hadn't planned on staying, but I felt bad leaving the waitress to a completely empty café, so I followed her. I could sample each cupcake, decide which was best, and buy another for Dad. I sat at a table where I could see out the back windows to a small footbridge that went over the river to the woods. It was only a couple of miles through there to my house—Emma and I had walked home on that path countless times.

The waitress made no move to leave and sort of hovered near my elbow. I sniffed the chocolate cupcake. It smelled rich, and it looked inviting, with a dark swirl of frosting on top— right up Dad's alley. I peeled back the paper wrapping and took a bite while the waitress watched my face.

To my surprise, the cake itself tasted like cocoa-flavored cardboard. And the frosting was too sweet, with an oily texture. I put the cupcake back on the plate and forced myself to smile.

"Your face is quite a sight," the waitress said, twisting her hands. "It's awful, am I right?"

I looked at her. She seemed barely older than Riya, with big blue eyes and a small pink flower pinned to her hair.

"I'm sorry," I said. "It's a tad dry. But let me try the other one. . . ." I quickly unpeeled the pretty purple cupcake and took a bite, which I regretted immediately. This cake was too moist—soggy and falling apart, like someone had soaked it in juice. The frosting, lovely as it looked, tasted like a sugary version of the papier-mâché paste that Jules had once tricked me into tasting when I was six, telling me it was mashed potatoes. This time I couldn't hide how disgusting it was and had to spit it out.

"Is this supposed to be a *grape* cupcake?"

"That's right. Oh dear, she'll be so angry now!" The waitress gave me a sheepish look. "It's not for lack of trying, but know-how."

"*You* baked these?"

"Yes, and no one likes them, don't you see? My—the owner is so very cross with me."

It seemed unfair to put this girl in charge and then be angry with her, since it was obvious she knew nothing about baking. "Isn't there anyone who can help you?"

She flared her nostrils. "The one who knows the most won't lift a hand. We struggle every day, you understand?"

Wait a second . . . was she *rhyming*? "But—"

"We try, and though we all must play the part—" She leaned toward me and whispered, "We have no clue of how to even start."

"Why don't you get a good book on baking? I can recommend a few I love," I said.

"Perhaps." She leaned toward me again. "You seem to know an awful lot. Could you perchance assist us with our plot?"

"But I'm not—"

"Oh, that would be *so* lovely. You're a dear. I'll go speak with the owner. Just wait here." She started toward the counter.

"But—"

She looked back at me pathetically. "Please tell me that you'll help us. 'Twould be awesome!"

I sighed. "What's your name?"

"Peaseblossom." She dipped a small curtsy.

What kind of parents saddled their kid with *that* name?

I held out my hand. "I'm Mimi. I don't know if I can help, but I'll try."

Peaseblossom took my hand and kissed it. She hurried to the back of the store while I rubbed my skin in confusion.

A few minutes later Peaseblossom reappeared and led me into a small office at the back of the café. I found myself standing before a beautiful young woman with a river of dark hair. She turned the pages of a book while seated on a velvet chair behind a worn wooden desk. A bowl of pink roses sat on the desk and filled the small space with a heady, sweet scent.

"*And, in the spiced Indian air, by night, full often hath she gossip'd by my side,*" the woman said in a low, melodious voice like a perfectly played oboe.

"Excuse me? Um—Peaseblossom said you wanted to talk to me."

The woman closed the book gently and looked at me with

bright green eyes that matched the flowing dress she was wearing. "I'm Mrs. T, the owner of the While Away. I hear you're quite the baking master." She sat very straight and still.

I shrugged. "I like to bake for my friends and family." Not that any of them noticed. Except for Mom and Dad, and they didn't count.

"Please, my dear, do take a seat." She motioned to a stool—more like a tree stump, I realized as I sat. "I don't doubt you're better than this sorry lot." She waved at what I assumed must be the door to the kitchen, where I could hear pots and pans being banged around, followed by a loud screech. Peaseblossom squeaked, then looked at the ground. There was an awkward silence.

"It's hard to bake if you don't know what you're doing," I said, and Mrs. T narrowed her eyes. Well, that sounded obnoxious. "I mean, my dad always says that baking requires precision."

"Your father is a baker of renown?"

"No, he's a food writer. He works for *Culinary Adventures*, the online magazine. He also sometimes writes features for the *Comity Journal*."

Mrs. T looked at me blankly. She was clearly *very* new in town.

"Anyway, he's a great taste tester. He helps me improve my recipes."

Mrs. T arched an eyebrow. Her moss-colored eyes bored into me like she could read my mind. "And what, pray tell, is your name, my young friend?"

"Mimi Mackson." I shifted in my seat so I didn't have to look her straight in the eyes.

"Well, Mimi Mackson, tell me what you like to bake."

"Lots of things—brownies, cookies, pies, tarts, scones. But cupcakes are my favorite. I like to flavor them with unusual spices and herbs."

"I see. And what's the last thing that you made?"

"Double-chocolate brownies with cinnamon and cayenne, to welcome someone home."

"And prior to that?"

"Cheddar-chive biscuits."

She waved her hand in front of her face like she smelled something bad. "No, no, my word, that will not do at all. Just *sweet* things, please." She stood and paced behind the desk. "Ha! Cheese and chives! I wouldn't dream of baking, eating, or even serving those, not to win the world."

Well, that was strange. Sweet isn't sweet without savory. One isn't good without the other—I thought everyone knew that. Even the most sugary dessert needs a dash of salt.

Mrs. T sat again. "So tell me then, young Mimi. The best *sweet* thing you've ever, ever made?"

"Hmm . . . lemon-lavender cupcakes, I guess. To celebrate

friendship. At least, my best friend, Emma, before she—"

"I dare say that's more like it! I do hope you will bring your baked goods here so I may judge them."

I pushed my hair out of my eyes. "For the contest?"

"Yes, of course. You'll have a chance to win extraordinary prizes." Her face lit up, and her smile looked like it could stop a war. Or start one.

This was the first good thing that had happened since Emma told me she was moving. I pictured myself spending hours creating masterpieces with butter and sugar, eggs and milk, nuts and spices. If I won the contest, everyone in Comity would talk about me, the eleven-year-old pastry prodigy. Maybe Puffy Fay would hear about it and feature me on his show. Maybe he'd even ask me to write a cookbook with him! I'd end up as the most famous member of my family, more impressive than my superstar siblings, and no one would ever call me Mimi Mouse again.

"Think how you could boast to all your friends!" Mrs. T continued, like I needed more convincing. "You must bring in your best work for the contest." She held her hand out as if showing me a ring. Behind her, Peaseblossom looked at me hopefully.

I reached out and shook her hand. "I'll get started right away. In the meantime, you should get a copy of *Mischief and Magic in the Kitchen*."

Mrs. T tilted her head. "What did you say?"

"It's a great baking book written by world-famous pastry chef Puffy Fay, who grew up right here in Comity. It has lots of foolproof recipes, including a fantastic one for chocolate cupcakes. No grape cupcakes, though." I smiled and tried to wink at Peaseblossom, but all I could manage was a large blink of both eyes. That's right, I can't even wink right. Peaseblossom seemed to understand, though, and wrinkled her nose sweetly at me. "It even features a recipe created by the winner of Puffy Fay's first *Big Time Bake-Off*. Kind of like your contest, but for grown-ups."

"P! Look into that at once," said Mrs. T.

Peaseblossom nodded vigorously, the flower in her hair quivering.

Mrs. T leaned back in her chair and looked down at me. "I have no doubt you'll win a Golden Leaf and join us for the final rounds on Midsummer's Eve. Go and prepare, my dear. Go bake something from your heart. Bring it here before June twenty-second. Oh, and there is a *theme* for the first round. Here, take this." She handed me a small piece of paper with a poem:

> *A game to seek the talents of this town,*
> *A treasure to safeguard from greedy thieves.*
> *A lofty tree bedecked in soaring crown,*
> *A lovely green-gold canopy of _____.*

Mrs. T leaned toward me. I shrank into the seat and looked at the poem again. A riddle! I read it again, more slowly, and mouthed the words to myself. Okay—*town* rhymed with *crown*, and the second line ended in *thieves*. So that should rhyme with the last word in the fourth line . . .

"Leaves?"

Mrs. T clasped her hands. "You're clever. We've had quite a few who had no idea, even with hints. You wouldn't believe some of the guesses. Yes, the theme for the first round is *leaves*."

Well, that was a weird theme for a baking contest. "Leaves. Right. I'll do my best." I hoped I could dazzle her with my flavors. I glanced at the clock on the wall; Dad would be home soon. I stood. "How much do I owe you for the two cupcakes?"

"Two cupcakes? Twenty dollars, please," Mrs. T said.

Twenty dollars? That was pretty steep, and it was all I had with me. Now I couldn't buy anything else for Dad. I reached into my pocket and handed the bill to Peaseblossom, who took it from me sadly.

Mrs. T beamed at me. "I have a special treat for you, my dear. I made it with my own two hands. I hope it inspires you to return soon and often."

"But I don't have any more money." And based on the cupcakes I'd tasted, I wasn't sure I wanted to eat anything else from the While Away today.

"No charge, of course." She fiddled in a desk drawer, blew

on something in her hands, and held out a tiny golden box.

"How beautiful. What is it?"

"A rare and precious chocolate."

"My—Mrs. T, don't you think—"

"Silence, P."

Peaseblossom grew quiet and looked at the floor.

"Thank you," I said as I accepted the box. "I'll take it home and eat it after dinner. I'll be able to enjoy it more that way." I didn't want to risk the chance that I'd spit it out all over her floor.

Mrs. T inclined her head regally.

I walked back into the café, followed by Peaseblossom.

This was an odd place for sure, but not necessarily in a bad way. I couldn't wait to start planning for the contest.

"We hope you have the sweetest of sweet days," Peaseblossom said as I went out the door.

Outside on the sidewalk, I glanced back as I strapped on my bike helmet. Peaseblossom and Mrs. T had disappeared into the back; the café was empty again.

But as I pedaled down the street, I couldn't shake the feeling that someone was watching.

CHAPTER 3

A STRANGE HOMECOMING

Dad's laptop bag was already sitting in the mudroom when I got home. I sat on the bench and scrutinized the chocolate box, which looked like a miniature treasure chest. I opened it, gingerly picked up the chocolate inside, and examined it from all angles. It was a work of art, embellished with minuscule vines and teeny purple icing flowers, and covered in a shimmering gold dust. But would it be delicious? *I hope Dad won't be too picky about how it tastes*, I thought as I put the chocolate back and sprinkled it with the golden powder left on my fingers. I wanted to enter the contest, and I didn't want Dad's opinion of the While Away to be ruined by a less-than-perfect confection. I snapped the lid closed.

I set the box next to me as footsteps thumped down the stairs.

"Daddy!" I jumped up.

"Mimi Mouse! I was wondering where everyone was." Dad dropped his running shoes and swept me up in a hug. I inhaled the familiar scent of cucumber shampoo in his sandy hair.

"How was Houston?" I asked as he set me down.

Dad's warm brown eyes crinkled with his smile. "Hot. But the food was great, and I've got a lot to write about."

"What was your favorite bite?" I asked.

"Savory or sweet?" he asked, grinning.

"Savory first, then sweet," I said, grinning back.

"Well, I had an incredible pork shoulder in a brown sugar–tamarind barbecue sauce. It was the perfect combination of sweet and sour." Dad has an amazing palate; he can tell whether the nutmeg in a soup has been freshly grated or not.

"That sounds delicious. And the best dessert?"

"Hands down, a piece of pecan pie. It made me think of you. I took notes—it was flavored with vanilla bean and cinnamon rum. But I bet we could make one even better."

"Ooh," I said. "Maybe with five-spice powder? I think that would go really well with the sweet pecans."

"That's my girl, the master of combining unusual flavors." He ruffled my hair.

"Especially when you help me," I said.

Dad sat on the bench, and I plopped down next to him.

"I couldn't wait for you to get back. So much happened while you were gone," I said.

"Tell me."

"Well, there's a new café in town."

He grinned and raised his eyebrows. "I bet you already checked it out. Is it Mimi-worthy?"

I paused. "Well, they're having a—"

"Hey, Dad." Sweaty, dusty Henry walked in the door.

Dad stood and hugged him. "Hi, buddy. What've you been up to?"

"I was next door helping the new neighbors move in."

"Well, that was generous of you." Dad clapped him on the shoulder. "Nice folks?"

"Yeah. The kid, Cole, is going to be a junior in the fall, like Riya. He's pretty cool."

"Where are Mom and the girls?"

"They're out at practice until at least six, I think," Henry said.

Dad glanced at his watch. "Then I can squeeze in a run before dinner. Have to work off all that food from the trip!"

And there went my chance to talk to Dad alone.

"I'll go get washed up," said Henry. "I've got to go over all my lines before play rehearsal tomorrow. *I go, I go; look how I go, Swifter than arrow from the Tartar's bow.*" He ran up the stairs two at a time.

I was bursting with everything I wanted to tell Dad. The song. The bird. The contest! But I sat silently and watched him tie his shoes. He was always in a great mood after a run.

Maybe that would be the best time to tell him about the While Away and ask for his help preparing for the contest.

"I won't be long," he said. "I've spent too much time sitting on airplanes lately." He noticed the chocolate box on the bench and picked it up. "That's pretty. Yours?"

"It's for you. I got it in town."

"I knew you'd have something waiting for me." He opened the little box, popped the chocolate into his mouth, and made a face. "Oh! That's bitter. Must be extra-extra-dark. But there's a very sweet center that tastes of almonds and honey, and . . ." He smacked his lips. "Something floral."

I was glad I hadn't eaten it myself. I hated bitter chocolate except as a garnish. "Love you, Dad. Have a great run."

Dad shook his head as if to clear it. "Love you, too, Mimi Mouse. I'll be back soon. " He kissed me on the forehead and jogged out the door to the yard.

I went into the kitchen to do some culinary research.

Later, I was perched on the porch swing with three different cookbooks open, when I heard familiar footsteps.

"That was fast," I said. "How was your run?"

"Exactly what I needed." Dad started to do some stretches.

"DADDY!" Jules raced to him from the driveway. She nearly knocked him over as she grabbed him in a ferocious embrace.

"Whoa, take it easy," Dad said with a laugh. "How's my soccer star?"

"Great! How was the festival in Texas?" Jules asked.

"Oh! Yes, the Dallas Beer and Barbecue Festival, with top local chefs. It was excellent, really excellent," Dad said.

"Awesome, Dad. I'm going to set the table for dinner. I'm starving!" Jules gave him a quick peck on the cheek and ran into the house, hauling her sports bags to the mudroom.

I turned to Dad.

"I thought you'd gone to Houston."

"Yes?"

"You just said Dallas."

"I . . ." Dad stared at me. "In any case, I was in Texas, and there was a lot of big food, and I'm going to write all about it." He rubbed his neck. "I should go unpack now." He stood still for a moment, looking confused. Riya glided across the yard, floated over to Dad, and presented the top of her head to be kissed without bothering to take her earbuds out.

"Paul!" Mom said. Her long black hair was up in a frizzy bun, and she balanced a stack of pizza boxes and several grocery bags. "So glad you're finally home."

"You couldn't be gladder than I am, honey." He took the bags from her and kissed her.

Mom smiled. "I worked like crazy all day, drove these two to soccer and dance, and managed to grab a few groceries before I picked them up again. I am so looking forward to this dinner."

"I'm really hungry, too," Dad said.

"Then let's get inside and eat right away," Mom said. She went into the house.

I picked up my cookbooks and held the back door open for Dad.

Everyone was distracted at dinner that night. Henry kept glancing at the script in his lap and muttering lines to himself. Riya wouldn't stop tapping on her phone, and Jules wouldn't stop glaring at Riya.

"Sangita," Dad asked Mom, "can you pass me another slice?" He was already on his fourth slice of pizza, and I wasn't even halfway through my first.

Mom leaned over to put a slice of pepperoni on Dad's plate, but not before looking at her phone, which buzzed repeatedly with work emails. "How was your trip?" she asked.

Dad stopped stuffing his face for a second. "It was great, but I'm so glad to be home. What's going on with everyone?" He shoved the rest of the slice into his mouth and reached for a fifth. He usually only ate two.

I wanted to tell Dad all about the While Away. "I went—"

"I need to have all my lines memorized for tomorrow," Henry said.

"*A Midsummer Night's Dream*, right?" Dad asked. "It's my favorite Shakespeare play. *The course of true love never did run smooth*, and so on. What part are you playing?"

"Puck." Henry raised his eyebrows. "Don't you remember? I found out before you left."

"Oh, right."

"Tomorrow I've got to whip the other girls into shape for the big number," said Riya, her almond-shaped eyes growing expressively large. "We've got to be in perfect sync, or it'll look terrible. And I need to work on the leaps in my solo." Riya's big dance performance was coming up in a couple of weeks.

"And I've got soccer practice again," Jules said. "We're gearing up for our game against Bridgeton. We've got to beat them this time."

My siblings chattered away about their plans as I slowly chewed my slice of pizza. *There's a new café in town*, I rehearsed in my head. *And there's a contest . . .*

Mom turned to me. "How about you, Mimi? I don't want you to be bored tomorrow. Do you want to have a friend over? Maddy? How about Victoria?"

I shook my head. "Maddy's on vacation out west, and Victoria's at camp for a month."

"I ran into Carmela Jones the other day, and she said Kiera would love to have you over."

I froze. That definitely didn't sound like something Kiera would say. And it sure didn't sound like something I would want to do. I didn't need to spend time with someone who said my hair looked like a bird's nest and made fun of my favorite purple-and-black sneakers. Especially without Emma around to defend me. "I don't know," I said, hoping Mom would forget all about it.

"Our new neighbors moved in," Jules interjected. "Cole is *so* sweet."

"He's sweet all right," Riya said. "Next time, don't ruin everything with your stupid soccer ball. And try putting on some makeup once in a while."

"As if you want to help me." Jules glared at her. "You always manage to sink your claws into everyone."

"I don't like Cole," Riya said, lifting her chin. "Not *like* like."

Jules clenched her fists. "Like I believe *that*. Is he already texting you?"

"Girls, please," Mom said.

Maybe I could give Mrs. T my entry without anyone else needing to know. But I really wanted to share my excitement.

Dad looked up. "Did the new neighbors move in?"

Hadn't Henry and Jules already told him that?

Mom nodded. "Isabelle Clark and her son, Cole." She addressed all of us. "Guys, I've got to put in a full day's work tomorrow, even though it's Sunday. The website launch is coming up, so I won't be able to relax until July." She scrolled through the messages on her phone and set it down again.

We'd been through this before. Mom did software consulting and had to work around the clock before big deadlines.

"We know," Henry said. "We can help out with laundry and meals."

"I can make dessert every night," I volunteered. It would be good practice for the contest.

"If you do that, I think I'm going to have deadlines more often," Mom said with a smile.

"Between work and rehearsals, I won't have much time to help," said Riya. "I've got to have *some* time to chill out so I can dance my best. There's a rumor that a professor from the New York College of Performing Arts will be coming to my recital!"

"Don't try to get out of helping." Jules scowled at Riya. "I'm one hundred percent focused this summer, so I can keep up my streak of no missed penalty kicks. But I can still help fold the laundry." Jules tapped on the table in a complicated rhythm. In addition to being a soccer star, she played drums of every type, from a standard drum set to the tabla and even African drums.

"Little Miss Perfect," sneered Riya.

"Look who's talking!" said Jules.

"Girls, *please*," said Mom with exasperation before glancing at her phone again.

Riya and Jules were momentarily shamed into silence, and I jumped at the chance to finally tell everyone about my plans.

"So I went to that new bakery in town today, the While Away Café," I blurted.

"Great name. How was it?" asked Dad. He plopped another slice of pizza onto his plate. Was he really going for slice number six? Or was he on seven by now?

"I liked it," I said. My heart thumped so loudly I was sure everyone could hear it. "And I got to meet the owner. They're—they're having a kids' baking contest this summer."

"That sounds like fun," said Mom.

"You're a shoo-in to win, Mimi Mouse," Henry said.

"I don't know," Riya said in her Oldest Sister voice. "Baking is über-popular with kids these days."

"Never mind her. Even Cole loved your brownies," said Jules as Riya rolled her eyes. "When is the contest?"

I swallowed. "Contestants have a few weeks to bring something in from home, and the top entries win a 'Golden Leaf' that gets them into the second round."

"How many kids will get a Golden Leaf?" asked Riya.

"I don't know," I admitted. I hadn't even asked!

"And then what happens?" Henry asked as he lifted the lids on all the empty pizza boxes. "Hey! Who ate all the pizza? I only got two slices, and I'm still hungry."

Everyone looked confused. Dad didn't bat an eye as he finished his last few bites.

"Have some more salad," said Mom, passing the bowl.

"Rounds two and three of the contest will be on . . . Mrs. T said . . . when is Midsummer's Eve?"

"June twenty-third," Henry said. "My play opens that night. In ancient times, people believed all kinds of magical creatures came out on Midsummer's Eve, so it's the perfect time for a play about fairies."

"Your play is about fairies?" Jules asked.

"Kind of. It's about a fight between the king and queen of the fairies, and the havoc it causes for a bunch of unsuspecting mortals."

"One of our numbers is a fairy dance," said Riya, fluttering her arms like she had wings. "You won't *believe* the gorgeous costumes."

I had nothing against fairies, but I'd been discussing baking. "Mom. The contest. Can I enter?"

Mom's phone buzzed again. "I don't see why not," she said distractedly.

"Dad, will you help me figure out a new recipe that will wow everyone?"

"Absolutely," Dad said, grabbing Riya's discarded crusts from her plate and munching on one. "In fact, why don't you get started now?"

I stood. "Want to help?" I could tell him about everything— the mysterious song, the bizarre bird, the funny waitress, the grape cupcake—while we baked.

"Not now, Mimi Mouse. I'd better jump in the shower. But I'd be happy to give you my opinion on the finished product." He stood and stretched. "I'm famished, and something sweet will hit the spot."

I wondered how Dad could possibly be hungry after eating almost an entire pizza by himself.

For a split second, Dad's face looked strange. It had something to do with his eyes, but I couldn't figure out what. I blinked and looked again. His eyes looked normal—a warm brown, the color of good medium-roast coffee, as he always liked to say. Just like mine.

I went into the kitchen and baked sixty peanut butter cookies with sea salt.

By the end of the night, Dad had eaten forty-nine of them.

CHAPTER 4

PRACTICE DOESN'T MAKE PERFECT

I jumped out of bed the second my eyes opened the next morning. The song from the woods echoed in my head, and I was sure I'd dreamed about it. But baking came first. I couldn't wait to get to work making something for Mrs. T.

I'd already told Mrs. T about Puffy Fay's *Mischief and Magic*, so I picked two other cookbooks instead and thumbed my way through them as I quickly ate a bowl of cereal. Chocolate chip cookies? Too simple. Angel food cake? Too insubstantial. Brownies? Too common. And how did any of them relate to leaves?

An hour later I paced the kitchen floor with the worst case of baker's block I'd ever had. I couldn't think of a single thing to make that wasn't boring or didn't make sense with a "leaf" theme. Or both.

Dad came into the kitchen and slathered butter on a slice of bread.

"Don't you want to toast it first?" I asked.

He stuffed a slice into his mouth. "It's fine," he mumbled with his mouth full. "I'm going to snarf these down before my breakfast meeting."

"But it's Sunday. I thought you could help me decide what to bake for the contest."

"Sorry, honey, I've got to run," said Dad. He gulped down a glass of orange juice and poured himself a cup of coffee.

"Maybe later, then?"

"Oh, Mimi Mouse. I've got a lunch meeting, too, and then an interview over coffee. Maybe after dinner?" He left the room with a mile-high stack of bread.

I sighed, disappointed. I hadn't expected Dad to be so busy after coming back from his trip. Thinking a change of scenery might help, I grabbed the latest *Bon Baking* magazine and plodded to the living room. I trudged past the grand piano, plopped myself down on the squashy blue sofa, and tossed the magazine onto the coffee table. The lead article was called "Ode to the Summer: Put Summer's Bounty into Your Baking." But it just discussed using lots of berries.

I flopped against the sofa cushion. "How am I supposed to

bake something related to *leaves*?"

"*If music be the food of love, play on,*" Henry said as he walked into the room with a stack of papers. "Can I help?"

I blew a stray strand of hair out of my eyes. "Unless you've suddenly acquired magical pastry skills, I don't see how."

"I know I don't bake, but I'm not completely useless. We can make a trade—I'll help you think of ideas for the contest, and you help me run lines for my play. Please?"

I couldn't say no to Henry. He's always busy, but never too busy to lend me a taste bud. He can be dramatic, but unlike Jules and Riya, he's not completely self-involved. And he doesn't just demand things—he asks. If he were a baked treat, he'd be a seven-layer bar—the perfect combination of sweet and salty, exotic coconut and homey caramel, and supported by a good, strong, buttery shortbread crust.

"Okay," I said. "Let's start with the play. I can't deal with thinking about recipes right now."

He handed me his stack of paper. "I'm Puck, the mischievous fairy lieutenant serving King Oberon," he said. "You can be all the other parts. You start off as a fairy who works for Titania, the fairy queen."

I scanned the script. "Wow, I can barely understand this. Do I have to read it all?"

"No, just read your first line and then the last line or two before mine."

"I guess I can do that."

"Great. Remember, you're a fairy. Try to act light-hearted and spritely, okay? I think I have the whole thing memorized. . . . Here goes." He stood up, cleared his throat, and looked at me with a raised eyebrow. "*How now, spirit! Whither wander you?*"

We made our way through the beginning, which was basically all about the king and queen of the fairies having a big fight. Henry recited all his lines perfectly, of course, and probably would have gone through the whole scene without stopping. But then I read:

> "*For Oberon is passing fell and wrath,*
> *Because that she as her attendant hath*
> *A lovely boy, stolen from an Indian king;*
> *She never had so sweet a changeling.*"

"So Queen Titania and King Oberon are fighting over a boy?" I asked.

"Yeah," Henry said, sitting next to me. He didn't seem to care that I'd stopped halfway through the scene. "He's human, the son of one of Titania's followers."

"What's a changeling?" I asked.

"A child that's taken from our world and raised by the fairies, who usually leave a fairy child in its place."

"Well, that's creepy," I said. "And in the play, he's *Indian*?" I started to giggle. "You'd better watch out the next time you're in the woods. Half-Indian is close enough. The fairies might be after you!"

Henry tossed a throw pillow at me, and I ducked. "Keep going," he said.

We went back and forth again for a while. I couldn't make any sense out of most of it, but Henry seemed happy.

"That's the end of my part in the scene. Want to go on, or take a break?" he asked.

"Break, please. So I didn't really get what was happening. What's Puck's deal?"

"Puck works for King Oberon. Oberon tells Puck to find a flower that makes people fall in love with whoever happens to be in front of them. Then to embarrass Queen Titania, they make her fall in love with a donkey-headed man."

I snorted. "What about Titania? Is she mean, too?"

"I'm not sure she's any better than Oberon. But Titania won't give up the changeling boy because she promised to take care of him after his mother died."

"Does the boy have a big part in the play?"

"No, he never even appears. They don't mention him much after the beginning. It's like after a while they forget why they were fighting and only know they're angry."

They sounded a lot like Jules and Riya. "But why did

Shakespeare make up a story about fairies?"

"My English teacher told us that tales about fairies and other magical creatures go way back before Shakespeare. People have always thought there was magic in the forests."

"I can see why," I said, looking out the window to the woods. "When Emma and I were out there, we used to tell each other stories about creatures who lived under mushrooms or flew like dragonflies. The woods make me feel like I'm miles away from the real world, and anything could happen. And recently I've been hearing this song coming from there. It's kind of familiar, like . . ."

Like it was an old friend, calling to me. I almost said the words out loud, but I didn't want Henry to think I was crazy.

Henry wasn't listening. "Have you noticed cell phones don't work in the woods?" he asked absently. "That makes me feel far from civilization."

I shrugged. He must have forgotten that I didn't have a cell phone. "Anyway, I've never seen any fairies out there. It's too bad—I bet they'd be fun."

"Maybe they're hard to see," Henry said, chuckling. He stood and rubbed his hands together. "Now for some baking inspiration before we do my next scene. Maybe music can help get you unstuck. Are you game?"

"I'll try anything." We both moved over to the piano, where Henry played a simple melody.

"Wish I could play like you," I said, watching his hands fly over the keys. Unlike the rest of my family, I had no musical talent whatsoever. When I'd tried the clarinet in fourth grade, I'd squawked like a cranky goose.

"If you want to, you can. It comes with practice. You didn't give the clarinet much of a chance, you know."

I rolled my eyes.

"Anyway, can you describe what you hear? What does this song make you think of?" asked Henry.

I looked at him, puzzled.

"Is it happy or sad, simple or complicated?" he asked. "How does it make you feel?"

"I guess it's . . . happy, and simple. It makes me think of summer, like sunshine on the creek, and birds singing to each other."

"Good!" Henry said. "Now think about that and see if it stirs up some ideas." He continued to play and added a meandering accompaniment.

I closed my eyes, trying to focus on feeling a summer's day with sunlight shining through a canopy of leaves, making bright spots and shadows dance across the forest floor.

"When I play music, I'm telling a story. You do the same thing when you bake," Henry said.

I imagined walking on a leafy forest path with Emma. We picked wildflowers and made necklaces. We climbed trees and watched birds and squirrels at work. We told jokes, and I made Emma laugh so hard she snorted like a petite pig. We collapsed in fits of giggles.

I pictured oval leaves, translucent and veined in gold and green.

"Nice song, Henry," Riya said. I hadn't even heard her come in. "Let me join you." She began to sing the melody in her glorious voice.

"You guys need more rhythm," Jules said from the doorway. She entered and started tapping on the coffee table.

Henry played chords on the piano to accompany them. They sounded great together. Perfect, in fact. Like always. Whatever arguments they had with one another melted away in the music. It was like they were conjuring summer in the room—the warm air, the bright sunshine, the sounds of the woods I loved. As usual, they'd forgotten about me. I didn't dare try to join them; I'd break the spell and ruin everything.

It would have been like deflating a perfect soufflé.

After a few minutes I crept out of the room, leaving my dejected-looking magazine on the sofa. My brother and sisters didn't even notice. I kept going. I had to get out of the house.

I stopped in the kitchen, threw my Puffy Fay cookbook into my backpack, and headed outside. Once I got onto the forest trail, I relaxed into the scent of pine needles and dirt. I'd walked this path for so long that I knew each rock and root along the way. But there were changes from day to day. Clusters of wildflowers popped up in sunny patches, or delicate tendrils of vines wound their way up mossy tree trunks. Mushrooms sprang up after a heavy rain, and sometimes branches or whole trees came down overnight. There was always something new in the woods.

After a few minutes of walking, I came to the clearing where Emma and I had built our hangout—a small lean-to made of an old tarp thrown over a bunch of branches, with a tattered rug covering the dirt floor. I sat inside, where the air was still cool and damp from the night before. A tube of Emma's favorite ginger lip balm lay on the floor. I took the cookbook out and flipped through it distractedly, squinting in the yellow light coming through the triangular entrance. What would impress Mrs. T—snickerdoodles or brownies, linzer cookies or coconut cupcakes? But Mrs. T deserved something that suited her, something special, something regal. Something to do with *leaves*. I was getting nowhere.

"I miss you so much, Emma," I said out loud. Even if Emma couldn't help me, she would have listened. *You don't need to be the best at anything, Mimi*, she'd say. *You just need to be yourself.* But being myself was lame. How much worse could this summer get? Emma had moved across the world to Australia. Right now she was traveling in the outback somewhere, and she wouldn't even get email until next month. Dad seemed to be too busy to bake with me last night or today, and I couldn't win the contest without his help.

A familiar melody wound through the air around me. There it was again! I strained to hear it better. It definitely wasn't a bird. It wasn't a person's voice, either. And why did I feel like the song was asking me a question?

I scrambled outside and headed farther on the path into the woods, following the song. Eventually, I had to leave the path and strike through the trees, pushing aside branches and scanning the ground for roots. The song seemed a little closer, a little louder.

And then it stopped. I froze and held my breath, hoping it would start up again.

It didn't.

Pu-de pu-de pu-de, called a cardinal, and its mate responded. A robin chirped, *Wheet, wheet, a-wheet*. Small animals scurried through the underbrush. But the song had disappeared completely.

Something snuffled faintly. I stared hard at the place where I thought it had come from, but I couldn't see anything but bushes.

Goose bumps erupted on my arms.

There was something out there. Something that was snuffling and watching me. I wasn't going to wait around and see what it was.

I backed up slowly, then turned and sprinted back to the path, trying not to look behind me too many times.

I was sweating by the time I arrived at the hangout. Realizing I'd left my backpack and cookbook inside, I stooped under the opening to grab them quickly before going home. My empty backpack lay on the floor like an open mouth, but the book wasn't in it. Even after getting down on my knees and groping around in the shadows, I still couldn't find it.

I was positive I'd left it there! Where had it gone? Mom and Dad had gotten it for me when we visited Puffy's New York bakery last year. It was signed by Puffy himself. This was turning into the worst day of the summer since Emma moved.

Something rustled in the trees nearby.

"Hello? Is someone there?"

No answer.

A flash of yellow feathers took off from a branch above me, and a leaf fluttered to the ground at my feet. I picked it up. It was unusual—quite large, oval and shiny, and green-gold in the light.

I searched my surroundings, but the area was filled with maples and oaks. There was no tree with gigantic oval leaves. There was something really strange going on.

"Where did you come from?" I asked the leaf.

The woods answered with noisy silence.

CHAPTER 5

LEAVES OF GREEN AND GOLD

Over the next week, I went to my hangout daily, but I didn't see the bright little bird. I kept hoping my Puffy Fay cookbook would somehow turn up, but it had apparently disappeared for good. And I kept hearing pieces of the song drifting from deep in the woods, but it never lasted long enough for me to follow it to its source.

Although I spent hours whipping up treats to practice for the contest at the While Away, I wasn't satisfied with anything I made. I kept coming up with stuff that I thought was good but likely not special enough to truly impress. Every time I finished one of my creations, I imagined Puffy Fay critiquing it like I was on his show. My nutmeg-caraway shortbread had too many conflicting spices, he would say. And of course, it had nothing to do with leaves. The lemon-raspberry cake decorated with lemon leaves was too tart, and the toffee cupcakes with leaf-shaped maple candy were cloying. And then I would hear him say those fateful words: "I'm sorry, Chef Mimi. You will *not* be the winner of today's Bake-Off. Please turn in your toque."

Mom sampled everything, but getting any kind of real feedback from her was impossible. Despite being a fantastic cook, she didn't know much about baking, and besides, as far as she was concerned, everything I made was amazing and delicious. What I really needed was Dad's input. I could trust him to be critical of my food if something wasn't working, or to suggest another flavor to enhance it. At least, I used to be able to. If only I could get him to say anything useful.

Since he'd returned from his trip to Texas, Dad had been eating everything in the house. He was supposedly working from his home office, but he must have spent most of those hours eating, too. Chips and popcorn disappeared from the pantry. There were never any leftovers in the fridge, not even the frittata that no one ever wanted the next day. And every time I baked, it was all gone by that night. I realized that even if I finally made something I felt was good enough to bring to Mrs. T, I'd have to hide it from Dad, or none of it would even make it out of the house. When he wasn't eating, he spent hours running in the woods.

Dad became even worse than Mom in the advice department—he never offered any suggestions for improvement on anything I made. He just said everything was "scrumptious." My dad, who wrote about food daily in exquisite detail, whose *job* was to describe smells, tastes, and textures precisely, had somehow been reduced to a single word.

The next Friday, almost a week after I first visited the While Away, I woke when it was still dark outside—which, given that it was the middle of June, meant *really* early. I tossed and turned for a little bit, but there was no way I could go back to sleep. So I went to the kitchen to try to bake my way to inner peace. I was in the mood for some savory scones—I couldn't eat only sweet things, no matter what Mrs. T said.

I cut cold butter into flour with my pastry blender, added minced sun-dried tomatoes, fresh Parmesan, salt and pepper, sprinkled in oregano, and then, on a whim, tossed in crushed fennel seeds. I mixed in an egg and some milk. I kneaded the dough a few times, cut out rounds, and plopped them on a cookie sheet. I brushed the tops with more milk and slid the sheet into the hot oven.

I sat at the kitchen table and gazed out the big window that faces the backyard. Branches swayed in a sky warming with the day's first light. It was summer in the woods I loved—the perfect inspiration for a leaf-themed dessert. I closed my eyes and let the red from the sunlight dance under my eyelids.

It seemed like only a few minutes had passed when the timer went off. The scones were golden brown and smelled wonderfully cheesy and herby. I pulled the pan from the oven and left it on the counter to cool while I cleaned up.

Dad wiped sweat off his brow as he came into the kitchen through the back door. He sniffed the air. "What did you make? It smells scrumptious."

"Come on, Dad, you know the rules. You've got to use your nose, and your mighty palate." I smiled at him hopefully. Dad and I always played a game at restaurants trying to identify the ingredients in each other's meals.

"Okay, Mimi Mouse, whatever you say, as long as I get to eat a lot."

"Here you go." I put two scones on a plate and offered it to him. "Tell me what you think is in there. Watch out, they're still hot."

Dad broke a scone in two and stuffed an entire half in his mouth. I could see steam coming off the piece in his hand and was sure he was burning his tongue, but he didn't seem to mind. He chewed a couple of times and then crammed in the other half. "Mmm!" For a second I thought he might choke. But then he swallowed and reached for the other scone.

I pulled the plate back. "What's in them?"

He smacked his lips. "Flour? Definitely butter."

"Oh, Daddy." I giggled, but Dad didn't laugh with me, didn't rattle off the right ingredients like he'd done a hundred times before.

Flour and butter. He was being serious.

I stared at him. "You can do better than that. You write about food all day! You can detect a pinch of cloves in a whole bowl of batter! You can taste the difference between white and black truffles!"

He looked around and glanced at the milk container on the counter. "Milk?"

"They're *scones*, Dad, of course they're going to have flour, butter, and milk. But what about the flavorings?"

"I'm sorry, Mimi," Dad said, not meeting my eyes. "I'm not sure what else you want me to say."

"But—"

He grabbed the other scone and shoved it in his mouth. "I may not know what you put in them, but they really are scrumptious. Now I'd better jump in the shower so I'm not late for work." He snatched two more scones from the still-hot cookie sheet and darted out of the room.

I flopped into a chair. Dad had been the only one with the patience and endurance to taste seventeen versions of my coconut key lime pie until we found the perfect balance of tart and sweet. And now all he could guess was flour, butter, and milk? I gently pulled apart a scone and nibbled. The sun-dried tomatoes were robust and sweet and played well with the salty

Parmesan. The oregano added a floral note, and the fennel made it energizing and playful. These scones were *good*— maybe even good enough to survive the opening round of one of Puffy Fay's Bake-Offs.

Puffy would be able to taste every little detail of my work. And so would Dad, under normal circumstances. Why couldn't he do it now?

But I didn't have time to think about that now. I had to keep going. I had to make something leaf-themed to impress Mrs. T, and I wanted to bring it in the next day, to make sure I didn't miss the window for the contest. I glanced at the oval leaf, which I'd propped in the window like a piece of stained glass.

It occurred to me that maybe I'd been making things way too complicated. As Puffy Fay liked to say, sometimes simple and sweet are all that you need.

Three hours later, I applied the finishing touches to my entry for the first round of the While Away Café's Midsummer Baking Contest: vanilla bean sugar cookies, decorated with green and gold royal icing. I didn't have leaf-shaped cookie cutters, so I used heart-shaped ones instead and paid careful attention to drawing stems and veins. They looked beautiful, and they tasted buttery and full of warm vanilla flavor. Now I just needed to hide them from Dad overnight so he wouldn't eat them all before the icing had time to set. I snuck them up to my room in batches and left them on top of my bookcase.

"Are you texting Cole?" Jules glowered at Riya across the breakfast table the next day.

Riya glanced up from her phone. "No, it's not Cole," she said. "I told you I don't like him."

"Then why does he keep making excuses to come over and talk to you?"

"If you want to know, it's—"

"Just shut up. I don't want to hear it. I really like him, and you're toying with him! I invited him over for dinner tomorrow night, so keep your claws off him!" Jules sprang to her feet and left the room in a huff.

Riya rolled her eyes and went back to her phone. "I invited someone, too."

A few hours later, I accepted Mom and Dad's offer to drive me into Comity Center. I didn't want to risk biking there and having the cookies crumble to dust in my backpack. I asked them to drop me off near the While Away while they ran errands. I didn't want them coming in with me while Mrs. T judged my cookies—succeed or fail, I wanted to do it without an audience.

I passed the other new food place in Comity, the Salt Shaker, which had a line snaking out its door. In contrast, the While Away looked relatively quiet. Gripping my platter of cookies in sweaty hands, I took a breath and stepped inside.

The café was busier than it had been the previous weekend. More than half the tables were occupied, and a bunch of people were milling around in the back. There was a short line at the pastry counter, where Peaseblossom stood helping customers.

"Hi, Mimi. Still wearing those shoes?" came a sneering voice.

Kiera Jones. Of course. The only person who could possibly make me feel more nervous. Even without her usual gang of hangers-on around her, Kiera looked like she was in charge. She tossed her perfect light brown hair with perfect gold highlights. It was always smooth and shiny, and never in her face.

"Hi, Kiera."

"I assume you're hoping to win one of these?" She fanned an oval-shaped piece of paper in front of my eyes so I blinked instinctively. A Golden Leaf! How had she already gotten one? "It has the clue for the theme of round two," she said. "I can't *wait* to get started."

"I didn't know you baked," I said.

"I've been baking for years, with my nana." Kiera sniffed. "Is that your entry? Are you going for a Green Valentine's theme?"

My face heated up like a broiler. "They're *leaves*. Isn't that supposed to be the theme?"

Kiera squinted at the platter. "Oh. I see. How . . . literal."

"What did *you* make?" I asked.

Mrs. T called from across the room. "Mimi Mackson! How lovely to see you again! Whatever took you so long?" She was seated at a long table at the back of the café.

I pushed past Kiera and made my way to Mrs. T. She had a large selection of baked goods on various plates, platters, and other containers spread in front of her like a smorgasbord.

"I've been working hard on my entry for the contest," I said.

"Of course you have, my dear. Do put your entry down, and sign your name on that clipboard. I'll judge it in due time."

In public? I thought she might judge entries back in her office. What if she hated my cookies? I cringed at the thought of the whole café full of people, and especially Kiera, watching my humiliation. I put the platter down, scrawled my name on the sheet, found a nearby seat, and looked around. Sure enough, there were a couple dozen kids hanging around, ranging in age from tiny second graders to middle schoolers like me, and a pair of taller girls who I assumed were thirteen-year-olds.

"If you ask me, Demetrius is the most interesting role in the play," came a loud voice from the door. I turned to look. It was Riya's friend Fletcher, who was as artificial as sour gummy candy. As he walked into the café, he ran a hand through his smooth blond hair, then jerked his head forward to make his hair flop in front of his eyes again. "He has the biggest *transformation*, loving Helena at the end when at first he only has eyes for Hermia."

"Um-hmm," said Riya, tapping on her phone as she followed him inside. Her hair was pulled back in a bun, and she wore a soft, loose cardigan over her tank top and leggings. What was she doing here?

"No offense, of course, Lily," said Fletcher, tilting his head so his hair flopped to the side.

Henry came in with his latest crush—Lily, a petite girl with long, wavy dark hair. "I'm not Hermia, I'm just playing her," Lily said with a laugh. "You're not offending me. And if I were going to be mad at anyone for what their character did, it would be Puck. Right, Henry?" She giggled and pulled Henry farther into the café.

"*If we shadows have offended, Think but this, and all is mended*," said Henry with a laugh. "I didn't mean to mess up everyone's lives, honest."

They must have come straight from play rehearsal. But why was Riya with them? Unless they'd given her a ride from the dance studio. Which was near the soccer field where . . .

"Move it, guys, it's hot out here," Jules said. She trudged in, sweaty from soccer practice, with her hair billowing like a storm cloud above her headband.

Every head in the café turned to them. A table of teenagers waved and chattered, and even some of the grown-ups nodded and smiled. As Comity's reigning Actor in a Lead Role, Prima Dancer, and Most-Likely-to-Go-Pro Soccer Star, Henry, Riya, and Jules were recognized by everyone in town. I was just an anonymous afterthought, the sister who tagged along and witnessed all their triumphs. Maybe I was the changeling in my family—only from the Land of the Lame and Untalented instead of the fairy world.

"Oh, hi, Cole!" Jules called. I turned and realized that sitting a few feet away from me was none other than our new neighbor, sipping a coffee and reading a book on robot design.

Cole looked up at Jules, and his freckly face flushed a deep pink. "Hi," he said softly.

"Mind if we join you?" Jules asked.

"Well, I—"

"There's lots of room. Look, we can pull up another table." Jules hauled over a nearby table, scraping it across the floor. She took a seat next to Cole with a grin. "Henry, get me an iced green tea, okay?"

Henry gave Jules a thumbs-up from the line at the counter as Riya and Lily joined Cole and Jules at the table.

How long were they all going to be here? I didn't need my sisters getting into an argument and embarrassing me in front of the whole café. And I didn't want to embarrass myself in front of them, like I had so many times before. I glanced anxiously at Mrs. T, but she was taking her time, asking questions of a tiny pigtailed girl and tasting the girl's green swirled cheesecake bars before giving her a Golden Leaf. I slumped in my seat and pulled my hair in front of my face to hide from my sisters while keeping a surreptitious eye on them.

"Hey, Riya, have you thought about what I asked you the other day?" Cole asked.

Riya nodded as she tapped on her phone.

Fletcher and Henry arrived carrying two trays of drinks and pastries.

"So, Cole," Jules said in a high-pitched voice that didn't sound like her. "Henry, Lily, and Fletcher are in the Comity Youth Theater's production of A Midsummer Night's Dream. Have you seen it before?"

"No." Cole laughed nervously and looked at Riya.

"Well, Carl, you have to come. It's going to be amazing," Fletcher said.

Jules turned pink. "His name is Cole."

"Henry plays the mischievous fairy prankster, Puck," Fletcher said. "And Lily and I are two of the young lovers."

Lovers? That sounded terrible. I sank further into my seat.

"There are two women and two men—regular people— who get caught in the middle of a fairy fight," Henry explained to Cole. "Both guys like the same girl at first, but the fairies—well, Puck, on orders from the fairy king—interfere and make them fall in love with the other girl. Everything goes crazy for a while, and it's hilarious, but it all works out in the end."

"And it takes place in the woods," Lily said. Given the strange things that were happening in my woods, it didn't sound that far-fetched.

"That's the best part," Fletcher said. "Not only is the play set in the woods, but we're actually *performing* it outside. We're running in and out of the trees the whole time—it's almost like the woods are another character in the story." He took a sip of his coffee. "Problem is, it's hard to see when the light gets dim. I nearly twisted an ankle the other day." He flopped his hair in front of his face again.

"I wish," Jules muttered.

"What about you, Charles? Do you act?" Fletcher asked.

"It's Cole. And I'm more of a math and science guy," Cole said.

"Oh. I'm sorry." That wasn't an apology for getting Cole's name wrong. Fletcher looked horrified to be sitting next to a nerd.

"*I* think math and science are fascinating," said Jules, smiling brightly at Cole.

Riya snickered.

"What?" Jules snapped.

Riya rolled her eyes. "It's a rather recent fascination, don't you think?"

Jules gripped her glass so tightly her knuckles turned white. "Why don't you—"

"Mimi Mackson." Mrs. T's clear voice rang through the café. "Please come up to be judged."

Henry, Riya, Jules, and their friends looked up in surprise as I approached Mrs. T's table, shaking like a flan, like a cup of gelatin.

Like a leaf.

CHAPTER 6

HOME

"My dear, dear girl, what did you make for us?" Mrs. T wore a gauzy white dress embroidered in tiny pink roses.

"They're vanilla bean sugar cookies," I said. "Decorated to look like—"

"Leaves. Yes, heart-shaped leaves like those of the empress tree. How appropriate," she said with a titter.

I guessed they weren't too literal, after all.

"And you intend these to . . ." She looked at me curiously.

I spluttered in confusion. "To win a Golden Leaf. I'd love to get to the next round of the contest." I gave her a tentative smile.

"I see." She chose a cookie, sniffed it delicately, and took a bite. "Well, they're not unpleasant. Very . . . vanilla."

The smile hardened on my face like old gingerbread icing.

"They're not *quite* what we're looking for, I'm afraid," said Mrs. T.

My stomach dropped to my sneakers. "But—"

"I told you to bring something from your *heart*."

"These cookies *are* from my heart. I love the woods, and that was my inspiration."

"Let me tell you a secret." She leaned toward me, carrying the faint scent of wild roses. "It's important that the While Away do well this summer, Mimi. *Exceedingly* important," she whispered. "I see potential greatness in you, but I need you to work harder. I need you to put *everything* you have into this contest."

"But . . ." I'd been thinking about nothing else for a week! I had racked my brains and done my absolute best.

"Mimi, Mimi, don't be disappointed. You can try again to earn a Golden Leaf. Next time, put *yourself* into your creation. I'm asking for courage. And loyalty."

"Loyalty? I don't—"

"Return with something from your heart, something only you in all the world could make, and you will succeed." She focused on the sign-up sheet. "Sam Blake! You're next!"

My ears started to buzz while I took my platter and shuffled away. The other kids waiting to be judged stared at me, and my siblings put their heads together and whispered. The edges of my vision turned gray as I threw myself into the nearest chair.

I thought the cookies had been tasty. They looked appealing, and smelled sweet, and tasted of luscious vanilla. But my idea wasn't good enough. My execution wasn't good enough.

I wasn't good enough.

Memories of my biggest failures boiled over in my brain like milk on a stove. There was the time I'd scored a goal against my own team in soccer. I hadn't meant to, but the ball had bounced off my leg. Kiera Jones had bellowed, "You're supposed to shoot at the *other* goal!" and looked at me like I was half a worm she'd discovered in her apple.

At my first and only dance recital, I'd tripped and stumbled into the girl next to me, causing a domino-like chain reaction and a pile of screaming dancers in fluffy chick costumes.

And at my first and only clarinet recital, I'd squeaked like a goose in mating season.

And here I was, a failure yet again.

In front of my brother and sisters. In front of their friends. In front of a whole café full of people.

Henry hurried over. "You okay?" he asked.

I nodded, not trusting myself to speak without crying.

"Those cookies are beautiful," said Jules fiercely. "That lady is crazy."

"I *told* you there'd be lots of competition," said Riya.

"Riya, this isn't the time," said Henry. "Want a ride home?" he whispered to me.

"It's all right. Mom and Dad will be here soon. Go back to your friends. *Please*."

Henry, Riya, and Jules went back to their table, but it didn't make me feel any better. Especially when Mrs. T handed a Golden Leaf to a red-haired boy who couldn't have been older than eight.

My parents walked in a minute later. "How'd it go?" Mom asked.

I shook my head.

Kiera pranced over and shook hands with Mom and Dad. "Mr. and Mrs. Mackson. How wonderful to see you!" She turned to me. "Don't be too disappointed, Mimi. Mrs. T said she wanted the *very* best, and loads of kids have been turned away today. Just not me." She gave an evil giggle and waved her Golden Leaf again. "I brought in the most glorious napoleons— you know, mille-feuilles, or 'thousand leaves' in French. Isn't that clever? And she loved them so much, she's serving them to the customers!"

I kept my eyes on Mom. "Let's get out of here," I said grimly.

"I spy some things I'd like to try," said Dad, eyeing the pastry case.

"Let's go, Paul." Mom grabbed his arm.

Dad allowed Mom to lead him to the door, but he kept

glancing back at the pastries. He grinned at me like I hadn't just been humiliated in front of the entire town.

As we exited the While Away, I thought I saw a tiny flash of purple in his eyes.

The ten-minute car ride home seemed to take hours.

"These cookies are scrumptious." Dad munched on his fifth one. "I don't understand why you didn't get through to the next round."

"What did the owner say again?" asked Mom.

"She wants me to bake something from my heart," I said dully. I swiped at the tears on my face. I might have won a Golden Leaf if Dad had helped me like he used to. And what was up with his eyes?

"Dad, are you feeling okay?" I asked.

"Never better, Mimi, never better." Dad reached for another cookie. He winked at me in the rearview mirror, and his eyes were their normal color. Had I just imagined that violet flash?

When we finally reached home, I went straight to my room and took a long look around at the lavender-colored walls with black butterflies, the bookcases under the windows that held all my cookbooks and baking magazines.

I *loved* to bake. But was I doomed to be terrible at it?

I opened my closet and reached into a dusty corner where

I'd stowed shoes I'd outgrown and extra poster board for school projects. I pulled out my clarinet case, which stared at me accusingly, and my old dance shoes, still shiny and unscuffed. My soccer cleats were tiny and barely used. Maybe I should cram all my cookbooks in there, too.

The library would be a better place for them—at least that way someone else could learn from them, someone who might someday be great. I was fooling myself about my baking abilities if Kiera Jones and two eight-year-olds could make it into the next round of the contest when I couldn't. I started to make a pile of books, but when I picked up *The Cupcake Codex*, I couldn't bear to part with it. It had given me the inspiration for my lemon-lavender cupcakes, the best ones I'd ever made.

I flopped on my bed to browse through it one last time. I couldn't pay attention, though—my mind kept drifting back to Dad. People's eyes didn't just start flashing purple. And what about his bottomless appetite? Did he need to see a doctor? Had he actually lost his food writer's sense of taste, or was it just that he didn't want to help me bake anymore?

The next thing I knew, I woke to the sound of knocking. I sat up and realized I'd drooled on my book. "Come in," I said. I closed the book and rubbed my eyes.

Mom carried in two small bowls. She glanced at the pile of books on the floor, then sat at the edge of my bed and handed me a bowl.

"I thought you could use a treat you didn't have to make yourself."

The bowl was warm, and I inhaled the comforting aroma. It was kesari bhath, a dessert Mom had learned to make from her mom, who'd learned it from hers in India, and on and on and on for who knew how many generations. It was made with semolina, sugar, milk, and ghee, flavored with saffron and cardamom, and studded with raisins and cashews. I tasted a spoonful of the thick, golden pudding. It was perfect.

"What about everyone else?" I didn't want to eat all of it, knowing how much the whole family loved it. Especially Dad.

"Don't worry, there's plenty more downstairs. But this is for you and me."

I sighed and put down the spoon. "I can't believe I failed. *Again.*"

Mom shook her head and looked at me with her beautiful eyes, so dark they were nearly black. "I wish you wouldn't take things so hard, Mimi. I know how much work you've put in, and you can always try again."

"But what if I fail again? What if I fail at everything, always?"

"Life isn't about succeeding or failing. It's about trying your best, and loving what you do, and being kind. I'd be so disappointed if you were a snide little snake, like that Kiera Jones. I don't care how many Golden Leaves she won."

I gasped in surprise. Then, against my will, I started to smile, and giggles bubbled through me until they burst from my mouth. Mom started to laugh with me, and all of a sudden, neither of us could stop. We laughed until tears ran down our cheeks. I couldn't catch my breath, and Mom clutched her stomach. We lay on the bed and took gasping gulps of air.

Eventually, we were able to control ourselves and sit up again.

Mom looked at me like I was the only person in the whole world. "You remind me of myself."

"But you're so good at everything, and you always know what to do."

She snorted. "You're a *much* better cook than I was at your age. You wouldn't believe my dreadful attempts when your dad and I were first married."

"Really?" I giggled again.

She nodded. "I burned more things than I can count, and we didn't have much money, so we had to eat it, no matter how bad it was. And I had a real talent for undercooking rice. But I kept at it, and read lots of cookbooks, and asked both your grandmothers for recipes, and eventually, I got better."

"You're the best cook I know."

"You're the best baker I know."

"Mom, don't make stuff up!"

"I mean it. Keep baking, honey. Because you love it. Contest or no contest, no one can take that away from you. And if you do want to try the contest again, I think you'll have a great shot."

"Thanks. But I'm not sure what I want to do."

"Whatever you decide, I'm proud of you. Now, move over," said Mom.

We propped up pillows and Mom snuggled next to me while we ate. I let the sweetness of the sugar and ghee, the sunniness of the saffron, and the gently grainy texture of the semolina play in my mouth. It was the perfect combination of sweet and savory, smooth and gritty, fragrant and the tiniest bit bitter.

It tasted like home.

CHAPTER 7

INTO THE WOODS

Humidity is the enemy of meringues, but it can wreak havoc on buttercream, too. The next day was the hottest of the summer, and by the time I finished piping purple frosting onto my pale yellow cupcakes, they were already starting to sweat. I'd decided to take a break from thinking about the contest and just bake something for fun. I wanted to bring the cupcakes to my hangout and let them inspire my letter to Emma.

I placed two cupcakes in my special carrier, snapped it closed, and put it in my backpack with a thermos of limeade and my notebook and pen. As long as I was careful and kept the container horizontal, the cupcakes would be fine.

I reached the hangout and took off my backpack. By habit, I glanced around for my still-missing Puffy Fay cookbook, and something caught my eye. I crawled to the far end of the tarp and picked it up.

It was a book. But judging by its size, not the one I was looking for. I brought it into the sunlight.

The book was smaller than *Mischief and Magic*, but it was much thicker, with a worn leather cover. It had no title on the front or the spine. Where had it come from? I opened it and leafed through its soft, translucent pages, pages filled with exquisite drawings of herbs and flowers in bright colors. It was a catalog of every plant I could imagine—and many I'd never heard of—and all their subtleties of flavor, scent, and use in cooking.

The ultimate cookbook! It didn't just list ingredients and give directions for recipes; it explained what each ingredient was good for. I sank to the ground and flipped to the beginning. An image of bright blue flowers caught my eye: *cornflower*, read the entry, *to alleviate discord and strife*. I'd love to sprinkle those into pancakes for Jules and Riya. Next to a picture of small oblong green seeds: *fennel, to promote strength and healing*. Fascinating! Then, a lifelike drawing of tiny purple petals on vertical blooms: *lavender brings luck and—*

I jerked my head up. There it was—a wistful melody, a question repeated.

The song!

I stowed the book in my backpack, hoisted it onto my back,

and followed the dreamy tune through the trees. I walked quickly—first on the path, and then off it—for a long time. The song steadily grew louder, and every few feet I thought I'd find whoever (or whatever) was making the music.

But then, almost as if the music maker had heard my thoughts, the song stopped.

Trees crowded together, thick with foliage. Brightly colored insects buzzed in the humid air. I'd come to a part of the woods I'd never seen. Ahead of me lay a large and unfamiliar pond. How could this be? Emma and I had explored every corner of its thirty acres over the past few years, and I would definitely remember if we had been here before.

A snorting noise erupted to my left, startling me. I looked, but there was nothing there. Then heavy footsteps (hoofsteps?) thundered closer. I peered into the trees around me: still nothing. But as the sounds grew louder, I sensed something large and hairy charging through the nearby leaves and brush.

I ran. This was no neighborhood dog. I glanced back and caught the flash of a white tusk and shiny, rolling eyes.

It was a boar.

The wild, hairy cousin of a pig. But a whole lot meaner.

That was impossible! Boars didn't live in these woods.

I sprinted. I rushed around trees and tried not to trip. A painful stitch gnawed at my side and sweat poured into my eyes.

I nearly collided with an enormous tree. It had a gigantic

central trunk and branches that reached down and became smaller trunks, like gnarled fingers grabbing the ground. I scrambled to climb up but couldn't find a foothold. The boar drew closer by the second.

"Help!" I cried in a panic.

A hand reached down out of the tree. It was a kid's hand, with skin tanned from the sun, attached to an arm that disappeared into the leaves of the tree. The hand opened, as if in invitation.

So I grabbed it.

The hand grasped mine with surprising strength and pulled me up. I clutched at the first branch I could reach and used my feet against the tree's enormous trunk to clamber up as the boar's hot breath blew on my ankles. Eventually, the hand let go and disappeared farther up into the branches. I sensed someone moving above me, but I had to keep my head down to avoid getting a face full of leaves.

"There's a big branch up here you can sit on," came a muffled voice. After several more minutes of climbing, I reached a large limb and hauled myself up to sit on top. And then I saw who the hand, arm, and voice belonged to.

It was a boy. He looked like he was about my age. He had brown skin and wavy black hair that brushed the collar of his T-shirt. He sat on the branch with his hands out, ready to steady me if needed. I wrapped my shaking legs around the tree limb. Then I looked up into the boy's face.

He had the most unusual eyes I had ever seen. They were bright brown, with bursts of gold in the middle, like sunlight shining through honey.

He flashed me a smile and watched me until he seemed satisfied that I had my balance. Then he relaxed his arms and leaned back against the tree's huge trunk. "Are you all right?"

I looked down; I couldn't see the ground, but I could still hear the snorting, combined with the occasional ugly squeal. "Oh-my-goodness-that-is-a-BOAR," I said. "Do you think it can climb?" I forced myself to slow my breathing.

"No, because it chased me up here a short while ago," he said.

"Good thing it did, or you couldn't have saved me from being eaten."

"Where I come from, boars don't generally eat people. They're more of a nuisance," said the boy. "But those tusks did look sharp."

"But what is a boar doing here? There are no boars in Massachusetts! The worst I've seen in these woods is a fisher-cat."

The boy shrugged. "I don't know. I've never been to these woods before last week."

"Well, thanks for the hand up." Why wasn't he more freaked out? "I'm Mimi."

"I'm Vik." He smiled. "And you're welcome."

Now that I was safe, I could finally appreciate the tree we were sitting in. It spread its huge, twisting limbs so wide that there were no other trees within at least twenty yards in every direction. Its leaves were enormous, oval, shiny, and green-gold. And when I ran my fingers over its bark, it felt more *alive* than any tree I'd ever touched, as if I could feel it breathing. "What kind of tree is this?"

"A banyan tree," Vik said.

I shook my head. "I've never seen anything like it."

"Some say the banyan is sacred. Each of these limbs can take root and form a new tree." He patted a branch. "This tree is immortal."

"Amazing," I said. "Where are you from? I haven't seen you at school."

"I was born in India, and I've lived in lots of places, but right now I'm staying here for the summer with my old aunt Tanya, who lives at the edge of the forest."

"Welcome to Comity," I said.

"Lovely town. Wonderful woods. And great food," said Vik.

How nice that someone else had noticed! "What are your favorite places?"

"Ronaldo's, and Deli-shush, the sandwich place. I'd love to get their harvest bread recipe and make it myself."

I gawked at him. "You bake?"

He nodded. "I cook, too, but baking's my favorite."

This was almost too good to be true! "Have you visited the While Away Café? Are you entering their contest?"

He paused, then shook his head. "No contests for me. Too much of a hassle."

"I'm entering," I said. "I'm trying to figure out how to make it to the second round."

"Good luck," said Vik.

"Someday, I want to be a professional baker. A celebrity professional baker, like my idol, Puffy Fay." I took my backpack off and laid it on the branch in front of me.

Vik plucked a leaf from the tree and examined it. "I just want to be a person," he said.

"What?"

Vik laughed. "I mean, a regular person. My—my aunt is kind of famous . . . in our country."

"You mean India?"

"I was born in India, but now I live in Lemuria."

"I've never heard of it."

"It's a beautiful but tiny island in the Pacific," said Vik. "There, Aunt Tanya's a celebrity. Royalty, even."

"That sounds glamorous."

"Less than you'd think," Vik said with a weary laugh. "We're always traveling—to Europe, Asia, America. All around the world. She has business interests everywhere. It can be exhausting."

That sounded like the kind of exhausting I would enjoy. "We don't go on many trips to places we can't drive to," I said. "I have a brother and two sisters, and it's super expensive for six people to go anywhere. I would love to visit India again." The last time we'd visited Mom's relatives was five years ago, and I was dying to go back.

"India is beautiful," Vik agreed. "And—"

"The food is amazing!" we both exclaimed.

"Anyway, you said you like Puffy Fay? I'm a fan, too," said Vik. "Have you been to his bakery in New York?"

I swung my legs back and forth. "Yeah, we visited last year, and I had a pumpkin pavlova that was insanely delicious." It had been one of the best days of my life.

"I love a good meringue," said Vik. He leaned toward me. "But I've never had a pumpkin one. I wonder how he kept the pumpkin from weighing down the egg whites?"

This kid definitely knew baking!

"Yeah, I wondered that, too. He's never published that recipe, though."

There was a brief silence. A bluebird called to its mate, and I remembered what had brought me out here in the first place.

"Did you hear a song playing a little while ago?" I had to know. Had I imagined it, like I imagined Dad's weird purple eye flash?

"What song?"

I whistled the tune. If Vik had heard it, maybe he could help me find out what made it. A rare bird? A strange lizard? Or maybe something I'd never even dreamed of. Up in a banyan tree, safe from a snorting boar, anything seemed possible.

"Oh." His face lit up. "That was me."

"You whistled it?"

"No, I played it—like this." And before I knew what was happening, he reached behind him for a small wooden pipe, and, balanced perfectly on the branch, he played the tune I had heard.

My heart inflated like a clafouti in the oven. So this was the answer I'd been searching for since I'd heard the first few notes of the song. A boy. In a tree! It was like being inside a story that Emma and I made up.

"I've been hearing bits of that song since the beginning of the summer! Did you write it yourself?" I asked.

"No, it's an old family song. I play it to keep myself company. And to remind myself of where I come from."

"Well, I love it," I said. "I can't get it out of my head."

"I can teach you, if you want."

I shook my head. "I'm no musician. It's enough to finally know where the song came from. Besides, we'd better eat these before they melt. To celebrate avoiding sharp tusks." I reached into my backpack and took out my carrier.

"Oh," said Vik. "Cupcakes."

He looked as grumpy as I felt when Grandma Kate served up stewed cabbage.

"I made them myself." I held one out to him. It was only slightly squished; the carrier had done its job.

Vik accepted the cupcake reluctantly. "I'm kind of sick of sweets." He peeled the wrapper down and took a small bite.

"I'd love to hear your opinion. I like trying unusual combinations of ingredients, like—"

"You made this?" Vik looked at me sharply.

"Yes," I said tentatively. Was it too weird? I knew I shouldn't have added that extra lemon zest!

"It's superb. Wow. I've never tasted anything like it. Lemon and . . . blueberries, right? No, hold on—blackberries, I think. And . . . lavender? Lavender, for . . . excitement? I think there's an old saying that lavender is good for something like that."

That sounded familiar. "Just a second." I took the book out of my backpack and flipped through the beginning again. "This isn't in alphabetical order, or any kind of order at all. Oh, here it is. *Lavender brings luck and adventure for those who choose to embrace it*," I said. "You were right."

"What book is that?" asked Vik. "It looks ancient."

"I just found it. It's got all these drawings and descriptions of herbs and spices."

"Cool! Can I take a look?"

I handed him the book, and he spent the next few minutes

leafing through it, but then returned to eating the cupcake.

"I love this. It's so different from the usual boring things people make. Although . . ." He took another bite. "I have a suggestion." He studied the cupcake. "The cake is light, fluffy, and complex, and the creamy, tangy frosting complements it so well. It might be even better with an edible garnish. Like a sugared mint leaf." He took another bite. "Or a sugared violet," he said with his mouth half full. "That would be lovely."

I gaped in surprise. He was right. It *would* be lovely! I'd thought about topping them with fresh, mouth-puckering black-berries, but these suggestions were so much more elegant. This kid shouldn't be hanging out in trees; he should be working in a restaurant. Or a bakery. Or writing reviews for a newspaper.

"It's the best cupcake I've ever had. Sorry for my initial reaction—I've had a startling number of truly terrible desserts lately." His gaze flicked to the other cupcake. "You should eat yours."

"Okay." My cupcake had changed him from grumpy to giddy in just a few minutes! I giggled and peeled back the wrapper.

"Now." Vik's eyes glinted. "Tell me the story."

"What do you mean?"

"The story of how you came up with this delicious cup-cake. I know you have one." He finished his cake and looked at me expectantly.

I took a bite and thought for a moment. Puffy Fay had a story for every recipe in his book—something about the inspiration for the food, or how he enjoyed it with people he loved. I cleared my throat. "I first made these last year, for my friend Emma's birthday. She lives—well, she lived—next door to me, and we've been best friends since before we could walk. Her favorite color is yellow. She's a sunny person—she loves jokes, and we used to laugh together every day. My favorite color is purple, so I thought about how I could bring the two together. And I had all this lavender in my garden begging to be used, so I put everything together and . . . this is what happened."

Vik had closed his eyes. "I can see it. But . . . did something happen to your friend?"

"She moved to Australia a couple of weeks ago."

Vik opened his eyes again. "That came through in your baking. What a great friend she was, and how much you miss her."

Speechless once more, I stared at the cupcake in my hand. I took another bite and chewed slowly. Could someone *taste* friendship?

"You should totally enter the contest," I said. "You know so much."

Vik shook his head. "I just like baking for fun. I don't need anyone to give me a prize for it."

"I bet you don't care because you've already won a bunch of

prizes. I've never won anything, ever."

Vik resumed looking through the book while I continued eating my cupcake. "Did you know there are stories in here?" he asked.

"No, I found that book just before I heard your song, so I didn't get a chance to read much."

He turned a few pages in the book, then stopped. "Here's a cool one," he said. "Want to hear?"

"Go ahead." I adjusted my seat on the branch. "Emma and I used to tell each other stories all the time."

Vik sat cross-legged and leaned over the book. "Once there was a girl with flowers in her hair. Flowers were what she knew and loved. She tended her garden and grew blossoms beyond all imagination, with colors bold and bright, and colors soft and yielding. But she felt that no one truly understood her." His voice was low and pleasant, and I could picture the girl from his story as if she were sitting in the tree with us.

He continued, "And then the girl met the Woodland Queen, the Queen of The Wild, who knows everyone's deepest desires."

Vik's eyes sparkled in the sunlight filtering through the golden leaves.

"To join the Court, the girl needed to give something worthy of the Queen. She offered the Queen the Love Blossom, with trailing vines and petals that blushed purple with love's wound. And the Queen was pleased, but asked for something more.

"Next, she offered the Queen the Herb of Refreshment, with tiny white buds and blue-green leaves that restored the senses and cleared confusion. And the Queen was pleased, but still she asked for something more.

"So one starry night when the moon was full, the girl presented the Queen with her heart's work, a perfect pink flower that resembled a tiny woodland dancer. It was something that only she in all the world could have wrought. And the Queen bestowed upon the girl a trowel of willow wood, unmatched in coaxing fragile roots to find their way. And so the girl was welcomed to the Court of The Wild and resides there still, tending to endless gardens that never cease to delight."

It was quiet; it felt like everything in the woods had stopped to listen to the story. "That's beautiful," I said. I finished my cupcake and licked the tangy frosting off my fingers. "Her heart's work. And the Queen gave her a special gift to help her with her garden! I wonder, was it magical?"

"Probably." Vik closed the book. "I bet it wouldn't make just anyone a master gardener, but it was the perfect tool for that girl."

What tool would the Queen give me? I wondered. *A whisk? A spatula?*

I glanced at my watch. It was getting late, and I'd promised

Mom I'd help with dinner. But I didn't want to leave. I thought for a moment. Mom would be happy I'd already made a new friend this summer. I didn't think she'd mind. And besides, it would be fun to have someone my age to talk to.

"Want to come home with me? We're having friends over for dinner. Would your aunt Tanya be okay with that?"

"I'd love to," Vik said. "As long as I'm home before dark, it should be fine."

I packed away the cupcake carrier and the book and hoisted my backpack. I looked down and hesitated. "Do you think it's safe?" The snorting had stopped, but who knew whether the boar had really gone?

"Yes," said Vik. He began to climb down.

"But how do you know?"

"Simple. We ate your lavender cupcakes. Remember? Lavender is for *luck*."

As we started on the path home, I found a large rock and picked it up.

Just in case.

CHAPTER 8

HONEYSUCKLE COOKIES

Every tree seemed leafier, every flower brighter, and every fleeting scent drew me here and there before vanishing into the humid air. I knew we should hurry home, especially since the boar might be nearby, but we couldn't help strolling off the path.

We came to a clearing and stopped. Dark green vines with oblong leaves and purple flowers in pairs grew everywhere—under our feet, around tree trunks and small shrubs, in a circle at least thirty feet wide. Fat green-eyed insects buzzed lazily around the blossoms. A heavy, luscious fragrance filled the air.

"Honeysuckle!" I plucked a couple of flowers and took a moment to appreciate the dark purple petals that faded to lavender and then white at their base. I brought one to my nose and sniffed. My cousins had a vine like this at their house in India. But these blossoms were gargantuan, each one the size of my palm.

I pinched off the green cap that held the petals together, pulled on the little string that was exposed, and tasted the small glob of nectar that glistened at the end. My mouth burst with sweetness. Vik did the same and beamed at me.

Some time later, when I found myself competing for the flowers with an irritated-looking hummingbird, I decided it was time to stop. I had an idea.

"Help me, will you?" Vik and I gathered a bunch of flowers, threw them in my backpack, and raced the rest of the way home.

Mom was working in the kitchen. "Mimi! There you are," she said, drying her hands on a kitchen towel. "Who's this?"

"I'm Vik." Vik placed his hands together and bowed. "Very nice to meet you."

"Namaskar, Vik," said Mom, putting her hands together.

"Vik's visiting for the summer. He's been all over the world," I said.

"Are you from India?"

Vik nodded. "Originally, yes. My family is from a small village in Tamil Nadu not far from the border with Karnataka."

Mom raised her eyebrows. "So is mine. Where are you from?"

I tried to silently signal Mom not to monopolize Vik, but she wasn't paying attention.

"Kothur," said Vik.

"Amazing! Our ancestors are from the same place. My family moved to Bangalore in my grandparents' time, though . . ."

"*Mom*," I said.

Mom winked at me and smiled. "In any case, I hope you're staying for dinner. I've made some old favorites."

"That would be great," said Vik.

"Can we help?" I asked.

"Thanks, sweetie, but everything's already done. We'll have watermelon for dessert, and I have some kulfi in the freezer."

"We're going to bake with these—we found them in the woods." I unzipped my backpack and took out a few flowers. They smelled sweet enough to cause cavities.

"Honeysuckle! How wonderful. And wow, these are the biggest blossoms I've ever seen." Mom took one apart and tasted the nectar like an expert. "Do you need help?"

"No, we're just going to experiment."

"Okay, sweetie. Then I'll go and answer a few emails, but I'll be back down soon." Mom kissed the top of my head and went upstairs.

Vik and I got to work.

I preheated the oven, pulled out a cookbook, *The Cookie*

Connection, and assembled ingredients: flour, butter, sugar, salt, baking soda, honey, cinnamon.

"I'm basing this on a honey cookie recipe," I said to Vik as I flipped to the recipe. "What else do you think would be good in them?"

"How about walnuts?" Vik asked. I grabbed a handful, and we toasted them in a pan and then chopped them up.

After some experimentation, we put hot water in a measuring cup and dissolved the honeysuckle nectar by swirling the stems around.

When we were done with all the flowers, I tasted the golden liquid; it was sweet and fragrant. There wasn't much of the solution, though—we'd have to make a very small batch if we wanted the honeysuckle to be noticeable.

We measured out the dry ingredients and Vik whisked in a pinch of ground cloves while I creamed the butter with the sugar, and then added honey. We poured in the honeysuckle nectar and combined everything. Vik and I tasted the dough: it was sweet and spicy, the flavors in perfect harmony.

"These are so good, they're going to cause trouble," said Vik.

"What's that supposed to mean?"

"People will fight each other to eat them first."

"Ha!"

I closed my eyes. I didn't want to face a night of Riya and

Jules antagonizing each other and Fletcher being mean to Cole. *If only these cookies could make people love each other. Be sweet and kind. No bickering sisters, no mean boys.*

We rolled little balls, dipped them in superfine sugar, put them on parchment-lined cookie sheets, popped them in the oven, and set the timer. I grabbed a notebook and pen and wrote down the recipe while it was still fresh in my mind. If these cookies turned out as good as I thought, I'd make some more and take them to Mrs. T. In terms of baking, Vik had done more to help me in a few hours than Dad had done in a week.

"So, Mimi, about these delightful honeysuckle cookies," Vik said in an excellent Puffy Fay imitation. He *was* a fan! "Tell me the story behind them."

"Why, yes, Chef Fay, I'd love to," I said.

"Please, call me Puffy," said Vik.

I snickered. "Well, you see, Puffy, my friend Vik and I found this beautiful honeysuckle in the woods, and it inspired me to rethink my honey cookies. Vik had the brain wave to add walnuts and cloves so the bitter and spicy flavors would enhance the sweetness of the honey and the wildness of the honeysuckle."

"Yes? Do tell me more," said Puffy-Vik. He rested his chin in his hands and looked at me intently.

"I hoped the sweet cookies would inspire people to be more

loving and kind to each other. And they did, and we had the most pleasant dinner ever in our house."

"Cookies for world peace? That's quite an accomplishment for such a young person," said Puffy-Vik.

"Well, I try," I said with a small bow.

"I could use a bright young mind like you. How would you like to work together? You could guest star on my show, and we could collaborate on a cookbook. We could go on a world tour and do cooking demonstrations."

"That would be a dream come true, Chef Fay," I said. Then I sighed. "Forget about meeting Puffy Fay. First I have to figure out how to get to the next round of the While Away's contest."

"You're clearly an awesome baker. What's the matter?"

"I can't figure out what to make that fits the theme of *leaves*."

Vik snorted. "Well, that's a weird theme."

"Right? Anyway, my leaf-shaped sugar cookies didn't go over well."

"You might be overthinking it. Bake what you like to bake, and figure out afterward how it fits with leaves."

"Maybe," I said.

The timer went off, and I peeked through the oven door. The cookies were ready.

I took the sheet out and set it on the counter. The cookies were golden brown and smelled of spices, with a faint flowery note of honeysuckle.

"It's too bad we didn't have more honeysuckle," said Vik. "Only a dozen cookies. But they smell incredible."

"Try one," I said.

But then Dad walked into the kitchen, scanning the counters for snacks.

I stood in front of the cookies and shielded them from view until he'd grabbed a jar of peanuts and left the room.

Mom came in. "Ready for dinner?" she asked.

Vik and I set the dining room table as everyone else trickled in. Cole and Fletcher had come, but unfortunately for Henry, Lily couldn't make it. The older kids said hi to Vik and me and then proceeded to ignore us completely. They sat at one end of the table while Vik and I sat at the other, snickering at Dad's relentless peanut munching while Mom finished up in the kitchen.

"Riya, we could use your help choreographing some of the more complicated scenes in the play. You have such an eye for movement. It's remarkable how awkward some of the cast is." Fletcher ruffled his hair and gave Riya a coy look.

"I doubt you need me. Your director is great," said Riya with a laugh.

Henry furrowed his brow. "Yeah. Don't complicate things."

"How's your summer going, Cole? Still working on robotics?" Jules asked in a weird high-pitched voice.

"Yeah," said Cole, staring at the table, then at Riya.

"Robots? How droll, Cory," Fletcher said.

"It's *Cole*. Stop being such a pig!" Jules said.

"Jules. Chill." Riya returned to tapping on her phone.

Jules spluttered, "*Chill*? Why don't you—"

"Here we go," said Mom. My mouth watered as she laid a serving bowl full of steaming kothu chapati on the table. It was a delicious dish made from sliced and shredded Indian flatbreads, or chapatis, garlic, ginger, vegetables, spices, and tonight, Mom's famous chicken curry. The shredded bread resembled noodles—crispy on the edges and full of flavor from the sauce soaked into them. "Can someone help me bring out the rest?"

Henry and I went into the kitchen with Mom and returned with green beans with coconut, lemon rice, and a salad called kosambari, made with cucumber, tomatoes, and soaked dal. Riya and Jules continued bickering, but they quieted down once Mom came in with a bowl of creamy homemade yogurt.

"This looks delicious," said Vik to Mom. "Thanks so much for letting me join you."

"It's our pleasure," said Mom. "We're always happy to welcome new friends at our table." Mom winked at me, and I gave her a Mimi wink back.

It was finally time to dig in. Everyone passed bowls around until there was a traffic jam in front of Dad, who had given himself almost half the kothu chapati.

"Dad, can you please pass the bowl?" I asked. He frowned and handed it to Henry.

It was my favorite meal. The slivers of bread were full of vegetables and tender chicken, salty and chewy and the perfect amount of spicy. The green beans were sweet with pops of pungent flavor from black mustard seeds and complemented the lemony rice. The salad and yogurt cooled everything off.

Everyone stuffed themselves and raved about the food. Henry and Fletcher chatted about the play. Riya tossed her hair and got up to twirl or saunter to the kitchen to bring back napkins and refill her water glass. Jules, doing her best Riya impression, tried to toss her hair, but it didn't have the same effect in a ponytail, and her attempts at sauntering were more like stomping. Cole chewed slowly, glancing at Riya from time to time. Vik took second helpings of everything.

"It's like being home again," he said with a wistful look.

I was almost done with the deliciousness on my plate when Dad started coughing. At first everyone ignored it, but when he didn't stop, eight pairs of eyes turned toward him. Dad's face turned red, and his nose ran, and beads of sweat formed on his forehead.

"Paul, are you okay?" Mom asked.

Dad waved her away and took a sip of water. Everyone went back to eating.

I thought about the contest again. Maybe I could make a batch of macarons in the shape of a leaf? Mom's phone rang, and she gave my shoulder a squeeze as she left the room to answer it.

Then I glanced at Dad.

His face had turned reddish-purple. He looked like he was trying to smile, but it quickly turned into a grimace, and he began shaking his head. He wasn't making a sound. He stood up abruptly, knocking over his chair, and put his hands to his throat.

"He's choking!" I cried. I stood up and knocked over my own chair. "Somebody help!" My body went cold and I felt like I couldn't get enough air either.

Cole and Fletcher didn't move a muscle. Riya froze with her fork halfway to her mouth like she'd been turned to stone. Jules ran out of the room. Henry jumped up, but Vik had already raced around to stand behind Dad and stretch his arms around Dad's waist. His hands were steady as he made a fist and wrapped his other hand around it, then pushed forcefully into Dad's belly. One push, then two.

Nothing happened. Dad's eyes bulged. I held my breath and felt my head pound.

On Vik's third try, Dad coughed up a wad of food and hunched over with his hands on his thighs, taking great heaving breaths. Dad put his hands over his face for the next few moments as he wheezed and coughed hideously. Jules burst into the room with Mom.

"Paul!"

"I'm okay," Dad said in a ragged voice between coughs. Jules gaped at him. Mom rushed to Dad and rubbed his back while Vik returned to his seat.

Once it was obvious that Dad was all right, Mom spoke. "Vik, we can't thank you enough." Tears glistened in her eyes. "You saved Paul's life."

Dad nodded, holding on to the table for support.

"Where'd you learn to do that?" Henry asked.

"It's nothing," Vik said, not looking at Henry.

"Well, it's a big deal to us," said Henry. Riya and Jules nodded.

I opened my mouth, but I didn't know what to say.

CHAPTER 9

WEIRD AND WEIRDER

After a few minutes, Dad declared himself back to normal.

"Are you sure you're okay?" I asked.

"I'm fine. You guys should enjoy the rest of the night. I insist," he said with a nod. "I'm going upstairs to shower."

The rest of us cleaned up. I used a paper towel to grab the wad of bread and chicken on the floor near Dad's seat. It was a lot of food; no wonder he'd choked on it. Something was really off with Dad. He used to savor foods' flavors, but now he was just shoveling everything down.

Mom went upstairs to check on Dad. Everyone else moved to the backyard, where the sun hung low in the sky like a blazing blood orange.

"Hey, Riya, can you think about what I asked you?" Cole said, ducking his head in an effort to get her to look up.

Riya nodded absently as she grabbed one foot and stretched while looking at her phone.

Jules found the soccer ball and kicked it to Cole. "Let's kick the ball around," she said.

"Sure." Cole wiped his hands on his shorts. "I'm not that good, though."

"I'll play," Henry said.

"Me too," Vik said. "How about you, Mimi?" He took the ball, dribbled it a few feet, and booted it to me.

I stuck my foot out and miraculously managed to stop the ball. "I guess so," I said.

Jules beamed. "Anyone else?"

"I'm fine right here," said Fletcher, watching Riya, who was making a show of rising slowly onto the very tips of her toes with her arms extended gracefully.

"Pass it here," Vik said.

"You might want to back up." Jules laughed. "Mimi doesn't know her own strength sometimes."

Low blow, Jules, I thought.

Vik laughed and looked to me.

I can do this, I thought. At least there were no platters to break this time.

I held my breath and kicked the ball toward Vik. It stayed on the ground, didn't go too fast or too slow, and came within a couple of feet of where I was trying to send it.

Maybe I wasn't that bad, after all.

Vik kicked the ball to Jules, who took a step back and prepared to send it to Cole.

"Dessert!" Mom called from the porch. She made her way to the patio holding a platter of watermelon and the plate of honeysuckle cookies. The older boys swarmed around her while Vik and I brought up the rear.

"Is Dad okay?" I asked.

Mom nodded. "He's fine. He asked about dessert, but I told him he'd had enough food for tonight."

I agreed.

"These smell incredible." Cole sniffed a cookie. "What kind are they?"

"Cinnamon-honey with a twist," I said. "Vik and I added honeysuckle we found in the woods."

"*Quite over-canopied with luscious woodbine, with sweet musk-roses and with eglantine,*" said Henry, taking a couple.

"Is that hygienic?" Riya asked suspiciously. "No thanks, I'll pass." She sat at the patio table and engrossed herself in her phone again while Fletcher grabbed cookies for himself.

"Guys! Come on, let's play," said Jules, still on the grass with the soccer ball.

"How about you, Vik? Mimi?" Mom asked.

As I reached for a cookie, I felt someone brush past my shoulder and lunge for the platter. "These are the most delicious things I've ever had," said Cole as he grabbed more cookies.

"Leave some for the rest of us!" Fletcher elbowed me out of the way and snatched what was left.

And just like that, all the cookies were gone. I frowned; I hadn't even gotten a chance to try the finished product. Oh well. At least I knew what the dough tasted like.

"Well then," said Mom, shaking her head in a bemused way. "I'll leave the watermelon here. I'll be inside if you need me." Mom set the platter on the patio table with some napkins and went into the house.

"These look super, Mimi," said Henry. His phone buzzed. "It's Lily. She feels bad she couldn't make it tonight. I'll show her what she's missing." He held his phone in front of his face and clicked while he took a bite.

"Come on. Back to soccer." Vik tilted his head toward Jules, and I followed him reluctantly.

"Wow." Cole shook his shaggy head at Jules, who was kneeing the soccer ball expertly.

"Wow, what?" said Jules, bouncing the ball off an ankle.

"You're an amazing soccer player."

"Thanks, Cole," Jules said. She blushed and bounced the ball faster.

"She made varsity as a freshman, you know," Fletcher said, smoothing his blond hair behind his ear and moving to stand between Jules and Cole. "And she didn't miss a penalty kick all year. She's the most talented player the school's had in years."

"Fletcher! I didn't realize you'd noticed," said Jules, heading the ball and then catching it with her ankle.

"I notice everything about you, Jules," Fletcher said. He flipped his hair in front of his eyes again.

Jules let the ball fall to the ground and put her hand on her hip. "Yeah, sure."

Jules was right to be skeptical. Since when had Fletcher paid any attention to her?

"I haven't known you as long, but I've noticed everything about you, too, Jules," Cole said, moving around to her side. "Like the way your smile is slightly lopsided when you're thinking, and how your hair shimmers in the light. May I?" He reached out and touched Jules's dark ponytail, and she looked like he'd given her a birthday present.

"Hands off, interloper. I saw her first," Fletcher declared.

Jules clearly didn't know what to make of this, and neither did I. *Interloper?*

"Your family is so entertaining," Vik whispered. "This is better than anything on TV."

"Ha," I said half-heartedly.

Cole and Fletcher each grabbed one of Jules's hands and pulled like she was the rope in a game of tug-of-war. She looked from one to the other as they spoke to her adoringly.

When Fletcher called her "my sweet," Jules looked over to Riya, who was still seated at the patio table but was now bent to one side, stretching. Jules wrenched her hands away from the boys. "*You've* always been under Riya's thumb," she said, glaring at Fletcher. "But *you*." She turned to Cole. "How could you?"

Cole stepped back and spread his hands. "How could I what?"

"How could you mock me like this?"

"But I'm not mocking you. Oh, Jules, you're perfect, divine!" Cole tenderly clasped her hand again.

"All you've done since we met is ogle Riya. Now I'm supposed to believe you think I'm *divine*?"

"I only looked at her because I was afraid," Cole said. "Afraid that if I looked at you, you'd be able to see straight into my heart and know how I felt."

Wow. That was a wild explanation. But was it true? Why'd he wait so long to tell her?

"Halt!" Fletcher said. "I've known the lady longer, so her hand is mine."

"No, it is not! You can have the witchy dwarf over there." Cole pointed at Riya, who finished stretching her other side and smiled at Fletcher.

Jules snickered, but then looked angry and confused again. She booted the soccer ball across the yard at Riya and knocked the phone out of her hand.

"Awesome," whispered Vik.

"Hey! Watch it!" Riya reached under the table to retrieve her phone.

"How did you do it, Riya? And why?" Jules broke away from the boys and launched herself at Riya but tripped and crashed spectacularly to the ground.

Riya rolled her eyes and tossed her hair as she looked down at Jules. "What are you accusing me of now?"

Cole and Fletcher rushed to help Jules. They picked her up gently by the elbows while giving each other dirty looks.

"Jules! My jewel," Fletcher said.

"Are you all right, my goddess, my nymph?" Cole asked, his eyes wide with concern.

Nymph? I thought. I wasn't even sure if that was a compliment or not.

Jules pulled away from the boys again and sneered at Riya. "Is this your idea of a joke?"

"Do you have brain damage from heading too many balls? I don't know what you're talking about." Riya crossed her arms. "Come on, Fletcher, let's get out of here."

Fletcher shook his head. "Not after you didn't help your beautiful sister off the ground. Why should I go, when love doth press me to stay?"

Wow. No one *ever* talked to Riya like that. Especially boys.

"Let's go back to playing soccer," I pleaded. I trotted behind the table to our overgrown herb garden. The ball had landed in a patch of thyme. I inhaled the woodsy scent, and a light bulb blinked on in my head. I jogged back to Vik in a daze.

Riya was still talking to Fletcher. "Jules is fine. And she's always accusing me of something or other."

"You must deserve it," Fletcher said. "My Jules is both fair of mind and of face. Fair Jules, who more engilds the night than all yon fiery oes and eyes of light."

Engilds? Oes? Why did Fletcher and Cole suddenly sound like they were in one of Henry's plays?

"What is wrong with you?" Riya snarled at Fletcher.

"Riya, come off it, tell them to stop!" Jules cried, yanking her arm away from Cole.

"You could charge admission for this," said Vik.

"This is a spectacular argument, even for them," I whispered. "But I just had an idea—"

"Jules, please do me the honor of stepping forth from here with me tonight," Cole pleaded.

"Desist! Unhand the fair maid!" Fletcher grabbed Cole's shirt, and Cole shoved him.

"Stop blaming me for all your stupid problems! I'm going inside." Riya stalked toward the house.

"You did this! You set me up!" Jules ran after Riya and tried to tackle her, but Riya jumped away, sprinted to the porch, and crouched behind the swing.

Vik gave me a look, and I shook my head in confusion. What had gotten into everyone?

"I didn't do anything! Why don't you ask *them*?" Riya nodded at the boys, who were engaged in a kind of vertical wrestling match.

"Why are you doing this to me?" Jules's voice got thick. "Do you hate me that much?"

"Of course not! And I was trying to—never mind," said Riya, sounding close to tears herself. She whirled and scooted inside, banging the screen door as she went.

Fletcher gave a push and smirked as Cole landed on his butt. "We're finally rid of the harpy," he said. He turned to Jules. "My love, my life, my soul! Let us go!"

"I say I love thee more than he can do." Cole scrambled to stand and stepped close enough that Fletcher had to tilt his head back to look at him.

"If you say so, come here and prove it, too," said Fletcher. "Jules has no interest in such nerdiness."

"Be quiet," said Cole.

"Betwixt you and me, I'm clearly the winner. Get you gone, you minimus, of hindering knot-grass made—"

"I said shut up!" Cole shouted.

I tried to talk some sense into them. "Guys, come on, let's calm—"

Fletcher punched Cole in the stomach.

"Oof!" Cole hunched over. Jules shrieked and covered her mouth.

Wow. I thought Fletcher only *talked* like a bully. I didn't think he'd resort to actual violence.

Then, faster than I could believe, Cole socked Fletcher in the face.

We had to stop this! "Henry, help!" I called.

But Henry stood in the middle of the yard, staring at his phone.

"Stop it, both of you!" Jules said, rushing to push the two apart. "Are you okay?" she asked Fletcher.

"I'b fide, fair Jules," said Fletcher, blood oozing through his cupped hands.

I grabbed a bunch of napkins from the table and handed them to Fletcher, trying not to stare at his rapidly swelling nose. He took them from me wordlessly and tried to staunch the flow of blood.

"I want you to leave. Both of you. Now!" said Jules in a shaky voice. She swiped at her tears and raced into the house without waiting to see if they listened.

Still clutching a bloody napkin to his nose, Fletcher headed for the driveway. "I will dot forget dis, Calvin," he called as he got into his convertible.

Cole looked longingly at the back door, but there was no sign of Jules. "I'll return tomorrow to woo that fair maid," he said to no one in particular. He spun and strode into his own yard.

"Truly incredible," said Vik. "Is it like this every night?"

I shot him an exasperated look. This night had been a disaster! "We don't usually have boys fighting over my sisters. At least, not over Jules," I said. "Right, Henry?"

Henry, still remarkably silent despite all the excitement, sat on the porch stairs staring at his phone.

"Where were you? Why didn't you stop that fight?" I asked him. "Do you think Cole broke Fletcher's nose? And I've never seen Jules and Riya that mad."

No answer.

Henry was still riveted to his phone.

"Henry? What is it?" I wasn't used to him being as phone-obsessed as Riya.

"Oh no!" he said.

"What?" What else could go wrong?

Henry touched just under his right eye. "Do you see—no, it's nothing, everything's all right."

"What are you babbling about?" I peeked at his screen. It reflected his face; he was using it like a mirror.

"I thought I saw the beginning of a wrinkle, but t'was a trick of the light," said Henry. "Well, good night, young Mimi. I must away to get my beauty sleep." He jumped onto the porch and disappeared into the house.

Beauty sleep? The sun had barely set. And since when did he care about wrinkles?

I stood and pushed my hair out of my eyes. "That was the weirdest dinner ever. What got into everyone tonight?"

"Maybe it's a little midsummer magic." Vik grinned, and then squinted at the sun hovering over the horizon. "It's getting late. I should get back."

"Do you need a ride? I can ask Mom," I said.

"I can walk. I'm just on the other side of the woods."

"Are you sure? What about the boar?"

"I'll be fine," Vik said.

"So, do you want to hang out again tomorrow? In the woods, and maybe bake something again? I . . . I have an idea what to make for the contest, and I'd love to get your opinion." I held my breath.

"Definitely," said Vik.

I let my breath out.

"Should I call you?" I asked.

"Why don't we meet at the banyan tree, like today? Just whistle the tune—you know, my song."

"Cool—like a secret signal."

"Exactly. I'll be there first thing in the morning."

"Great. And Vik—thank you for today. For helping me escape the boar, and baking with me, and saving Dad's life."

Vik smiled. "You're the first friend I've made here. And I

loved baking with you. And about your dad . . ."

"Yeah?"

"I did what I had to. I know what it's like to lose a father."

And with that, he stepped away and disappeared into the woods.

CHAPTER 10

A TIME FOR THYME

The next morning, I woke up and went straight to the herb garden. I stripped a few tiny thyme leaves from a stem and crushed them between my fingers to release their potent aroma.

Leaves! I'd told Mrs. T that I loved to flavor my creations with unusual herbs and spices, but all I'd given her was a pile of bland vanilla cookies. No wonder she hadn't been impressed! And what are herbs but leaves? I cut more stems of thyme and skipped into the house. I knew what I wanted to bake. But first, I wanted to get Vik's opinion. I wrapped the thyme in paper towels and tucked it in my backpack.

Jules stumbled into the kitchen and took a yogurt from the fridge. She yawned nonstop, and dark circles bloomed under her eyes.

"What happened to you?" I asked.

"Hardly slept." She massaged her forehead and handed me her phone. I scrolled through the messages and saw that Cole had texted her all night long. "Lovely Jules, I count the minutes till we meet again," one said.

"I eventually shut it off, but then I kept dreaming it was buzzing." She yawned again. "I can barely put one foot in front of the other. I don't know how I'm supposed to do penalty kick drills with fourth graders today."

"But aren't you glad Cole's finally paying attention to you?" Even if he was acting strangely enthusiastic.

"I guess so, but it's so weird how all of a sudden he's crazy about me. I wish I could be sure it's because he actually likes me, and not because . . ."

Riya slunk in silently and seemed to suck all the sound out of the room. She filled the kettle and put it on the stove.

"Fletcher won't leave me alone, either," Jules said loudly to Riya's back. "Ugh! He's so full of himself." Jules showed me Fletcher's texts—they were a lot like Cole's. "I am true, true as the sky is blue."

Had Riya told Cole and Fletcher to pretend to be infatuated with Jules? It didn't seem like the kind of thing she'd do, or that either boy would agree to. But what else could have made two guys who were nuts about Riya one minute suddenly start fighting over Jules the next?

Jules scarfed the yogurt and filled her water bottle. "I've got to pack up my gear. See you tonight, Mimi." She shuffled into the mudroom.

The kettle whistled. Riya poured boiling water over a forlorn tea bag and took her mug to the back porch without saying a word. Even if Riya had been behind the boys' weird behavior, she seemed miserable now. She didn't even have the energy to argue with Jules.

Henry strolled in and retrieved a pint of blueberries from the fridge. "Antioxidants, Mimi," he said in a booming voice. "Excellent for the skin. And the brain." He threw a bunch of berries in his mouth and chewed while he put the rest in a bag. "Well, off I go to share my genius with some lucky kids at theater camp. Yesterday, one of the little guys asked, 'Are you THE Henry Mackson?' And I said, *Thou speak'st aright; I am that merry wanderer of the night.*"

Henry's funny Shakespeare talk was getting seriously annoying.

Dad made himself breakfast before he drove the girls to their jobs. "Mimi Mouse! Want to visit the While Away with me this afternoon? I'm going to review it for the *Comity Journal*."

"Sure," I said in surprise. So he was finally willing to make some time for me. I missed sharing foodie opinions with him.

Dad toasted four bagels and topped them with a startling combination of almond butter and pickled peppers.

"Dad, are you okay?" I asked.

"Of course, Mimi Mouse. Why do you ask?" He slurped at a stray pepper that threatened to fall out of his mouth.

"Well, you usually put lox and cream cheese on your bagel. You know, with tomato, capers, red onion."

"I'm trying new flavor combos," Dad said mid-chew. "Want a bite?"

I looked away. "No, thanks."

After Dad left I cleaned up everyone's breakfast things, shouldered my backpack, and walked to the edge of my yard. Was it too early? Would Vik already be at the banyan tree? Now that I thought about it, I wasn't quite sure how to get there. I'd never found it in all my years of wandering through the woods with Emma.

I scanned the woods: no boars in sight. I stepped onto the forest trail and followed it to my hangout.

There, sitting at the top of the lean-to, was the bird. Now that I could see it up close, I realized it had even more colors than I had seen earlier—the lower part of its belly was red, as was the underside of its stubby tail. The black stripe extended over both eyes like a tiny mask. It was beautiful.

"What kind of bird are you?" I asked out loud. "I've never seen anything like you."

"*Wheeet-tieu*," it called with its little head thrown back. "*Wheeet-tieu*." Then it turned sideways and stared at me.

There was no doubt: it was staring at me.

It hopped off the tarp to the ground, then regarded me again. I took a few steps toward it, and to my surprise it stayed put. No bird had ever let me get this close.

It continued hopping on the path, always a few feet ahead, looking back often as if to make sure I followed.

It brought me to two hemlocks leaning on each other like a pair of tired green giants, then flew away.

"Now what?" I said.

A breeze ruffled my hair, and with it floated the song.

Vik stood at the base of the banyan tree playing his pipe like he didn't have a care in the world. "No boars today?"

I shook my head. "Thank goodness. Just a small bird that seems to like me. I've never seen one like it—it has a yellow chest, red belly, green wings, and a black mask."

"A pitta? They're smart little birds. It must know you're a kindred spirit, someone who loves the woods."

I laughed. "Well, it led me right along until I heard your song. I'm glad you played it, or I would never have found you. I still have no idea how to get here on my own."

"I bet you'll have the way memorized in no time," said Vik. He rubbed his hands together. "What would you like to do today?"

"First things first. I wanted to show you my idea." I pulled the bundle of thyme from my bag. "Here."

Vik sniffed appreciatively. "You're going to bake with this?"

"Yes. Last night, it finally occurred to me that herbs are *leaves*. And I have a fantastic recipe for chocolate chunk thyme cookies."

"Sounds delicious! But—" He snapped his fingers. "I know a bank where some wild thyme grows. It might be even better. Want to see?"

"Definitely." Vik was the perfect foodie partner! Who else noticed wild herbs in the forest?

We skirted the pond for a while and then took a path farther into the woods. We passed through patches of fragrant greenery and berry-bright bushes until we came to a sunny, relatively treeless patch with lots of low plants and flowers. The whole area smelled heavenly, and when I looked closer, I saw why.

The ground was covered in herbs.

"Do you have that book with you?" asked Vik.

"The Book," I said with a laugh. "Capital *T*, capital *B*. Of course I do."

We walked among the different plants and by using The Book, we did our best to identify them and understand how to use them. Some were easy—spearmint, "for refreshment, strength, and healing," and rosemary, "for remembrance, and the prevention of nightmares." We also found a swathe of sage, which could be used "to cultivate wisdom and intelligence." When I came across a bunch of plants with dark green leaves and tiny white flowers, it took us quite a while to identify it by its drawing in The Book: gotu kola, an herb that could "restore the senses and clear confusion."

"Oh, look at this one," I said. "*Saffron, for success.* I should probably bake with that."

"If only it grew here," said Vik.

Finally, on the bank of a small stream, we found gigantic thyme stems, almost two feet tall and topped with plump clusters of purple flowers. "What's thyme good for?" I asked Vik as I plucked a dozen stems and inhaled their herbaceous scent.

"*Thyme attracts affection, loyalty, and the goodwill of others,*" read Vik, "*and can foster strength and courage when needed.*"

"That's exactly what I need—courage," I said. "And the While Away could certainly use some goodwill and loyalty."

"Then you've already chosen the perfect herb," said Vik. "Now all you need to do is create your masterpiece."

I wiped the sweat from my face. "Want a drink?" I asked.

We sat with our backs against a big maple and passed my thermos of limeade back and forth.

"So, Vik," I said.

"Yes?"

"About . . . about last night. What you said right before you left."

"I know what it's like to lose a father."

"Is it true? Did your dad die?"

Vik nodded once. "My dad and my mom. From an illness that nearly killed me, too. Aunt Tanya's been looking after me since I was very young."

"I'm so sorry. Do—do you have any brothers and sisters?"

"I had an older sister. She was already married and had a family of her own when my parents died. And then she died, too, of the same illness. Half the village died."

"That's awful!" I couldn't imagine losing my entire family like that. I'd never met anyone who was an orphan. I didn't know what to say.

Vik looked at me like he'd just remembered I was there. "You have a wonderful family."

I snorted. "Wonderful, if you don't mind people arguing all the time. And everyone's always giving me advice because I fail at everything."

"You're obviously great at baking."

I shook my head. "Everyone's happy to eat my stuff, but I'm not even good enough to win a Golden Leaf on my first try. Henry, Riya, and Jules are *famous* in Comity—the best actor, the beautiful dancer, and the soccer star. And they're all musical, too—Henry plays the piano and guitar, Jules plays the drums, and Riya sings—while the music genes completely skipped me. Anyway, they're all so busy being the best at everything that they forget about me. Sometimes I feel like . . . like I don't belong with them. Like I'm in the wrong family."

There. I'd said it. I held my breath and steeled myself for Vik's advice, which I was sure would be like Mom's, Dad's, and even Emma's. *Of course you belong. They're your family, and they love you. They don't mean to make you feel bad.*

"I know what you mean," said Vik, plucking idly at a stem of thyme. When he had picked off all the leaves, he let it fall to the ground. "Hey, enough thinking about sad stuff. Want to read another story?"

"Sure."

Vik leafed through The Book again. "Here's a fun one." He leaned forward. "Once there was a girl who was a weaver," he said in a low voice. "Weaving was what she knew and loved. She wove fabrics to delight the senses, fabrics that shimmered and shined, fabrics that comforted and cuddled. But she felt that no one truly understood her."

I closed my eyes and pictured the girl from the story.

Vik continued. "And then she met the Woodland Queen, the Queen of The Wild, who knows everyone's deepest desires.

"To join the Court, the girl needed to give something worthy of the Queen. So the girl offered the Queen a luxurious cloak of softest goat's hair, lustrous and just the shade of winter's first snow. And the Queen was pleased, but she asked for something more.

"Next, she brought the Queen a gown of glimmering gossamer silk, reflecting the light of the stars that shone when it was woven. And the Queen was pleased, but still she asked for something more.

"So one stifling day when the sun burned the sky, the girl presented the Queen with her heart's work, a clever basket made of marsh reeds holding water from an icy spring. It was something that only she in all the world could have wrought. And the Queen presented her with an ebony loom, unmatched in weaving the most intricate fabrics. And so the girl was welcomed to the Court of The Wild and resides there still, weaving fabrics both humble and ethereal."

Humble and ethereal. Now that was something to think about.

And another magical gift! If I ever met the Queen, what would she give me? And what would I give her?

I stood. "We'd better get home and start baking. I told Dad I'd go with him to the While Away this afternoon. Want to come?"

Vik jerked his head back, and his eyes widened. "Sorry, Mimi, I can't come today. I'm—I'm busy this afternoon."

Why did he seem so startled? "Don't you want to bake the chocolate-thyme cookies with me?" I asked.

"I can't." He looked genuinely disappointed. "But I'll be around tomorrow."

I'd have to settle for that. "Same time, same place?"

"Absolutely. Tell you what—I'll send you off with a song."

And Vik pulled out his pipe and played his beautiful song. It followed me the whole way home. And I didn't hear a single snort.

It had been a perfect morning in the woods. Hopefully, the baking would go just as well.

CHAPTER 11

BACK AT THE WHILE AWAY

I got to work as soon as I got home. I creamed butter and sugar, then added eggs and vanilla. I sifted in flour, baking soda, sea salt, and two heaping tablespoons of finely chopped wild thyme leaves. *These are truly from my heart,* I thought as I sprinkled the fragrant herbs. *I wish Mrs. T, and the While Away, nothing but success.* I figured it was hard to run a business given all the failing restaurant shows I'd watched on Food TV. After everything was mixed well, I stirred in chocolate chunks and the zest of a tangerine for brightness.

After putting the cookies in the oven, I washed my mixing bowls and spoons and tried to distract myself from my nerves. Would these cookies earn me a Golden Leaf? I didn't think I'd have the guts to try a third time. Finally, the timer went off, and I took three pans of cookies out of the oven. They smelled fresh, green, chocolaty, and citrusy. After the cookies had cooled, I tasted one. Now, *this* was how I liked to bake. The sea salt set off the sweetness of the chocolate, and the tangerine zest woke up all the flavors. The thyme was subtle but definitely noticeable. They were good. Really good.

For the first time in a long while, I felt brave.

I broke out in a sweat as Dad parked the car and we walked to the While Away. I kept telling myself to calm down, but my body didn't want to listen. I was extra-anxious to be visiting the café with Dad, who'd been acting so weird. Would he eat half the store and not even notice what the food tasted like? I was grateful, though, that he finally wanted to spend time with me. And I looked forward to seeing sweet Peaseblossom again. I gripped my cookie container and hurried along beside him.

We passed the snack shop, the Salt Shaker, which had a slow-moving line that snaked around the block.

"Hi, Darla," I said to a girl with glasses and stringy brown hair.

"Oh, hi, Mimi," she said.

"This place must be excellent, if it's worth waiting in this line."

"Their food is ridiculously good," said Darla's mom, an extremely fit woman who always wore yoga pants. "It's a tiny place inside, barely enough room to fit two people. You have to know your entire order and say it as quickly as possible, or they won't serve you."

Dad laughed. "You've got to be kidding. That might work in Boston, but in Comity?"

"I'd stand in line for an hour just for the fries and onion rings, but they're nothing compared to the potato chips," said Darla's mom.

"Really?" I asked. How could they make chips that much better than what I could buy in a bag?

"They're amazing. Like magic." Darla gazed at the door like a potato chip might try to escape and she'd be able to grab it.

I giggled and glanced at Dad. To my surprise, he was rubbing his chin and looking back at the line like he was contemplating standing in it.

"Dad. The While Away. The *review*," I said, tugging at his sleeve. "Bye, Darla. Bye, Mrs. Moody."

Dad kept looking back but allowed me to lead him away.

As we passed the front of the line, I could hear voices from inside the snack store.

"Three bags of the Super Green Chips, please, sir," a boy asked.

"The Super Green, for athletes everywhere," said a voice that creaked like branches in the wind.

For *athletes*? Jules wouldn't touch potato chips within forty-eight hours of a game, saying that they slowed her down too much. And Riya hadn't eaten anything fried in years.

Dad held the door for me as we entered the café. It was a little busier today. The dreamy music still played, and the café still had that wild smell. There were new shimmering table-cloths on the tables and iridescent curtains in the windows.

A waitress greeted us. It wasn't Peaseblossom, though.

This waitress was ready for Halloween in the middle of June. She was tall and thin, with dark skin and asymmetrical black hair with gray tips. She had at least five piercings in each ear, and a nose ring. She wore thick combat boots, a tiny black skirt, and a poncho that looked like it was made from spiderwebs.

She spotted Dad and sighed. "And will it be the usual for you?" she asked.

Had he eaten here before?

"I'm here on official business this time," said Dad. "I'll need to sample everything." He cleared his throat and stood up taller. "I'm writing a review for the *Comity Journal*."

The waitress raised her eyebrows and nodded at me. "And now you'll tell me I must feed her, too?"

"I'm his daughter." I held up my container of cookies. "I

have something to show Mrs. T. For—for the contest. Can you please tell her Mimi is here?"

"Oh, Mimi's here! Let's give a cheer." The waitress rolled her heavy-lidded eyes. "Won't win the contest, I sadly fear," she said under her breath. She turned and stomped to the back office.

Well, that was rude. And rhyming wasn't nearly as charming when it was sarcastic. I turned to Dad, but he wasn't even looking in my direction.

"Come over here, Mimi. This is my favorite table," said Dad, steering me to one with a view of the woods.

"I thought you hadn't eaten here yet," I said.

"Oh, I've stopped here a few times after my runs," said Dad. He grinned and rubbed his tummy like a little kid.

"I'm going to check out the pastry case," I said.

"Okay, but they're going to bring us some of everything," he called after me.

Peaseblossom greeted me from behind the counter as I put down my cookie container.

"Dear lovely Mimi, what have you brought today?" she asked with a smile.

"Chocolate-thyme cookies with fresh citrus zest," I said.

"My mistress even now comes o'er this way." Peaseblossom gave a deep curtsy as Mrs. T emerged from the back office wearing a green dress the shade of first spring leaves.

"Mimi Mackson! You've returned." Mrs. T inclined her head gracefully and examined me with her bright green eyes. "Have you brought me something from your heart?"

"I think so," I said, opening the container.

She selected a cookie and sniffed it in rapid, shallow bursts like an extremely elegant rabbit. "Quite lovely," she said. "I think I can detect . . ." She took a small bite. "Thyme, correct? And orange? How unexpected." She quickly devoured the rest of the cookie.

"Thyme, and tangerine. I told you I like to combine interesting ingredients."

She gave me a swift, piercing look. "Methinks this one will save us all from ruin."

"I'm sorry?"

"Mimi, this is extraordinary. Peaseblossom, try one."

Peaseblossom shook her head. "My—"

"Try one, P. I *insist*," said Mrs. T.

Peaseblossom took a cookie with a shaking hand. She nibbled delicately, and then, her eyes wide with surprise, ate the rest in two bites.

"We'll give out free samples, don't you think?" said Mrs. T.

"Samples? Of my cookies? But—"

"These are *just* what we need at the While Away. Don't you agree, P?"

Peaseblossom nodded, making the pink flower in her hair tremble.

"Come sit down, dear Mimi. We'll let you have a variety of treats—no charge, of course—while we hand out your *stupendous* cookies."

"I should sit over there, with my—"

A plate crashed. Dad had knocked something off his table, now overrun with desserts. He didn't seem to care, though, and kept eating. "Mmph," he said, waving at me.

"Oh. *He's* here," said Mrs. T. "I do hope he doesn't choke again. At least, not before he's paid."

Apparently, Dad had been choking in a variety of places.

"Um, that's my dad."

"*That's* your father? Food writer of repute?"

I nodded. "He's here today to review the café for the newspaper."

Mrs. T looked back and forth between us a couple of times and seemed to recognize the resemblance. "I see," she said. "I must go greet him properly, and see he has all he needs." She hastened to Dad, her dress floating behind her like a cloud. I followed as quickly as I could. The lady sure could move; her slippers barely touched the ground.

As we approached Dad, I noticed what was left on his table: snickerdoodles, linzer squares, brownies, oatmeal-raisin cookies, coconut cupcakes, and a crème brûlée. They were some of Puffy Fay's signature desserts.

"So you did get Puffy Fay's cookbook," I said.

Mrs. T briefly furrowed her eyebrows. "Indeed, my dear.

How did you come to know?"

"Those are all desserts from the first chapters. I told you they'd be good."

Mrs. T sighed. "They're good, but I need *brilliant*." She addressed Dad. "Welcome, Mr. Mackson."

"Call me Paul," said Dad, revealing a mouth full of half-chewed snickerdoodles.

"I hope you are enjoying yourself." Mrs. T gazed at him intently despite the gross globs of wet crumbs on his chin.

"Oh, yes." Dad sprayed bits of cookie all over his shirt as he talked. "You wouldn't have any potato chips, would you? It's good to get a break from the sweet stuff sometimes."

"Potato chips?" Mrs. T winced like she'd gotten a mouthful of wasabi. "Certainly not!" She rooted me to the spot with a scathing look. "You haven't been to that *horrible* snack shop, have you, Mimi?"

I shook my head.

"Not yet, but it's on my list," Dad said, reaching for a brownie and downing half of it with a single bite.

"Mimi, Paul, you're such discerning . . . people," said Mrs. T, nudging a plate away from the edge of the table. "Don't you agree that sweets are infinitely better than salty snacks?" The green intensity of her gaze made me slightly dizzy.

I loved desserts—in fact, I was obsessed with them. But everyone needs a break from sweets sometimes. I didn't want

to upset her more, though, so I nodded.

"Of course sweets are my favorite," said Dad in a sugar-addled voice. He reached for a napkin and blotted his lips. Unfortunately, he missed most of the crumbs around his mouth; splotches of brownie had joined the snickerdoodle crumbs to make a kind of revolting cookie beard. Dad pointed to the decimated pile of desserts on the table. "Especially since all of this is free, because I'm a member of the press writing a review." He scarfed the other half of the brownie.

I wanted to look away, but I couldn't. Why was he being such an obnoxious mess in front of Mrs. T? And I could have sworn I saw a glimmer of purple in his eyes again. I rubbed my own eyes. Was I imagining things?

"Ah, yes," said Mrs. T. Her eyes widened, and a slow flush crept up her neck. "Well, I look forward to reading your piece."

Dad jotted something in his notebook. "It should be out next Thursday. I've got a tight deadline, so if you'll excuse me, I'll go back to my research." He started in on the crème brûlée.

"Mimi, come to my office, please," said Mrs. T, laying a surprisingly heavy hand on my shoulder. "I'd like to have a word."

I broke out in a sweat again as I followed her. Was Mrs. T so completely disgusted with Dad that I wouldn't get a Golden Leaf?

When we arrived at the office, Mrs. T took a seat in the velvet chair behind the desk and motioned for me to sit on the tree stump stool again. I perched there and chewed a strand of hair.

She reached into a drawer and pulled out another golden box. "May I offer you another chocolate, Mimi?"

"No thanks," I said, twisting my sweaty hands together.

"Did you eat the last one I gave you? Or did you give it to your father?" she asked softly.

How did she know? I gulped. "It was very generous of you, but I was so full that day, and I knew Dad would enjoy it."

"Did you look at the chocolate? Did you remove it from the box, I mean?" She leaned forward and scrutinized me.

"Yes—and it was beautiful. I loved the tiny purple flowers and the gold dust sprinkled on top. It looked like a little jewel. I hoped Dad would love it. As a food critic, he can be quite picky. But he thought it was delicious."

Mrs. T tilted her head and stared past my ear like she was trying to work out a difficult math problem. After a few seconds, the most beautiful smile spread across her face, like spring had returned after a long, snowy winter.

"Mrs. T?"

She stopped looking so distracted, but the smile remained. "Yes, Mimi?"

"I'd love to learn how to do decoration work like that. Would you teach me, sometime? And—and have I made it to the next round of the contest?"

"Of course, my dear Mimi, of course!" Her lovely eyes twinkled. "Here you are, my dear." She gently laid something in front of me. "You truly deserve this." She looked at me like I was the only person in the whole world.

The Golden Leaf glowed warmly in the light. I had made it to the second round! My chest puffed up like a buttery brioche, and I blinked back tears. "Thank you so much, Mrs. T."

I turned the leaf over and found another poem:

> *Oh, leaves and flowers glorious to behold,*
> *Oh, hearty nuts and sweet, refreshing fruits!*
> *We'd never hear your precious story told,*
> *Without the strong, deep nourishment of _____.*

Bring your Second Round entry by 9 a.m. on Saturday, June 23!
A special judge will choose THREE to compete immediately
afterward in the Bake-Off!

Another poem! Okay, this word had to rhyme with *fruits*. Something that was strong, and deep, and had to do with plants.

"Roots," I said.

Mrs. T smiled at me affectionately. "Yes, my brilliant girl. I'd so love to see more of you. Do visit us again, and soon. Tomorrow, perhaps? And bring more cookies if you can."

I hesitated. Was she serious?

"Of course, of course, you're busy, I'm sure. But do say you'll try," she said.

I laughed. "Sure. As Puffy Fay always says, the best way to avoid baker's block is to keep baking. I'm not going to let up before June twenty-third."

"Puffy Fay . . . you do love him, don't you?"

"Of course. He's not just the best pastry chef to come from Comity," I said. "He's the best pastry chef in the world."

Mrs. T looked away for a moment, and then snapped her fingers and leaned closer. "Mimi, can you keep a secret?"

There was a knock at the door. "Mrs. T? The crowd in here is growing rather large. It's very urgent that you come take charge," came Peaseblossom's worried voice.

"I'm sorry. I must go." Mrs. T looked at me regretfully and opened the office door. "But come by tomorrow. We'll be making an announcement. For now, please join your father and enjoy the best the While Away has to offer."

I carefully folded the leaf, put it in my pocket, and went to Dad, who was still gorging himself.

I chose a linzer cookie off a plate at the edge of the table. Like everything at the While Away, it looked perfect, with dark, glossy raspberry preserves nestled in an almond cookie sandwich with the barest dusting of confectioners' sugar. I tasted. It was good, but if I had to critique it I'd say that the cookie itself was a bit dense, and it was obvious the preserves were store-bought instead of freshly made. Even using Puffy Fay's recipes, they weren't executing them perfectly. They really could use my help. Maybe, if I won the contest, they might take me on as an intern, and I could teach Peaseblossom about flavors? And they could help me learn all about presentation and publicity. But I wasn't sure whether Mom and Dad would let me do that. They'd already signed me up for summer camp in July. I sighed and decided to tell Peaseblossom to get *The Cupcake Codex* and *Tutti Fruity: All About Fruit in Baking* as resources.

Voices rose in the café around us.

"Mrs. T, we'll be back with the whole family. And all our friends. And any strangers we can convince," said a mom with two young daughters. "What a delightful café!"

"Another round of cupcakes over here!" came a man's voice.

"Do you have any more of those fantastic chocolate chunk cookies?" said a woman.

"Now, now, dear customers, I told you we were out. But we have lots of other delicious treats, never fear. Call your friends! Call your family! Tell all you know to come to the While Away Café!"

In the time it had taken me to eat half a cookie, the line at the pastry counter had grown so long that it stretched to the door.

Dad ate up the last bits of a coconut cupcake, made a note,

and picked up my discarded linzer cookie. I had a terrifying thought: What if Dad trashed the While Away in his review? Would they still let me compete? I tried to read what Dad had written in his notebook, but he snapped it closed and moved it to the other side of the table.

"No peeking. You'll have to wait for the review like everyone else. I can't tell you all my secrets, can I?" said Dad.

I sighed. I wondered what Mrs. T had almost told me in her office. Did the secret have anything to do with Dad?

"For you, Mr. Mackson, a gift from Mrs. T," came a familiar voice. Like a malevolent spirit with perfect hair, Kiera Jones set down a chocolate box. "Do you need anything else?"

Dad shook his head and kept writing as he popped open the box and downed the gold-dusted chocolate.

"I spend a lot of time here, helping out," Kiera said in answer to my unasked question. "Hope I'll see you at the Bake-Off." Kiera gave me a snarky smile and tossed her shiny curls. "That is, if you've managed to earn a Golden Leaf by then."

"I'll be there." I waved my Golden Leaf at her.

"How nice," said Kiera, not looking pleased at all. "Of course, I'll be spending my time until then baking *and* perfecting my look." She fluttered her eyelashes and smirked.

"It's a baking contest, not a beauty pageant," I said, surprising myself.

Kiera cackled. "You're right! I've been learning *so* much the past few weeks. In fact, Mrs. T says that I'll be the one to beat. Well, good luck, 1 guess. See you soon!" She scrunched her nose like a rat and pranced back to the counter.

CHAPTER 12

THE SONG

Kiera Jones was the least of my worries. At home, each day dangled on the brink of disaster. Jules and Riya filled the house with such silent misery that I wished they would yell at each other like they used to. Jules turned her phone off permanently and started biting her nails again. She stopped going into the yard to practice her footwork after Cole cornered her and professed his love three days in a row.

Riya spent all her free time at the dance studio. When she was home, she barely talked to anyone, and a cloud of gloom followed her everywhere.

Fletcher (whose nose had returned to its normal size) showed up every afternoon asking for Jules. After two days of seeing Jules dissolve in tears as she struggled to send Fletcher away, I sat at the window watching for him so I could scurry

147

outside and fend him off. He became harder and harder to turn away, until one day in a fit of desperation I splashed a glass of cranberry juice all over him so he had to go home and change. I kind of felt sorry for him, but I couldn't let him get to my sisters. It was bad enough to see Jules crying, but I had a feeling Riya would beat him up, or at least kick him in the shins.

Henry constantly admired his profile in the nearest reflective surface. He spent hours doing voice exercises and making faces in the camera of his cell phone. He wouldn't eat a bite of any treats I baked, saying he was "watching his boyish figure."

Dad, on the other hand, managed to do what I hadn't thought possible: he stuffed his face even more than before, continuously snacking in a way that made me never want to eat again. Somehow, the hours he spent running in the woods were still managing to prevent him from gaining weight. I avoided looking him in the eyes so I wouldn't be freaked out by the more and more frequent flashes of purple. I tried to talk about Dad's disturbing behavior, but my sisters were too miserable to listen, I could barely get a word in edgewise with Henry, and I didn't want to bother Mom, whose work schedule made her exhausted.

Judging by the number of tiny chocolate boxes strewn all over the house, Dad visited the While Away frequently. He kept asking me to return with him, but I didn't want to be embarrassed in front of Mrs. T (and Kiera) again. I did happen to stroll past the outside of the café once, and noticed that the poster for the contest had been updated:

Attention Bakers Ages 8–13!
Enter the
While Away Café
Midsummer Baking Contest!
First Round: Bring in your BEST baked goods
to earn a Golden Leaf!
Second Round: On Midsummer's Eve, June 23,
The Golden Leaf Winners will bring more
treats to be judged, and
will be narrowed to THREE,
who will immediately compete in the
Third Round: A Live Bake-Off!
Your Delectable Delights could win you
Enchanting Prizes!
Grand Prize: Spend three days in New York City baking
with Guest of Honor and Judge,
World-Famous Pastry Chef Puffy Fay!

I couldn't breathe. *Puffy Fay!* The Master of Madeleines, the Sultan of Soufflés, the Cream Puff King from Comity!

My wildest dream had come true—I would bake for my

culinary idol. And I could win a chance to work with him in New York!

My baking needed to be beyond excellent. It had to be perfect.

I considered going in to talk to Mrs. T, but the line stretched around the block, and I spied Kiera greeting customers at the door. Although it infuriated me to imagine Kiera worming her way into Mrs. T's heart, I decided to wait until June 23 to wow Mrs. T and Puffy Fay together.

I went to the woods every day to meet Vik and escape the mayhem at home. It was almost like having Emma back. I followed Vik's song and met him at the banyan tree. We strolled around the pond, or swam in it, climbed trees, and explored other parts of the forest that I'd never seen before. Vik read more stories from The Book about the forest and the Woodland Queen. I wondered where The Book had come from. I looked in the library for cookbooks and herb manuals and did an Internet search, but I couldn't find any record of a book like mine. It was almost as if the forest itself had decided I needed it.

Vik and I discussed Puffy Fay and the baking contest for hours at a time, and Vik helped me prepare. I made some mistakes: my lemon bars were a little too mouth-puckering, and my lava cakes didn't ooze. But then I made black pepper almond brittle ("astounding," according to Vik), chocolate mint wafers ("invigorating"), and apple sage cakes ("inspiring"). Vik helped me think of ways to make them all better. We discussed herbs, spices, and flavorings, and I taught Vik about the million miraculous ways to use eggs, including a cool way to make sugar-dusted herbs and flowers with meringue powder. With a little over a week left before the contest, I felt reasonably optimistic about my chances.

But there was something else, something I'd been wondering about since the day I'd heard the first notes drifting to me in my yard. I rummaged in the back of my closet and pulled out something I hadn't touched in nearly two years.

I asked Vik one clear afternoon after we'd snacked on almond-tarragon shortcakes.

"Could you teach me your song, the one we use as our signal? I brought my old clarinet." I pulled it out of my backpack.

Vik looked surprised but pleased. "I can certainly try. It's called 'Come with Me.'"

"Okay, I'm ready—play the first note."

Vik played it, and I experimented until I found the same note on my clarinet. Then I wrote it in my notebook on a makeshift staff.

"What are you doing?"

"I'm transcribing the notes so I can play the song later."

He touched the page. "You can write music?"

"Yeah, can't you?"

"No, I've only learned by listening."

"You're like Henry. If he hears something once, he knows how to play it."

"But Mimi, being able to read and write music is so useful. You can learn things so much more easily, and you can share music without having to play it. It's like giving someone a recipe, instead of just handing out food."

I shrugged. "Sometimes notes get in the way. Henry says music is made up of notes, but what it actually does is tell a story. And I do the same, when I bake."

Vik nodded. "Henry's pretty wise."

I sighed. He used to be, before he got glued to mirrors.

We continued picking out the tune on the clarinet, and I transcribed as we went.

"Now why don't you try playing it?"

"Sure, but don't laugh."

Vik put on what he might have thought was serious expression, but instead he looked like he was trying to part his hair with his eyebrows. I giggled.

I tried playing the tune once—I was rusty, but there was no hint of a goose squeak. "Not bad," I said.

"Not bad at all," said Vik. "The rhythm in the second part should go more like this." He played the section for me, and I was miraculously able to replicate it.

"That's it! Now play it again, and I'll play something else on top of it, okay?"

I played, and Vik played a harmony on his pipe, a counter-
point that meandered in and around the main melody like a
vine.

"There are words to the song. Want to hear them?"

I nodded.

"You play, and I'll sing this time."

I played, and Vik sang gently:

"Come with me
And watch the sun rise
In our place
Watch it paint the world in gold and pink

For you and I once met each other
Under the banyan tree
You and I can stay forever
Won't you come with me?

Won't you come with me?
Won't you come with me?
Won't you come with me?"

His voice was sad, and happy. The song was a memory, and
an invitation.

"My mother taught me that song," said Vik. "It always
reminds me of her."

I leaned against the tree. "When I was five, we had a concert in our yard one summer night after dinner. Henry, Riya, and Jules had set up a band—Henry played guitar, Jules drummed, and Riya sang. They were brilliant, even when they were younger. They played this beautiful song. I thought it was the most enchanting song in the world, and I never wanted them to stop. I spun around in circles and asked them to play it over and over. Dad told me that some day, I'd be just like them."

Vik smiled.

"It never happened. It's okay, Vik," I said when he started to protest. "I've never been able to play with them, to be a part of the music they make. But your song—it reminds me of that song. It's like magic. And now I can play it."

He looked out over the pond. "Want to try it again?"

And we played the song together, over and over, until I felt the music fill my heart like it had always been there.

I got up and brushed myself off. "Tomorrow's an important day for my sisters," I said. "Jules has a soccer game against her team's biggest rival, and Riya has her dance recital. I want to bake something special for them and their friends."

Vik chuckled. "Do you always bake for everyone in your family? Sounds exhausting."

"Like I told you, they've been having a hard week." I packed up my clarinet. "And sometimes food is the best way to show someone you love them."

"Definitely," said Vik. He looked at me curiously. "Mimi, I'm going away for the weekend."

"You're going on a trip? With Aunt Tanya?"

"Yeah. To . . . visit some other relatives. Not very far. I wish I didn't have to, but—you know."

I shrugged.

"Don't worry, I'll be back in plenty of time for the contest." He smiled, and I blinked at the sunlight reflected in his eyes.

I'd gotten used to having a best friend again. When I was with Vik, Emma's absence faded to a dull ache, and I could forget about the weirdness at home for hours at a time. How would I survive without his company? Without his help? "Thanks for today," I said. I managed a small smile as I walked away.

When I got home, I gently laid my clarinet on the table near the piano.

I went to the kitchen and gathered ingredients. Whatever happened this weekend, I'd have to face it alone.

CHAPTER 13

THE EPIPHANY

I'd had such high hopes for Saturday.

The temperature and humidity were already soaring as we headed off to Jules's soccer game, but that didn't dampen our excitement. Mom put her phone in her purse so she wouldn't be tempted to read emails and pulled out her fancy camera instead. Henry had an all-day tech rehearsal for his play, but Riya came with us "under protest"—she hid behind sunglasses and earbuds and made it clear she cared more about listening to her recital music than watching the game.

Ignoring Mom's complaints that he was eating too much junk food, Dad brought his own cooler packed with snacks.

I'd made a batch of cannoli ice cream sandwiches filled with chocolate chip ricotta ice cream to share with Jules's team after the game. The frozen treats reminded me of Jules—sweet and universally liked, if sometimes stiff and unyielding. I'd stashed them in a separate cooler so Dad wouldn't eat them all himself.

Jules's team, the Comity Chameleons, was facing their biggest rival, the Bridgeton Badgers. While Jules had always been a great soccer player, she'd morphed into a truly remarkable one while playing on the high school varsity team. Jules was one of the highest scorers, had a record number of assists, and, as Fletcher had pointed out the other night, she'd managed to make every penalty kick all season.

The score was tied 2–2 as the final minutes ticked down. Jules looked unstoppable as she took a shot, but she was fouled with seconds to go. She looked completely focused as she lined up for her penalty kick, sizing up the goalie and calculating where to place the ball. Even Riya took off her sunglasses, put down her phone, and started to watch.

A murmur ran through the crowd, and then it erupted in laughter.

"Seriously?" Riya said next to me.

A man-sized soccer ball with "I Heart J" printed across the front bounced from the sidelines across the field. I soon realized that it had legs—it was an enormous inflatable soccer ball *costume*—and I could make out some shaggy hair. It was Cole! A small part of my brain was impressed with his ingenuity—how did he get that costume? Did he decorate it himself?—but mostly I was horrified. Within seconds he'd loped all the way to Jules and, after some wobbling and rolling, managed to get down on one knee in front of her. Cole grasped her hand while she stood frozen for a moment with her mouth gaping. Then Jules came to her senses and tried to haul him off the field.

The refs descended in a burst of whistles and flags. They rolled Cole to the sideline and deflated him. "Jules! My Jules!" he bellowed. "I shall return!"

Jules lined up for penalty kick again, and the other players stood behind her outside the penalty box, some of them giggling to each other. Jules looked rattled, and I could see her body trembling as she readied her shot. She took a deep breath, made a few quick strides up to the ball, and struck it.

The ball arced . . . it sailed toward the goal . . . and kept going, missing the net completely.

Jules had missed her first penalty kick in a year.

"I think she was still distracted after that prank," said Mom. "Riya, do you know anything about it?"

"Don't ask me. I don't have a clue about anything anymore," said Riya, hiding behind her sunglasses again.

We all watched helplessly as the Chameleons lost in overtime.

No one wanted my ice cream sandwiches, so I gave the cooler to Dad, who grinned like Christmas had come early.

On the drive home, Jules stared out the window and bit her nails until they bled. On my other side, Riya sighed and looked out her own window.

"What did Cole say?" I asked Jules.

She shook her head and mumbled something.

"What?"

"He asked me to the prom," she said. Her eyes were unfocused. "You know, the prom that's like eleven months away, at the school he hasn't even been to yet." She threw a hateful glance at Riya, then turned back to the window and started in on the nubs of her nails again.

Riya had devoted months to rehearsing for her dance recital. As we piled into the car, she reminded us for the millionth time that a professor from a New York arts college was rumored to be attending.

Riya performed in seven different dances, but my favorite was the number just before the grand finale—Riya's solo, which she had choreographed herself. It was technically modern dance, but it included elements of bharatanatyam, the Indian classical dance she'd studied since she was four. Riya wore a sleek green costume and ankle bells that jingled with each step to emphasize the rhythm of her footwork. The piece, set to Indian music with a lot of dreamy flute, was a tale of a wood

nymph who falls in love with a young man and convinces him to make the forest his home. Riya didn't need words to tell a story. She danced the young man with a proud posture and dynamic kicks. Flowing arms and a graceful tilt of her head transformed her into the wood nymph. But most of all, she told the story with her eyes, which changed from scared to suspicious to lovelorn in the space of seconds.

Halfway through Riya's solo dance, I sensed a presence to my left. Fletcher stood at the end of our row with an enormous bouquet of flowers.

"Jules," he murmured. I shook my head. Jules was sitting right next to me, her eyes glued to Riya like her life depended on it.

"Go away," I whispered. The couple behind me shushed. I pointed at Fletcher, and they turned their annoyance on him.

"Jules," said Fletcher in a louder voice.

Jules still wouldn't look at him. "Get lost!"

"Come with me," Fletcher pleaded.

"No way," said Jules, turning her back on him and looking sideways at the stage.

"But—"

"She said get lost!" said a droopy-mustached old man at the end of the row. "You're distracting me from the dancing!"

"I must talk to you," Fletcher said to Jules. "I heard word that cad Cole ruined your game."

Mom tried to wave Fletcher away while still recording Riya with her phone. Dad reached into a bag and snuck out one of the chocolate-hazelnut palmiers I'd made for the dancers.

Fletcher edged his way toward Jules, but the man at the end of the row braced his knees against the seat in front to block him. Fletcher began climbing over him but instead stepped on the man's foot and fell into his lap.

"Young man, this is unacceptable!" the man shouted through his quivering mustache. "Get off!"

Jules hid her face in her hands, but I looked back at the stage, hoping the outburst hadn't bothered Riya.

Riya had stopped dancing.

And then, as if in slow motion, she leaped off the stage like a deer. The audience gasped. Mom let out a small screech and covered her mouth. Riya landed lightly and stalked through the rows of the audience as her dance music continued to play. She came to a stop at our row, where Fletcher had gotten to his feet, leaving a pile of mangled petals on the floor. Riya's glare at Fletcher blazed hotter than a kitchen torch.

She slapped him sharply across the face.

As Fletcher fell to the floor, his eyes flashed purple for a split second, just like Dad's.

"I don't understand. Is that part of the performance?" asked the mustache man.

Riya pirouetted and ran like a gazelle to the wing of the

stage, her jingling ankle bells growing fainter with each step.

Riya danced perfectly in the finale with everyone else, but I could tell that underneath it all, she was furious. After the recital, she didn't want to stay for the reception, and dragged us all to the parking lot.

As it turned out, Dad ended up eating all the palmiers, too.

We had a silent dinner. I tried to make small talk, but no one paid any attention to me. After an entire day away from work, Mom had to catch up on her email, and Dad didn't stop eating long enough to say two words. Afterward, he dug into a pile of desserts he'd bought from the While Away. Eventually, Mom went upstairs, Dad went for a run, and my sisters slumped off to their rooms. It didn't look like I could help anyone, so I took some more notes for the baking contest, which was now only a week away.

Roots. What kind of theme was that? I supposed I could make carrot cake, but I figured a lot of kids would think of that. Should I make something with parsnips? Beets? Potatoes? None of those sounded particularly appetizing. And I also needed to memorize recipes I could make quickly if I made it to the live Bake-Off.

I was still writing when Henry came home.

"What happened? I thought your rehearsal was supposed to go late."

Henry shrugged and grabbed a yogurt from the fridge. "They sent me home," he said. "I was only trying to help."

"Help who?"

"The other actors. After all, I can play all their roles better than they ever could." He started spooning yogurt into his mouth.

"What?"

Henry waved the spoon around. "No one is truly channeling their characters like I am. We must *embody* our roles, or no one will believe us. We must broadcast our *intentions*. So I instructed everyone, trying to help them improve."

"You were playing all the characters?" No wonder they'd made him leave. What had happened to my sweet and thoughtful brother? He'd always been dramatic, but never obnoxious or unkind.

"Opening night's only a week away! And Mark—he plays Oberon—needs to put so much more *emotion* into his role, you know?"

"I guess so."

"Case in point: Oberon needs us to feel *love* when he speaks of the love flower: *Yet mark'd I where the bolt of Cupid fell. It fell upon a little western flower, Before milk-white, now purple with love's wound.* Mark was acting like these were just like any other lines."

I froze. That sounded eerily familiar. "What did you say?"

"He needs to emote more about the love flower."

"The love flower?" A chill ran through my body. "And it's purple and white?"

"Yes. He needs to say the lines with *feeling*—after all, it's the flower that makes people fall in love with the first person they see. It's a critical moment!"

I racked my brain. What was in the story from The Book, the story Vik had read the day we first met? He'd mentioned the *"Love Blossom, with trailing vines and petals that blushed purple with love's wound."* I pictured a grove filled with vines and purple flowers.

"I've got to go."

"Ridiculous, right?" Henry finished the yogurt and looked at his reflection in the teaspoon. "Amateurs."

And in his eyes, a tiny flash of purple glimmered.

I ran to my bedroom, locked the door, and pulled on my hair as I looked at the window, where all I could see was my own horrified face.

The love flower from Henry's play was purple and white. The love blossom from the story in The Book was purple and white.

And so was the honeysuckle I'd put into my cookies the night of the big dinner.

CHAPTER 14

MAYHEM MANAGED

I paced the floor. Could my cookies have actually made people fall in love? It was one thing to hear stories about fairies and magical plants, but it was something else for *me* to do something that made people act loopy. And there were certainly plenty of people doing plenty of loopy things.

Fletcher and Cole had been eating my cookies when they both became obsessed with Jules. I plopped on my bed and pushed my hair out of my eyes.

What about Jules and Riya? Other than not talking to each other, they seemed to be their normal selves. Jules had been too busy getting everyone to play soccer to bother with the cookies. And Riya hadn't eaten any because she'd been grossed out that I'd used an ingredient I'd found in the woods. I buried my face in my hands. My sisters would *kill* me if they discovered I was the reason why the boys were acting so zany. Not just because I'd messed up their love lives, but because Cole's and Fletcher's behavior had ruined the stuff that Jules and Riya excelled at, the stuff they cared about most, that made them who they were.

And Henry? He'd been so obnoxious and self-centered lately, so obsessed with his own reflection. What had he been doing when he ate his first cookie?

He'd been taking a selfie.

I slapped my forehead. I'd made Henry fall in love with himself! I put a pillow over my head. He'd been annoying enough at home since this happened; I bet that Lily and the other kids in the play were really fed up with him.

But . . . Vik, Mom, and I had all tasted the honeysuckle nectar, and Vik and I had even eaten some of the cookie dough, and we seemed to be fine. Or at least I thought so. And Dad had been acting weird since he'd come back from his trip to Houston—way before I'd found the honeysuckle.

I chewed on a strand of hair and turned the possibilities over in my mind until I thought my head would explode.

Bizarre as it was, the honeysuckle being the love flower was the only explanation that made sense. It couldn't just be a coincidence.

I burrowed under the covers and curled up into a ball. I

had *poisoned* everyone. It was the absolute worst thing a cook could do. This was way worse than making people throw up from pasta salad that sat in the sun too long. And based on the way the boys were acting, the effects weren't going to wear off anytime soon.

I needed to fix things. Now!

But how?

My first thought was to ask Mom for help. But what could I tell her? I didn't have any proof, and she would probably think I was hallucinating. And given how hard she was working, I didn't need to add more stress to her life.

Maybe the boys needed to see a doctor? But I didn't even think I could get Henry to go, let alone Cole and Fletcher. And what would they tell the doctor? *Uh, Mimi thinks she's poisoned us with a love flower. . . .*

I started to hyperventilate. I couldn't leave everyone like this! At this rate, no one in my family would be talking to one another in another week.

If only Emma were still here, or even reachable by phone. And Vik! Why'd he have to go away now?

Emma couldn't help me. Vik couldn't help me.

I had to figure this out on my own.

I raced downstairs, preheated the oven, and pulled out flour, sugar, and butter. Baking always helped me get my thoughts in order.

As I pressed a tart crust into a pan, it dawned on me: If food had gotten me into this mess, maybe food could get me out. There were plenty of foods that cleansed people's palates; I needed something to cleanse their minds.

I needed something refreshing to wipe away the confusion caused by the honeysuckle cookies. I covered the crust in parchment paper, poured pie weights on top, and slid it into the oven. Then I grabbed my notebook and started writing.

Mint—that was good for refreshment. What else? Lemon, menthol—no, too nasty. I thought about recipes that Puffy Fay had described as refreshing. In his cookbook, he had a great lime sorbet recipe and a pomegranate syrup that was tart and delicious on ice cream. And there was always chocolate, which dominated other flavors and was universally loved. I felt calmer after making my list, and I started to put together a plan.

While my tart crust baked, I gathered some mint from the large pot on the patio, chopped it up, and added it to a steaming mug of chamomile tea. I let it steep for a few minutes, strained it, and added some honey and an ice cube to cool it. I took a tiny sip—it was plenty sweet and very refreshing. Good. I pulled the tart crust out of the oven, set it aside to cool, and plopped a few shortbread cookies from the cookie jar onto a plate. I took the tea and cookies up to Henry's room. I burst in to find him strumming his guitar.

"What's up?"

"I have a treat for you." My hands were shaking so much that I had to set the mug on his desk.

"Oh, Mimi, you know I'm watching my—"

"Your figure." Ugh! "Right. Well, you don't have to eat the cookies—they're for me. But I thought you might like some tea with honey. You know, to soothe your throat since you've been rehearsing all day."

He smiled. "That's thoughtful of you. Sure, I'd love some."

I nodded at the mug, not trusting myself to pick it up again.

Henry set his guitar down and took a sip while I held my breath and tried not to pass out.

"Mmm . . . nice."

"Glad you like it. Go ahead, drink it up. I'll snack on these." I grabbed a cookie and nibbled it half-heartedly while Henry drank the tea. My mouth felt dry and numb, like I was getting a filling at the dentist's.

Henry drained the mug and set it back on the desk. "Thanks, Mimi. It does make my throat feel better."

I smiled at him and wondered whether his brain felt better, too.

"Want to hear the song I'm writing for Lily?"

I nodded. Now, that was encouraging; Henry hadn't talked about anyone other than himself all week.

Henry picked up the guitar and started playing gently.

"Lily, dear Lily, don't you see?" he sang.

Nice! My breathing got easier.

Henry continued: *"How lucky you are to be with me? I'm the hottest and the star-est, the playing the guitar-est."*

I sprang to my feet. "Henry! Are—are you sure that song's for *Lily?*"

"Yeah. I mean, she should know how fortunate she is, right? To get to work with *me?* The most awesome actor-singer-guy anyone's ever seen? And maybe, if she plays her cards right, I'll ask her out."

He smiled, and his eyes glinted purple.

I hurried to the door. "I'll stop bothering you. Good luck with the song."

Out in the hallway, I leaned against the door as Henry continued to sing the most self-centered love song ever.

"I'm the cutest and the sweetest,
The guy you'd always want to meet-est . . ."

Mint obviously wasn't the solution.

It was time for Idea Number Two.

Early the next morning, I snuck next door and peered through a back window. I was relieved to see Cole alone, so I knocked.

He let me in, and memories flooded my mind as I entered

Emma's old kitchen. They hadn't changed it much—just some new dishcloths and different pictures on the walls. Emma and I had baked hundreds of cookies here together. This was where we'd talked about opening a bakery someday. I'd be the baker, and she'd be the manager, we'd said . . . but it was pointless to think about that now. I had to concentrate on fixing the problem in front of me.

"So, Cole." I displayed the tart. "I brought you a treat."

"Where's Jules?" He peered around me like I might be hiding her behind my back.

"Oh, she's out," I said. Jules had another game, and she had made it clear she didn't want anyone else to come with her. "But she helped me make this last night, and she wanted to be sure I brought it over, first thing."

Cole looked at the tart. "That's just like her—so thoughtful and kind."

"We think it's perfect for you. A lime tart with pomegranate glaze."

I put the tart on the counter. The crust was the perfect shade of golden brown, and as I cut into it, the bright red glaze contrasted beautifully with the pale green lime custard filling. I served him up a large slice.

"Go on, try it."

Cole took a bite, and his mouth puckered. "Wow. It's very—"

"Tart. Yes, that's how it's supposed to be. A *tart* tart, ha-ha. Make sure to eat it up, or you'll hurt Jules's feelings."

He kept eating dutifully, smacking his lips from time to time. The lime curd and the pomegranate glaze *were* quite sour—I'd made them that way on purpose and hadn't added too much sugar. I wanted to clear his palate, and his mind, as much as possible. After all, this wasn't for the baking contest; it was kind of like medicine.

I scrutinized him as he chewed. Did I see a sparkle of clarity in Cole's hazel eyes? Was that dawning realization on his face?

Cole finished and poured himself a glass of water.

"Well, that was . . . something," he said. "Please tell Jules—"

"Yes?"

"Tell her I'd love to see her as soon as she returns. And I've got a gift for her," he gushed.

I scrambled to the back door. "I'll let Jules know, Cole. Keep the tart. Share it with your mom. Bye!"

I ran home and locked the door behind me.

It didn't look like lime and pomegranate were doing the trick, either.

What could I do? I needed help, but who could help me? I sat down heavily at the kitchen table and gazed out the windows to the woods. If only I hadn't found that stupid honeysuckle patch in the first place. If only I had recognized it for what it was. If only the Queen of The Wild would appear at my door and hand me a gift that would help me fix the mess I'd made.

If only . . .

I shot up in my seat. I *did* have something that could help me. Something that detailed everything about plants and how to use them.

I opened The Book. I leafed through its pages and finally came to the entry I needed.

I scooped it into my backpack and flew out the back door.

I had to get to the woods.

CHAPTER 15

THE QUEST FOR THE REMEDY

I ducked my head inside my hangout in the woods. Like I expected, there was nothing there: no Vik, no help of any kind.

"Wish me luck," I said to the empty tarp. I shouldered my backpack and hurried down the path.

I hummed Vik's song to myself and eventually came to the two hemlocks standing like a green gate. I ran through them and raced to the banyan tree.

"Vik! Are you here? I need help," I called, gazing up at the mass of green-gold leaves.

But the only answer was the birds calling to each other. The day was humid and oppressive, without even a breath of wind.

"Vik? It's an emergency!"

Still nothing. Clearly he hadn't returned from wherever he'd gone with Aunt Tanya. I squared my shoulders. I really was on my own. I decided to walk around the pond to see if I could find what I needed. After a while, I came to an area that seemed familiar. Spearmint plants had overtaken a large expanse. I crushed a leaf in my hand and inhaled the refreshing scent: invigorating, but mint hadn't brought Henry to his senses. Then I came to some fragrant bushes growing nearby—rosemary. I picked a stem and inhaled its piney aroma. *Rosemary, for remembrance.* Maybe this would help everyone recall what they used to be like, before I poisoned them? But that wasn't what I needed.

And then I saw it: a patch of shiny heart-shaped leaves with tiny white flowers. I matched them to the illustration in The Book: gotu kola. Hope blossomed in my chest. *An herb to restore the senses and clear confusion.*

"This better work." I took off my backpack and gathered bunches of leaves. They smelled a lot like basil, and I knew how I could use them. My family loved my orange-basil brownies, and I didn't think swapping one herb for another would be that noticeable. Not that they were noticing much these days.

When I thought I'd gathered more than enough, I zipped my bag closed and threw it over my shoulder. I sprinted back around the pond and past the banyan tree, heading for the path home. There was no time to lose. I was nearly at the hemlocks when I tripped over something lying across the ground but managed to catch myself before I wiped out.

A growling moan startled me.

Uh-oh. The boar was back again—at just the wrong time.

I strained my ears, trying to figure out where it was. But there were no hoofsteps. No snorting or squeals.

Just another hissing roar, this one even closer.

In front of me rose a monstrous hooded snake, tan except for two symmetrical black spots on its chest. Taller than me, it swayed back and forth, dancing to music I couldn't hear.

I stayed rooted to the spot, mesmerized by its terrible beauty.

It was a cobra.

It was impossible! Cobras didn't live in Massachusetts.

My eyes darted to look for an escape. Ten feet away was a large tree I thought I could climb.

The cobra continued to sway and growl. I inched sideways toward the tree.

When I was a few feet away, I broke into a sprint, got a foot on a low branch, and climbed for my life. I wondered if I'd feel the burn of a bite, how much cobra venom hurt, and how long I'd last before . . .

I reached a large branch and looked down. I was *way* up in the tree, at least twenty feet high. And I didn't see the murderous snake anymore. I let out a shaky sigh. When would it be safe to climb back down?

Rustling came from the branches below.

Apparently, unlike boars, cobras could climb trees.

"Help!" I cried. But there was no one to hear.

The impossible snake slithered toward me. My breathing grew ragged as I gripped the branch tighter. Just when I thought I could turn things around, it was all going to end. And what made me saddest was not the thought of missing the baking contest in front of my culinary idol. Not even the thought of dying in the middle of the woods that I loved. It was leaving my sisters hating each other, and my brother loving only himself, and Dad eating everything in sight and not appreciating any of it.

But I wasn't giving up without a fight.

The tree had large, hard green fruits almost as big as my head. I plucked one and got ready to throw. I would probably only have one shot.

"*Wheeet-tieu, wheeet-tieu*," came a call. I looked around for the source, and in a flash of yellow, the colorful little bird landed on my shoulder, feather-light but warm and alive. What had Vik called it? A *pitta*.

"Can you help me, little pitta?" I whispered.

The bird turned its head and regarded me with a shiny black eye.

The cobra reached my branch and glided toward me. Its tongue flicked in and out as it wended its way along the branch. I poised the fruit in my hands, aimed, and threw with all my might.

The heavy fruit hit the middle of the snake and knocked its tail off the branch. For a split second, it looked like it would just drop to the ground. But the cobra coiled the rest of its body so it didn't fall. It slithered toward me again, faster now, and reared up with its hood extended. I closed my eyes in anticipation of its bite.

And then the little pitta on my shoulder began to sing. Not typical birdsong, but something else, something that felt familiar. It sounded like the memory of all the creatures of the forest—birds and beasts, streams and plants, every growing thing. It sounded like an invitation.

When I opened my eyes, the cobra had gone.

"Don't require your assistance at this time, huh? Wait till you come begging for my help when all is lost! Talk about ungrateful! They'll never win without me, never. And then what will become of—"

"Vik? Is that you?" I called. "Watch out! There's a cobra!"

There was a pause. Then, "Mimi? Where are you?"

I twisted and stuck my head out of the leaves. I glimpsed Vik's dark hair. "Be careful! Look around you!"

It sounded like Vik was walking around the tree. "Mimi, there's nothing here. Come down."

I stayed put.

"Mimi? Really, there's nothing down here. You can come down now."

I carefully made my way down the tree. I reached the ground and couldn't stop trembling. "This is way weirder than the boar, Vik. There aren't supposed to be any poisonous snakes here! And certainly no cobras!"

"Are you sure it was a cobra?"

"It was a gigantic tan snake with a hood. It made this horrible growly roaring noise." I shuddered.

"Well, whatever it was, it's gone now," said Vik. "What were you doing out here?"

I clutched at my backpack strap; it was still there. I grabbed Vik's arm and pulled him on the path home.

"Come on," I said. "Let's get out of here."

We arrived at my yard. I dropped my backpack and collapsed onto the grass, exhausted and drenched in sweat. Vik plopped himself next to me.

"What was a cobra doing in my woods?"

"How do you know it was a cobra?"

"How many other snakes look like that?"

"Okay," said Vik. "Well, it's gone now. What do you want to do?"

I thought for a moment. "When there was a fox in the neighborhood last year, people called animal control. They observed the fox, made sure it wasn't acting like it had rabies, and taught people how to be careful around it until it eventually moved on. I should call them now. Maybe they can trap it?"

We ran into the kitchen, and I thumbed through the phone book for the town directory. I found the number and waited impatiently for someone to pick up.

"Hello? I'd like to report a dangerous wild animal," I said.

"Are you in danger now?" asked the woman on the phone.

"No, I'm safe at home."

"What type of animal, and where did you see it?"

"It was in Comity Woods. A cobra."

There was a pause. "Is this a joke?" said the woman.

"I'm not kidding. It really was a cobra. It chased me up a tree, and climbed the tree and—"

"Cobras don't live in Massachusetts. You probably saw a green snake."

"It wasn't a green snake! It was a gigantic hooded—"

"Young lady, you shouldn't be making prank calls like this. This line is for emergencies."

"But I'm not—"

"I'm hanging up now. I need to keep this line clear."

"But I haven't even told you about the boar! Please listen—"

There was a click. I exhaled through pursed lips and hung up the phone.

"What happened?" Vik asked.

I pushed my hair out of my eyes. "What do you think? She didn't believe me." I shook my head. "*I* barely believe me."

"What should we do now?" asked Vik.

I grabbed my backpack from the floor.

"Now we bake brownies."

We washed our hands, and I pulled out the gotu kola. We stripped the dark green heart-shaped leaves off the stems, and I rinsed and spun them dry. I tore off a piece and tasted: it was mild, kind of like basil, but with a slightly bitter edge, which would be masked by the chocolate I was going to use.

"What is this?" asked Vik.

"Gotu kola. Remember? From The Book? This will fix everyone. I hope."

Vik looked puzzled, so I explained what I had deduced about the honeysuckle and my hope that the gotu kola would reverse the effects.

His eyes grew wide. He opened The Book and flipped through pages. "*Honeysuckle,*" he read. "*To be used to promote infatuation and love.*"

I sighed. "I wish we had looked it up before we baked with

it. There are other magical ingredients in the woods!"

"But Mimi," said Vik. "Do you really think that's true?"

"It's the only explanation that makes sense," I said. "Why else would the guys suddenly act so strange? Anyway, even if I'm wrong, I have to try to fix things. Do you believe me? Will you help?"

Vik nodded. "Of course."

I took my recipe binder off the kitchen shelf and flipped to the brownies section.

We preheated the oven and lined a pan with parchment paper, and I put a bowl of chocolate and butter over a pan of simmering water on the stove. I left Vik to stir as they melted while I took the gotu kola leaves and walnuts and chopped them into tiny bits in the food processor.

Dad strolled into the kitchen. "What're you making?"

"Double-chocolate brownies," I said. "I'll give you one when they're ready." *Please let it work*, I thought.

"Better make it two, or four, or eight," said Dad, chuckling and ruffling my hair so it was in my face even more. "I'm going to grab a snack and go for a run. Nice to see you, Vik."

Dad proceeded to make himself the largest sandwich I'd ever seen: a triple-decker with salami, pickles, two types of cheese, mustard, coleslaw, and peanut butter. Vik watched him with his mouth hanging open. I was sure he was wondering the same thing as me: Who could possibly run after eating that? I had no idea whether the gotu kola brownies would work on Dad, but I had to try something before he exploded.

Dad took an enormous bite of the sandwich. "Save me some," he said with his mouth full.

"Promise," I said as he left the kitchen.

Once the chocolate and butter had melted, we stirred in sugar, salt, eggs, and the gotu kola mixture. We sifted in flour and added chocolate chips. *Please let this clear everyone's minds and return them to their normal feelings,* I thought as I stirred. I tasted the batter—it was super chocolatey with a subtle herbaceous undertone.

I poured the batter into the pan and slid it into the oven. We cleaned up, and I wrote my recipe notes while they were still fresh in my mind.

The oven timer finally went off. The brownies looked great, with a classic papery, cracked top. I pushed a toothpick into the center of the pan to test if they were done, and it came out with bits of crumbs clinging to it. Perfect—rich and fudgy.

"I hope everyone likes these," I said as I put the pan on a rack to cool. I needed them to be so delicious that no one could resist them. "And I hope they work."

"The Book says the gotu kola should work," said Vik.

I nodded my head but couldn't shake the sour churning in my stomach.

Once the brownies had cooled enough to eat, I cut them

and inhaled the heady scent of fresh herbs and chocolate. I placed one on a napkin and handed it to Vik, then took another and bit into it. I'd learned my lesson: I was never giving anyone anything without tasting it first myself.

The brownie was luscious and moist. The herbs brightened the deep chocolate in a way that reminded me of mint.

"What do you think?" I asked Vik.

"Delicious," he said. "Like I knew it would be."

"But do you think it will cure everyone of their . . . honeysuckle madness?"

Vik rubbed his hands together. "Only one way to find out. Who did you say is on the list? Your sisters?"

"No, just the boys. Henry, Cole, and Fletcher. Oh, and Dad, of course. He's been the weirdest of all."

A car pulled into the driveway next door and a shaggy-headed guy got out. Luck was finally with us.

"Let's try these on Cole first." I covered the brownie pain in foil so Dad couldn't gobble them all before everyone else had gotten one.

"Sounds good," said Vik. "But is he your highest priority?"

"Are you kidding? He showed up dressed as a giant soccer ball and made Jules miss her penalty kick at her game yesterday!"

Vik snickered. "Oh, that is excellent. Why do I miss all the fun stuff?"

"Trust me, it isn't fun when you're actually living it. I have to stop him before he does anything worse! Come on, let's go."

We rushed next door. Cole sat at the kitchen counter, bent over something small.

"I've got another treat for you," I announced. I put a brownie on the counter.

Cole finished adjusting something with a screwdriver, then sat back and assessed what he'd done.

I saw that Cole had been working on a small robot with wheels instead of legs. It blinked with cheerful blue lights.

"What a cute little guy," I said.

Cole picked up the brownie and sniffed. "It does smell delicious." He took a nibble, then another, and then finished it off in seconds. "Wow," he murmured as he reached for another, which he inhaled just as quickly.

"How do you feel?" I asked anxiously.

"Fine, I—" He rubbed his head. "Man, what the heck have I been doing?" He looked at the robot in dismay. "I programmed it to wait for Jules in the yard and follow her around your house singing love songs. What was I thinking?"

I giggled. "Yeah, I don't think she'd appreciate that."

"Don't tell her," Cole said. "And . . . did I mess up her game yesterday?"

I let out the breath I'd been holding. What a relief—he was back to normal! "She missed the penalty kick, and her team lost."

Cole jumped up. "I can't believe how stupid I was! She's the most wonderful person I've ever met—I need to make it up to her!" He grabbed the robot and ran out of the room.

Well, not quite normal. I turned to Vik. "At first I thought it worked, but he still likes her!"

"Maybe—"

"Maybe he needs more gotu kola. Maybe we need to rethink this whole operation!"

"Mimi—"

"What?" I snapped.

Vik sighed. "Why don't we try the brownies on someone else and see what happens? Is Henry home?"

"I think so," I said. "It's certainly going to be harder to get him to eat them, but I guess it wouldn't hurt."

What choice did I have?

CHAPTER 16

THE WORST SONG EVER

Vik and I paused outside the door to the mudroom and listened to Henry strumming his guitar and singing:

"Some say my eyes are dreamiest, so brown and warm and bright,
Some say my skin is creamiest, like cinnamon in the light,
I know my acting is the best, but if I had to choose,
I'd say my voice is loveliest, what I'd never want to lose . . ."

Vik laughed so hard he started choking and coughing. I looked at him through narrowed eyes, then steeled myself and opened the door.

"Henry! Just who we were looking for."

"I'm heading to rehearsal early so I can give everyone my

individualized notes before we start," Henry said. "And so I can sing my song for Lily."

Vik collapsed onto the bench next to Henry.

"Henry, you have to try these." I held out the pan. "They're the best brownies I've ever made."

"Now, Mimi, I know you love to bake, but I've got to be in top shape for the play," Henry said, trying to peek at himself in the mudroom mirror. And I needed to be in top shape for the contest, which was the same day. But I couldn't do that until everyone was back to normal.

"But these are healthy brownies."

"How so?" said Henry. He stopped trying to be sneaky and stood in front of the mirror, guitar still strapped to him, and raised his eyebrows as he looked at his face from different angles. "What do you think is my better side, my right or my left? I want to make sure I use the best angle when I sing for Lily."

Vik fell over in silent laughter, and I gave him a death stare.

"Uh . . . both your sides are great. I don't think you need to worry about that. But seriously, try a brownie. They're full of healthy green things, with, you know, anti—anti—"

"Antioxidants? Really?" Henry's reflection looked intrigued.

"Yeah, you can't taste them, but they're in there. Right, Vik?" I asked pointedly.

Vik nodded, tears leaking from his eyes.

"I'll give you a small piece. Please, Henry. I value your opinion so much, and you know the baking contest is only six days away."

Henry smiled at me affectionately. "Oh, all right, I'll try one. I should use my prodigious skills to help my littlest sister. *Come hither: I am here.* Right, Mimi Mouse?" He winked at me.

I plastered a smile on my face. This had to work, for Henry's own health, because he was making me want to kill him.

"Here you go," I said, offering him a brownie. Vik lay on the bench and shook with hilarity.

Henry took a bite. "Mimi, this is delicious." He kept chewing and finished the brownie, licking the crumbs from his fingers.

Then all of a sudden, he shivered. His guitar made a jangly noise as he hastily set it down.

"Good grief," Henry said. "What have I been doing?" He clasped his hands on top of his head.

"You look pale," I said. "Maybe you should sit." I poked Vik so he would move over.

Henry dropped onto the bench and rubbed his eyes. "I wrote a song for Lily . . . but it was about *myself* . . . and it was *terrible* . . ."

"Yeah, it was," Vik agreed.

"Stop it!" I whispered to Vik. "Henry, do you feel all right?"

"And I was . . . telling everyone what to do last night . . . and . . . oh my goodness! Lily! I've got to call her!" Henry pulled his phone from his pocket and ran from the room.

"Stop laughing!" I shoved Vik's arm.

"I thought he was supposed to be a musical genius!" Vik slumped against the wall.

"He is!" I said. "But you can't hold it against him if he wrote a bad song while he was in the middle of . . . honey-suckle madness!"

Vik chuckled. "I don't, but still, that was the funniest song I've ever heard!"

Now that I knew Henry was going to be okay, I couldn't help smiling myself. "Can you imagine if he had played it for the girl he likes?"

But I couldn't relax yet. I had two down, maybe. I still wasn't sure about Cole. Two to go.

I picked up the brownie pan. "Let's go up to my room," I said. "We've got more planning to do."

"Cool," said Vik, looking around my room and taking in the lavender-colored walls with black butterflies. "We're doing well so far."

"I don't know about Cole," I said, chewing on a strand of hair.

"I wish I'd been at the soccer game. A giant soccer ball—sounds hilarious. And Henry's obnoxious song! I'd love to hear others."

I raised my eyebrows. "It's less fun than you think living with these people while they act strange."

"I guess so. What's next?"

"Well," I said, "there's Fletcher. He's Riya's friend and used to be all googly-eyed around her, but since he ate the cookies he's been lovesick for Jules."

"How do we get to him?"

"I don't know. He's in Henry's play. Maybe I should ask Henry to give him a brownie at rehearsal?"

"But Henry might eat the brownie himself," said Vik. "I would—they're mouthwatering."

I scratched my head. "Maybe I should go to the rehearsal? But would that be weird?"

"Actually, I don't think you'll need to." Vik pointed out my window. "Fletcher's here."

"What?" I ran to the window and saw Fletcher striding across the back lawn. "Wait, is he wearing a suit?"

Vik started to snicker again, but I grabbed his shoulders and shook him. "We have to cure him before he does something idiotic, like . . . like asking Jules to marry him!"

"But it's so entertaining." Vik had tears in his eyes again.

"Riya ruined her own dance yesterday to leap off the stage

and slap him! He might have destroyed her chance to go to her dream college! If she ever finds out I'm the one responsible for all this insanity, she'll kill me!"

"Okay, okay," said Vik, wiping his eyes and straightening up. "What's the plan, boss?"

"Let's intercept him before he talks to anyone else."

Vik bowed.

We scrambled down the stairs. When we got to the kitchen, I was dismayed to find Riya at the counter drinking a glass of lemonade.

"What're you guys up to?" She tapped idly at her phone.

"Not much," I said. "We're going outside." We hurried to the back door.

But Fletcher stepped in before we could head him off. He wore a dark blue suit and a fat red tie and held an enormous box of chocolates.

"Hey!" Vik said, grabbing a brownie out of the pan I was holding. "Thanks for helping Cole out." He took the brownie and shoved it into Fletcher's gaping mouth. Fletcher's eyes widened, but he chewed.

I glanced at Vik in confusion, and he raised his eyebrows and tilted his head toward Riya. Oh! "Yeah, thanks," I said to Fletcher. "Jules appreciates it, too."

"What is going on?" asked Riya, standing and crossing her arms. Her eyes looked catlike and dangerous. "Fletcher, why are you here? Don't you know you're not welcome? And why would you be helping Cole with anything? Aren't you still fighting over Jules?"

Fletcher swallowed the brownie, put the box of chocolates down, and pushed his floppy hair out of his eyes. "I —"

My mind whirled. "I can explain. Fletcher learned how much Jules liked Cole, and he figured the only way to get Cole to make a move was to pretend to like Jules himself," I said. I grabbed a napkin and handed it to Fletcher.

Riya's expression softened. "Well," she said, still looking at Fletcher, "if you had asked me about the Jules-Cole situation, you would know that I've told him over and over since the day he moved in to just go talk to her." She snorted. "He acted like she was some sort of movie star or something. I told him that she'd be thrilled if he asked her out, but he said he was too intimidated. Since when has Jules been intimidating?"

Wait a minute. Cole liked *Jules* from the day he moved in? Vik raised his eyebrows in an I-told-you-so kind of expression.

"I—" said Fletcher, shredding the napkin in his hands.

"And Fletcher was sick of Cole hanging around you all the time," I said. "Right, Fletcher?"

"Uh—"

"So you really should be thanking him, Riya. Here, have a

brownie." Feeling reckless, I handed her one.

To my surprise, Riya started eating it. "Mimi, why don't you stop interrupting and let him speak for himself?" Her laserlike gaze was still on Fletcher.

"I brought these for you," Fletcher said, moving past me with a grateful glance to stand next to Riya.

Riya finished the brownie and put down her phone. "For me?" She looked skeptical.

"To say how sorry I am about yesterday. I didn't mean to cause such a commotion and mess up your recital."

"Commotion? You wrecked my solo dance," Riya said.

"I know, I know, and I don't know what I was thinking. I just felt compelled to . . . um . . . I don't have an explanation," he said.

Riya looked at him coldly while he shredded the napkin and stared at the floor.

"It was good for me," said Riya quietly.

Vik and I shared a confused look.

"I'm tired of having guys fall all over me," said Riya, smoothing her hair away from her face. "It was . . . illuminating to feel what it's like to have the guy you like pay attention to someone else." She smiled ruefully.

"You mean you like me? Still?" asked Fletcher.

Riya laughed. "Fletcher, you're the only guy who's ever treated me like a *person*, who's been my friend before trying anything romantic. I wasn't even sure if *you* liked *me*."

"Can we try again? To be friends, I mean—at least to start. I'm so sorry I ruined everything. Can you forgive me?" He handed her the box of chocolates.

I could tell Riya was trying not to smile. "I should kick you out of here. But it turns out you did me a favor," she said, taking the box.

"A favor?" I asked.

"The mustache guy sitting next to Mimi was the art school professor," said Riya, holding up her phone. "He thought Fletcher was part of my dance—the tripping, my leap off the stage, and the slap." She shrugged her shoulders. "He thought it was the best performance art he'd ever seen. So believable." Riya giggled. "They want me to attend an exclusive dance program with them next month!

"So if you promise me you won't act erratically like that again . . ." Riya tore open the box and pulled out a chocolate. "Then yes, we can start over, as friends."

"I promise," Fletcher said.

I grabbed Vik's arm. "Come on," I whispered. "Our work here is done."

We walked out onto the porch in time to see Jules returning from her game.

Something rolled up to her, and she bent to look at it.

"Oh, what's this?" she said.

Cole's little robot stood on the grass in front of her.

"You're so *cute*! And what do you have for me? A note?" She took an envelope from the robot's hands, ripped it open, and read it quickly. She looked around, picked up the little robot, and ran to the porch.

"It's Cole," she said breathlessly. "He apologized for everything! He wants to start over. He said that if and when I want to, I can call him." She tilted her head and smiled. "I might give him another chance after all. And what an awesome game we just had! It started off rough, and I had no idea how we'd recover. But we pulled it out in the end." She gave me an exuberant hug and barreled into the house.

I high-fived Vik. "Looks like we pulled it out in the end, too."

CHAPTER 17

ON THE SWING SET

"Now I need to wait for Dad," I said.

"I'll hang out with you," said Vik. "Want to wait over there?" He pointed at Emma's old swing set. "We'll have a good view of your whole yard."

We walked to Cole's yard. I put the half-finished brownie pan at the top of the slide, sat in a swing, and rocked back and forth with my feet on the ground, keeping an eye out for Dad. Vik did the same, and then, with a grin, he started to swing in earnest. I grinned back and pushed off myself. I remembered swinging with Emma, pretending that we were on a rocket ship to Mars, or gymnasts making dismounts off the uneven bars.

"Beat you to the moon," said Vik, swinging higher and higher.

"You wish," I said, pumping my legs harder and letting my head fall back as my feet reached for the sky. It felt so good to be here with a friend again, knowing that Henry, Cole, and Fletcher were back to normal and my sisters were happy.

Then, upside down, I saw Dad jog into our yard.

I straightened up and let go, flying out of the swing and landing in a heap. "Dad!" I called as I scrambled to stand. "I've got something for you!"

Dad stopped and looked at me in surprise. I ran up the slide and grabbed the brownie pan as Vik jumped off his swing and joined us.

"Here. I saved a bunch for you, like I promised." Still panting, I held them out to Dad.

"These look fantastic, Mimi. Thanks!" said Dad, leaning over the pan and taking a couple.

"Everyone says these are the best brownies they've ever had," said Vik. "Mimi is so talented."

"We're all very lucky to have her," Dad said through a mouthful of brownie.

"So what do you think of the flavors, Dad?" I asked. I held my breath.

Dad finished chewing and smacked his lips. "Well, they're . . . full of . . . you know . . ."

"Yes?" Come on, Dad—chocolate and herbs.

"Chocolate, for sure," said Dad, with a momentary purple

glint in his eyes. "Scrumptious! Can I have more?"

My heart sank. "Uh—"

"I'll take the rest of these. They're the perfect snack after a long run." Dad tucked the pan under his arm and jogged into the house.

I turned to Vik. "I guess the brownies didn't fix Dad."

Vik looked at me with concern. "Yes, but why not? Did he have a honeysuckle cookie, too? What's he in love with—food?"

I shook my head and plunked myself down on a swing again. "He's been weird since he came home from his trip a couple of weeks ago. It's not just that he's eating everything in sight; he doesn't seem to care whether anything's delicious or disgusting, and he can't comment on flavors. And he's a food critic! It's literally his job to do that. When he's not eating, he's in the woods running for hours. And . . . his eyes are different. Like, a different color sometimes."

"Oh," said Vik, sitting on the swing next to me.

"Oh, what?"

"I'm not saying I know anything about what's happening with your dad, but my friend's dad—it was last summer, when I was in Portugal—started acting weird, too."

"Yeah?" I leaned forward. Could Vik know something that would help me figure out what was wrong with Dad?

"It was little things at first. You know, like he had meetings late, or forgot when my friend was in a game or a concert. But then he got a new haircut. And started working out a lot more."

"Okay," I said.

"And he got colored contacts lenses, too."

"So his eyes looked different! And then what happened?"

Vik looked at me sadly. "Then he left them."

A chill went down my back and my heart skipped a few beats. "What do you mean he left?"

Vik looked at the ground and nodded. "He told his family he had some things to work through, but it turns out he had a new girlfriend, and that's who he wanted to be with."

I didn't know what to say.

That was terrible. But it wasn't what was happening to my family. It couldn't be.

Or was it?

I blew a strand of hair out of my eyes. I couldn't believe Dad wanted to leave us. I just couldn't. I had to think. I had to come up with a plan. "I need to go. Catch up with you tomorrow?" I said.

"Okay." Vik looked at me anxiously. "You know, I'm sure the whole thing with your dad has nothing to do with him leaving you. I've seen your family—you all love each other. Forget I said anything."

"It's all right," I said. I walked back to my house in a daze.

But it wasn't.

Was it possible? Was Dad leaving us? Did that explain his

weird behavior? I walked into the kitchen like a zombie and stared blankly at the empty brownie pan on the counter. But becoming a glutton didn't mean Dad wanted to abandon us, right? Unless that was part of a plan to make us all disgusted with him? But then I thought about Dad losing his sense of taste and not wanting to bake with me anymore—was it all an act, so that he could break away from me, from all of us?

I threw the pan into the sink with a clatter. It was time for desperate measures.

I stood at the bottom of the stairs and listened. I could hear the shower running in the upstairs bathroom, and the door to Mom and Dad's room was closed. Henry had probably already left for rehearsal. There was no sign of Riya or Fletcher.

I tiptoed into Dad's office, next to the kitchen. It was a small room, but cozy, and always a little messy. Piled on top of his scratched-up desk were receipts from the past month or two, business cards, a mug smelling of old coffee, gum wrappers (cinnamon currently), photos of us kids, pens, broken pencils, sticky notes with lists, and lots of crumbs.

The nicest part of the room was the window that faced out back—it captured the evening sun and magnified it so that everything glowed golden at the end of the day, when Dad said he did his best writing. Dad always said that "poets need time to stare out of windows," and although neither of us was a poet, I understood what he meant.

His laptop case was on the desk. I silently slid the zipper open and took the laptop out. When the password screen appeared, I typed in: mimimouse527.

An error screen appeared. Wrong password. Wrong password? Maybe I just made a mistake. I tried again, carefully typing: mimimouse527.

Error.

Why had Dad changed his password? I finally admitted defeat and put the laptop back.

I felt terrible about snooping through Dad's stuff, but I had to know if there were any clues to his strange behavior. I unzipped an outside compartment of the laptop case, but it was empty. No brochures, and no handwritten notes.

I eased open the other outside zipper, felt inside, and fished out a book. A library book, judging from the plastic stretched over the cover. As I turned it over to get a closer look, a piece of paper fell out and fluttered to the floor. Just a boarding pass. I glanced at the cover—*Ghostwriting for Dummies*—and put it on the desk. I reached down to pick up the boarding pass when Mom called me from upstairs.

"Mimi?"

I snatched up the boarding pass and dashed back to the kitchen. "Yeah, Mom?" I called.

"Want to go to the movies with me? That chef film you wanted to see is playing in Bridgeton in an hour."

"Sounds great. Thanks!"

"Want to invite Vik?"

I glanced at the paper in my hand and froze.

"Mimi?"

"Uh, sure, I can try and ask him," I said in what I hoped was a normal voice.

I sat down hard and looked again.

The boarding pass said that Dad had flown home from Chicago two weeks earlier.

But he was supposed to have come from Houston.

CHAPTER 18

A REVIEW TO REMEMBER

I spent the next several days in a stupor but noticed several things that made me even more worried. While Henry, Jules, and Riya ran around happily, busy with their jobs and practice and rehearsals and going out with their friends, I couldn't say the same for Mom and Dad.

Mom worked all day and late into each night. Like Henry had promised, we tried to help her with cooking, laundry, and stuff—but Dad didn't pull his weight at all, except in the eating department. I caught Mom muttering to herself in an annoyed way when a whole shelf of leftovers disappeared in an hour.

Dad didn't appear to be bothered by Mom's increasing irritation. But his persistent cheerfulness made me suspicious that he was living in an imaginary place in his head, a place that didn't include the rest of us. I tried to talk to him, but he never had any time to spare for me. I carried the boarding pass around with me like an unlucky talisman but couldn't find the right time to ask him about it. Part of me was terrified to find out the truth.

Vik and I met every day, and I confided my worries in him while he tried to convince me that everything would be all right. I did my best to concentrate on baking something with *roots* for the While Away's contest, which was growing closer every day, but my heart wasn't in it. Not even for Puffy Fay. I was too worried about what Vik had said. *He left them.*

Late Thursday afternoon, two days before the contest, two things arrived at our house: *The Comity Journal* and a flyer for the While Away's contest.

I grabbed them from the mailbox and ran into the kitchen. First, the While Away's flyer:

Congrats, Golden Leaf Winner!
Only two days until the
While Away Café
Midsummer Baking Contest!
Bring your delectable baked goods by 9:00 a.m.
on Midsummer's Eve, when
the holders of the Golden Leaves
will be narrowed down to THREE,

who will immediately compete in
a Live Bake-Off!
Grand Prize: Spend three days in New York City baking
with Guest of Honor and Judge,
World-Famous Pastry Chef Puffy Fay!*

*Also, a Mandatory Internship at the While Away!

I shivered in excitement. Not only could I win a baking weekend with Puffy Fay, but also an internship at the While Away! I wasn't sure why they had to make the internship "mandatory"—who wouldn't want to work there? I folded up the flyer and tucked it in my pocket.

Next, for Dad's review. I didn't know what to expect. Would he trash the While Away? Would Mrs. T hate me forever as the girl whose father ruined her reputation? Or would it be a glowing review that helped launch the While Away as a Comity institution? I flipped to the back of the small newspaper and found it in the features section:

A WHILE REVIEW
By Paul Mackson

The While Away Café and Bakery, an enchanting addition to our lovely town, is located on Main Street, bridging the area between the town center and the woods. And what a welcome addition it is!

They make a lot of food! Most of it comes out of the ovens! I've eaten a lot of scrumptious things there this summer, and you should, too!

They have cakes, pies, cookies, and lots of other things that are baked! And did I mention that they are scrumptious?

The waitstaff is sometimes cranky, but that shouldn't dissuade you from going. The owner, Mrs. T, is as lovely and gracious as can be.

Oh, and there's going to be a contest for kids on June 23—my daughter, Mimi Mouse, is hoping to win, so let's all go cheer her on!

I'm sure all the food at the contest will be scrumptious!

Stay tuned—next week I'll review that scrumptious-looking snack shop, the Salt Shaker!

The paper fell from my numb fingers. Something was seriously wrong with Dad. That had to be the worst review I'd ever read. What kind of reviewer says, "They make a lot of food! Most of it comes out of the ovens!" How many times could someone use the word "scrumptious"? And of course, he snuck in a bit about the Salt Shaker, the While Away's chief competition. Mrs. T was going to be furious! And why did he mention *me*? He called me *Mimi Mouse*! I'd never live that down. I folded the paper back up and stuck it under the pile of mail to hide it from Mom, who had strolled into the kitchen. She scooped tea leaves into a small teapot and put the kettle on to boil.

The phone rang, and Mom answered it.

"Hello . . . Oh, yes, Charlie, how are you? . . . No, he's not home right now, but he should be back soon. . . . Is everything okay? . . . I will. . . . All right, thanks. Bye."

Dad came in the back door, breathing hard from his afternoon run.

"Paul," said Mom, "Charlie just called sounding upset. He wants you to call him as soon as possible."

Dad waved her off. "Oh, he can wait." He opened the fridge and started pulling out containers.

"Well, since he's your boss, maybe you shouldn't make him wait too long," she said.

"I know what it's about. I left him a message this morning saying I quit."

My stomach dropped.

"You *what?*" Mom slammed down her teacup. "Why on earth did you quit?"

"I'm tired of that job, Sangita. I'm sick of traveling and writing what other people tell me to write about. I want to . . . I want to . . . well, I want to eat this, for starters." He held up a takeout container and poised his fork.

"But you didn't even discuss it with me!" said Mom. She glanced at me, then back at Dad. "We've got a lot of bills coming up," she said quietly.

Dad started scarfing lo mein. "Oh, it'll all work out, don't worry," he said between slurps.

"Don't worry?! I can't believe you're being this nonchalant!" Mom cried. "How could you do this to us?"

I chewed on a strand of hair. I wished I could say something, anything to make things better. But I couldn't.

"I don't understand why you're so upset," Dad said.

"This is our family we're talking about," said Mom. She looked close to tears. "I've been working so hard, and I can't believe you . . . you . . ."

The kettle whistled. Mom turned off the burner but made no move to fill the teapot.

"What's going on?" said Henry, walking through the back door with Jules and Riya. "Why's everyone yelling?"

"I'm not yelling," said Dad, "but your mom's—"

"I'm furious, and I have every right to be!"

"Now, Sangita, calm down . . ."

"I will not calm down! Not until you explain yourself!"

I looked back and forth between my parents. They had their arguments from time to time, but I couldn't remember the last time they had actually yelled at each other. This was scarier than the cobra, and worse than Emma moving to the other side of the world.

I fished the boarding pass out of my pocket and threw it on the counter in front of Dad.

"Dad, why'd you go to Chicago?" I asked.

No one said anything. Dad stared like he was surprised to see me but kept slurping from the container. He rapidly finished the noodles and started on a slice of cold pizza.

Mom picked up the crumpled boarding pass. She looked pale, and her voice shook. "Well, Paul? What's your explanation?"

My worst fear was coming true. Dad held his finger up as he finished swallowing a huge bite. I was petrified of what he might say, but I also needed to know.

"It was just a connection," Dad said, turning the slice around and starting on the crust. "I wanted an earlier flight out of Houston, so I had to connect through Chicago instead of flying direct. I can show you my flight confirmation if you want." He chuckled and turned to me. "Where'd you get that, Mimi? Have you been fishing through my stuff?"

The guilt must have shown on my face.

"Oh, Mimi," said Mom. "Really?"

"He's been acting so weird!" I said, raising my voice. "All he does is run and eat!" I blinked my stinging eyes.

Everyone gaped in stunned silence while Dad finished the

pizza and dug something out of his pocket—one of Mrs. T's chocolates from the While Away. He popped it in his mouth and immediately started to unwrap another.

"But what I really want to know," said Mom, "is why you quit your job."

"I . . ." Dad finished the chocolate and took out a third.

"Wait, Dad quit his job?" Henry asked.

"I'm waiting, Paul, and so are your children." Mom put her hands on her hips.

"I . . ."

"Dad, are you all right?" Riya asked. "Mom, don't you think his face looks flushed?"

"Is he choking again?" asked Jules, sounding terrified.

"I'm fine." Dad unwrapped a fourth chocolate and chomped on it as his eyes flashed purple.

"Didn't anyone else see that?" I cried.

"See what?" asked Henry.

"Your cheeks do look red," said Mom. "Do you have a sunburn?" Mom put her hand on Dad's face and snatched it away like he was a hot stove. "You're burning up!"

"I said I'm fine." Dad reached for another chocolate.

Then his eyes rolled back in his head, and he collapsed on the floor.

CHAPTER 19

THE LULLABY

"So how is he? . . . Uh-huh, okay. That's good. . . . They think what?" Henry said. It was hours later when Mom finally called with an update from the emergency room.

I jumped up and down.

Henry held up a finger. "That's great. Should we come now? What? Oh, okay." He paused. "We're all fine. Yes, we ate. Don't worry. Love you, too. Bye."

"Can we go now?" Riya asked.

"Mom said not to bother. They're going to keep Dad overnight to make sure, but the doctors say he's going to be fine. Mom's coming home soon."

"Do they know what's wrong with him?" I asked.

"Lyme disease. At least that's what they think, given how

much time Dad spends running in the woods."

"Can Lyme make someone that sick?" Jules asked.

"I guess so," Henry said.

"Does Lyme disease make your eyes turn purple?" I asked.

Henry did a double take. "What?"

"Never mind." Apparently no one else had noticed.

"Can they cure him?" Riya asked.

Henry nodded and ran a hand through his curly hair. "Yeah. They're giving him antibiotics now, and he's already improved."

"I'm going to call Cole and let him know what's going on," Jules said. She bounded upstairs.

"I'm going to jump in the shower," Henry said. "What a night!"

"I'm going upstairs, too. I'll be back soon." Riya put a gentle hand on my shoulder.

Now that I was alone, I let out a long breath that I hadn't even realized I'd been holding. Although it was scary to have Dad in the hospital, I was relieved that everyone else could finally see there was something seriously wrong with him. I wondered, though, whether Lyme could really explain everything. Emma had Lyme two years ago, and her eyes and appetite had stayed normal—all she'd had was a rash. And Cole, Fletcher, and Henry had purple in their eyes, too, and they didn't seem to have Lyme.

I wandered into the living room and found myself at the table next to the piano. My clarinet gleamed in the waning light.

I picked it up and sat on the edge of the sofa, looking out the window at the woods. It was the summer solstice, the longest day of the year, and the sun had only just dipped below the horizon. I brought the mouthpiece to my lips and began to play Vik's song. I closed my eyes and could feel the summer sunlight shining on me, wavering through a canopy of trees. I heard birdsong. *Come with me*, the song said. I played it over and over; I got lost in the music.

I opened my eyes to the sound of a guitar. Henry was in an armchair across from me, damp hair shining, smelling of shampoo and strumming away. He played the chords flawlessly, as if he already knew the song. He caught my eye and nodded at me.

For the first time in my life, I didn't feel embarrassed making music with my brother. Surprising myself, I sang:

"Come with me
And watch the sun rise
In our place
Watch it paint the world in gold and pink

For you and I once met each other
Under the banyan tree
You and I can stay forever
Won't you come with me?"

Jules came into the room and started tapping on the coffee table in a syncopated rhythm. The heavy top of the table made a deep, dull thud, but the sides sounded lighter and more hollow. I went back to the clarinet, feeling the rhythm of Jules's drumming in my bones. Then I heard Henry take up the song:

"Come with me
And feel the noon sun
In our place
Feel the world grow strong

For you and I once played together
Under the banyan tree
You and I can stay forever
Won't you come with me?"

My heart leaped. I was astonished at Henry's ability to come up with lyrics that felt so right. But then Jules started to sing:

"Come with me
And smell the evening
In our place
Smell the dim, purple scent

For you and I once loved each other
Under the banyan tree
You and I can stay forever
Won't you come with me?"

My skin tingled, and the clarinet trembled in my hands. How did she do that? I gaped at Jules, who winked and put extra enthusiasm into her drumming. Then the thought came to me: there was a fourth verse. Who was going to sing it?

I heard a woman's lovely voice, meandering through the air like a vine. I thought briefly of Mrs. T, but then I realized who was singing.

"Come with me
And hear the starlight sing
In our place
Hear the world grow sleepy

For you and I once rested there
Under the banyan tree

You and I can stay forever
Won't you come with me?
Won't you come with me?
Won't you come with me?"

Riya faced the window as she finished singing. There was a moment of complete silence.

"How do you all know that song?" I whispered. I felt like the four of us were trapped in a bubble that wasn't letting in enough air.

"Same way you know it," Henry said, smiling. "Mom used to sing it to us every night when we were little. Don't you remember?"

"She said her mom used to sing it to her. I bet it goes back generations," said Riya.

"It's fun to make music with you," said Jules. "You've never stayed to play before."

And then I remembered: rocking in Mom's lap, her soft voice in my ear, her arms holding me close as I fell asleep to that melody. "She only hummed the song to me. She didn't sing the words," I said. "At least, I don't think so."

"Well, that's the family song," said Henry, ruffling my hair. "An oldie but a goodie."

"Vik taught me that song," I said.

"How could he know it?" Jules asked.

"I don't know. That's how I found him—he was playing it in the woods," I said. "He has an old wooden pipe." Vik said this was a song from his family—I wondered how we were related!

"So you're still spending all your time in the woods," said Riya. She looked at me curiously. "I thought that would end once Emma left."

"I love the woods," I said. "It's where I feel most like myself."

"But now that Dad's got Lyme disease, shouldn't we all stay away?" Jules asked.

I shook my head. "I always use bug spray and check for ticks. I'm fine, and I'm going back."

"But Mimi—"

"Leave her alone, Jules. Let her be happy," Riya said.

I was more than mildly surprised at hearing Riya stick up for me. "Thanks," I said. "The woods are a part of me, and I can't let go of them. I just have to be careful."

"What does that mean? Of ticks? Poison ivy?" asked Henry.

"No," I said, blushing furiously and trying to drive away thoughts of boars and cobras and delicious but dangerous honeysuckle.

"What are you hiding?" Riya's eyes bored into me like she could see into my brain.

"Nothing," I said.

"Mimi, are you okay?" Jules asked.

"Is there anything you want to tell us?" Henry asked.

I shook my head.

"Come on, Mimi," Jules said. "We want to help."

I scrambled for something to say. "I'm just . . . I'm just nervous about the baking contest." Which was true. Partly.

"So," said Riya. "Are you prepared? Have you planned out all the steps?"

I blinked. "Well, I've been so worried about Dad—"

"What's on your menu?" Henry asked.

"I've almost finished—"

"You need to know exactly what you're making, and how long it will take," said Jules. She tapped her foot. "The contest is the day after tomorrow, right? Cole is coming with us to cheer you on."

"That's nice of him. I don't know exactly what I'm making, but—"

"Kids! Where are you?" came Mom's voice.

"In the living room," called Henry.

Mom's hair curled crazily around her shoulders. She looked relieved, though, and wrapped us all in a hug.

"Oh, kids," she said. "He's going to be okay."

If only I could feel so sure.

CHAPTER 20

THE GOODBYE

Cream puffs. If I did a good enough job, Puffy Fay would love them. I felt confident about my choux pastry—after all, it was based on Puffy Fay's recipe. With a little patience, the puffs came out perfect every time. I combined water, sugar, salt, and butter in a saucepan and brought them to a boil. I added flour to the butter mixture, then stirred and cooked for several minutes until it was no longer raw. I moved the dough to my mixer, let it cool for a bit, then mixed in four eggs, one at a time. I piped the dough onto my baking sheet and slid it into the oven. Soon I had perfect little puffs, dry and hollow in the center to hold my filling.

This was the last day I had to prepare for the contest, and I was determined to use it wisely. I spent all morning making different fillings and trying them out on Mom. There are lots of root vegetables, but not all of them translated well into pastry cream.

"Nice, but heavy," Mom said when she'd tasted my sweet potato cream. "Also, kind of one-note?"

"I'm sorry, but ick," she said after trying a tiny taste of green garlic cream.

She tried a spoonful of beet cream. "It's gorgeous-looking, but . . . a little muddy-tasting? Keep trying."

"Now *that's* delicious," she said of my carrot pastry cream. "Sweet and carroty . . . and so unusual!" I'd decided to add some cinnamon, "*for prosperity*," according to The Book. I finally had a winner.

Vik's song floated through the open kitchen window as I finished my final shopping list.

I ran upstairs and handed the list to Mom, who was making a quick grocery run before getting back to work. After spending all morning taste testing with me, she'd brought Dad home from the hospital. He was exhausted but seemed fine otherwise and was fast asleep in bed. Lying next to him was a basket of get-well chocolates sent by the While Away, and he'd only eaten one. That reassured me that he'd truly recovered from whatever had made him act so weird. And that Mrs. T didn't hate him for mentioning the Salt Shaker in his review.

"Thanks for getting these ingredients for me. Are you sure

you have time? I could ride my bike into town."

"It's no problem." Mom smiled. "Do you need more help preparing?"

I shook my head. "You already helped me a ton by being my taste tester. Sorry I distracted you from work."

She brushed my hair out of my eyes and put her hands on either side of my face. "Dad's illness reminded me that nothing is more important than our family, Mimi. Compared to you, work doesn't matter. I'm incredibly proud of you. I love you so much, honey."

"Thanks, Mom. I love you, too," I said as she kissed me on the forehead and gave me a hug. It was so good to have things back to normal.

Once Mom left, the song wafted through the window again, and I could feel the woods calling me. I hoped Vik would still be there when I got to the tree.

I grabbed The Book, put it in my backpack, and flung it over my shoulder. The song echoed through the forest as I ran to the banyan and called Vik's name.

"I've got so much to tell you!" I said as he jumped down.

"All good, I hope?" Vik said with a quirk of his mouth.

"Well, kind of. Dad had Lyme disease—that's why he was acting so strange. But he went to the hospital, and they put him on antibiotics, and he's much better now."

"Oh," said Vik. "That's great!" He furrowed his brow. "I

mean, about him being better, of course. Come, let's walk while we talk. I've got something to show you. And something to ask you." He started on a path leading away from the pond.

"Where are we going?"

"I'll tell you when we get there," said Vik.

I couldn't wait any longer; I was bursting to tell him. "I know why your song seems so familiar," I said.

"Yes?" Vik made his way around a scrubby young pine.

"'Come with Me' is my family's song, too! At least, my mom's family. Mom used to sing it to us as a lullaby when we were little. She learned it from my grandmother."

Vik stopped and stared at me like I'd told him I was flying to the moon. "You can't be serious."

I nodded. "It's true. And my brother and sisters knew like three more verses. Anyway, I thought . . . maybe we're related." I nearly jumped up and down with excitement.

Vik stared at me for a moment longer, but I could see his thoughts were far away. He abruptly shook his head as if to clear it. "Let's keep going." He walked so fast I had to jog to keep up with him.

Well, that was strange. "But isn't that cool?" I asked.

"Yes, sure, I suppose," said Vik.

That wasn't the reaction I expected. "But—"

"What else has been happening?" Vik asked. "You said you had lots to tell me."

"Oh!" I reached into my pocket and found the flyer from the While Away. "As if I needed more to be excited about—I mean, *Puffy Fay* is the judge, and the winner gets to bake with him! But the winner also gets an internship at the While Away! It's just what I was hoping for this summer. If I win, I'm sure I can convince my parents to let me skip summer camp next month. I don't know why they had to make it mandatory, though. Who wouldn't want an internship?"

Vik stopped midstride. "Mandatory? Can I see that?"

I handed Vik the flyer. He read it with narrowed eyes and mumbled something under his breath.

"Is something wrong?"

Vik handed the flyer back to me. He crossed his arms and looked me in the eyes. "Has it ever occurred to you that they're taking advantage of you?"

"Who?"

"The While Away. The owner, and those who work there. They're the ones who benefit the most from this contest."

I blinked. "They're giving me this huge opportunity! I mean, Puffy Fay!"

"Yes, and they've been doing a brisk business, haven't they, ever since word got out about the contest? Didn't you tell me that their original baked goods were awful? I hear they've been a lot more successful selling their contestants' entries to customers."

"They gave away my chocolate-chunk thyme cookies for free. People loved them," I said. "I didn't have a problem with it. Anyway, Mrs. T could give away or sell everything I've ever baked, if it means I get to meet Puffy Fay."

"And what about this internship? Another demand."

"Demand? It's a chance to learn—"

"Change of plan," said Vik, turning back on the path and accelerating again. "Let's go a different way."

"Where are we going?" I struggled to catch up with him.

But Vik didn't say another word and sprinted like the boar was chasing him. I didn't know how much longer I'd be able to keep up, and I struggled to catch my breath, when Vik finally stopped.

He had brought us to my hangout. That was odd.

I flung myself to the ground and dumped my backpack next to me. "Why did we run all that way to just come here?" I asked.

Vik stared into the middle distance with knit brows.

"Um, Vik? Will you come to the While Away tomorrow? It would mean a lot to me."

Vik shook his head. "I don't think so. And I don't think you should go, either."

I couldn't have heard him right. "What? But you've been helping me. Don't you want to see how I do? And . . . cheer me on?"

Vik laughed. "I've just been kidding around; I didn't think you'd take me so seriously."

"What are you talking about?"

"I'm leaving," said Vik.

"But—"

"I don't belong in this little place," said Vik. I understood that he didn't mean my hangout; he meant Comity, and the beautiful woods around us. My woods.

"I'm not the one who—"

"I told you I was only here for the summer," he said, eyeing me coldly. "I hope you didn't think we were going to be best friends."

"I . . ." I didn't know what to say, and angry tears sprang to my eyes. I refused to blink.

"All that time we spent talking about food—it was just a way to pass the time while I was stuck here. I don't actually think you're that talented. I've met loads of kids who are much better bakers than you."

A few traitor tears trickled down my face before I hastily wiped them away. "But you said—"

"I said what I thought you wanted to hear," Vik said in a flat voice. "That's all."

"But—"

"Don't come back to the woods," said Vik. "And if I were you, I wouldn't compete in that baking contest." His eyes glittered like golden ice. "You won't win. Don't make a fool of yourself in front of everyone. Like you did before."

I watched helplessly as he spun around and disappeared into the trees.

CHAPTER 21

PUFFY FAY

The birds woke me. The sky lightened and a rose-colored streak appeared on the horizon as I looked out my open window. The dewy-fresh air did nothing to soothe the molten lava cake of dread in my stomach. If only I could disappear into the woods and never have to face anyone again.

But I couldn't.

I might run into Vik.

I dragged myself into the kitchen and set out my ingredients. But for the first time in my life, the prospect of baking didn't make me happy.

You won't win. Don't make a fool of yourself.

I pounded the counter with my fist, tipping over a mixing bowl and engulfing myself in a cloud of flour.

After all the hours we'd spent together, all the stories we'd shared. All the *food* we'd shared. What had happened? Why would Vik suddenly be so cruel?

And he'd also done something else, something I'd discovered when I'd picked up my strangely light backpack to trudge back home.

He had taken The Book. Just when I needed it most! I wanted to have it as a reference if I managed to make it to the Bake-Off.

Now I was completely on my own.

It didn't matter. I was going to compete. I dusted myself off and got to work. While I was baking my cream puffs, I had second thoughts about my filling. Too many people were going to use carrots. They were clearly the easiest root to cook with. I wouldn't win by playing it safe—I'd learned that the hard way, with the vanilla cookies.

I looked through the pantry and the fridge, hoping to come up with some last-minute inspiration. No luck.

And then I opened the freezer and saw what was sitting there.

I was going to take a risk.

There should be a word for being grateful and terrified at the same time . . . terriful? Grateified? Because that's how I felt having the whole family come to support me. They were taking my baking seriously now, so it would be even worse when I messed up. *If* I messed up.

By the time everyone was ready to leave, I was filling the last cream puff with pale green pastry cream. I licked a bit off my finger. It was good—an intriguing mix of warm pistachio, floral cardamom, and invigorating ginger. And ginger, of course, was a *root*. I only wished I knew what The Book would say about it. And was it good enough? Spotting the last of Mom's batch of kulfi—Indian ice cream made of thick sweetened cream and flavored with pistachio, ginger, and cardamom—had inspired me to make a pastry cream with the same flavors.

I gently put the tops on the puffs and pressed ground pistachios onto the sides of the filling. I piped small dots of white icing on the top and pressed a piece of candied ginger onto each one.

"These look great. What are they, petit fours?" asked Henry, peering over my shoulder.

"Petit fours are miniature cakes. These are cream puffs," I said with an attempt at a smile. "Puffy Fay's favorite. It's how he made his name in the Food TV world—he won a competition with his cream puffs."

"Cool, since his name is Puffy," said Jules, finishing the last of her orange juice.

"That's not his real name, dummy," said Riya, rolling her eyes. "Right, Mimi?"

"Yeah, he has a funny name," I said. "It's Pyramus, but he abbreviates it as P." I took a deep breath. "I know I'm taking a risk making cream puffs. If I messed up in any way, he'll hate them, and I won't make it to the Bake-Off. But I've added my own twist, and I hope he thinks they're interesting, at least."

"Ready, Mimi?" Dad lifted my three-tiered dessert stand and headed to the mudroom. Since he'd come home, he'd had no fever and no purple eyes. He'd even thrown out the rest of the get-well chocolate package. I guessed all he needed was antibiotics after all. Mom grabbed the car keys and my backpack loaded with baking supplies that I'd need if I made it to the Bake-Off.

I placed the cream puffs in a box and snapped the lid closed.

I took a deep breath and walked out of the kitchen.

It was time to meet Puffy Fay.

We parked down the street and passed the Salt Shaker as we hurried to the While Away.

"Try our famous sports chips?" A muscular teenage boy was handing out free samples. "And inside, we're serving a special avocado toast that really helps with computation."

Computation?

"No thanks." Dad shook his head and kept striding toward the café.

I caught my breath as we passed a glossy black limousine parked in front of the While Away. Puffy Fay was here already! I thought we were going to be early, but there was a line out the door. Thankfully, it was moving fast.

Peaseblossom stood at the entrance. She wore a flowing white dress and a circlet of delicate pink flowers in her hair and carried a tray with cups of golden liquid. "We bid you welcome to our sweet café," she said, her cheeks flushing prettily as she gave a small curtsy. "On this, our first midsummer's contest day." We each took a cup as we passed and drank the sweet chilled beverage—it was refreshing and tasted like ginger ale with a swirl of summer peaches. Then Peaseblossom waved us through the open door.

"Wow," said Henry.

We stepped into an enchanted culinary forest. The walls had been painted to look like a thicket of trees, and the ceiling resembled the summer sky in the woods, complete with overhanging branches. There were topiaries and baskets overflowing with wildflowers. The tables were grouped to one side, still draped in their shimmering coverings. Dreamy music floated through the air, and piney, herby scents wafted on gentle currents. Butterflies flitted around and landed on people's heads

and shoulders. And everywhere we looked, there were trays of baked goods—most of them, I realized, straight from the pages of Puffy Fay's cookbook. The pastry case and the counter near it were hidden behind curtains that looked like a wall of evergreens.

The cranky goth waitress I'd met before was seated at a registration table that appeared to be chiseled from a mossy stone. Her stand-up headband looked like a stretched spiderweb. I tried not to stare.

"How many in your party?" she asked, peering behind me.

"Six," I said.

"How sweet. Now where's your Golden Leaf to compete?" She held out a long-fingered hand.

I handed her my leaf. She examined it carefully, holding it up to the light as if looking for a counterfeit. She seemed satisfied and passed me a piece of paper.

"And now you'll sign this form, for if you win, your mandatory training will begin."

"What?" said Dad. "What kind of contract is this?"

"It's an internship, Dad. The grand prize winner gets to bake with Puffy Fay *and* gets an internship at the While Away!"

"But what about camp?" Mom interjected.

"Mom, Dad, *please*. It would be a dream come true to work here for the summer," I pleaded.

Mom and Dad looked at each other. Mom gave a tiny nod.

"Okay," said Dad.

"Thanks for understanding, Mom and Dad." My hand shook as I signed the form and got my entry number.

At the far end of the room, in front of the windows that looked out onto the woods, was an enormous table with platters of homemade baked goods with a couple of dozen kids milling around it. I searched in vain for Puffy Fay's starched white chef's jacket and perky toque. Maybe he was dressed in normal clothes, since he wasn't actually baking today?

I took the dessert stand from Dad and hurried to the table, still looking for Puffy. Once I got there I tried to arrange my cream puffs in the most attractive way possible. They did look lovely—golden pastry and pale green filling, like the café around us. I hoped Puffy Fay would agree.

Don't make a fool of yourself, Vik's voice echoed in my head.

"Stop it," I whispered.

"Hi, Mimi Mouse." Kiera's syrupy voice came from behind me.

I turned slowly and tried unsuccessfully to smile. "Hi, Kiera." She wore a watermelon-colored skirt and a creamy vanilla top and looked perfect as always. Her shiny hair was pulled back in a sleek ponytail. I noted she was wearing sandals, a big no-no in kitchen safety.

"What a sickly shade of green," said Kiera, peeking at my cream puffs. "No chocolate, huh?"

"Thought I'd do something different," I said.

"Me too," said Kiera. She pointed to the tall gilded dessert stand next to mine. It held the most spectacular carrot cake I'd ever seen, three-layered, ridiculously lofty and even, and topped with swirls of creamy frosting. I knew the layers would be moist and spiced and the frosting tangy and sweet. It looked worthy of a professional pastry shop. My stomach dropped to my dusty sneakers, which I shuffled awkwardly.

"That looks beautiful," I said, trying to keep my voice even. "I guess you've learned a lot working here."

"Especially about *presentation*," said Kiera. She took in my outfit of rumpled T-shirt and shorts, glanced at my cream puffs again, and looked smug.

I looked anxiously at my puffs. Were some of them uneven? Had I made a mistake by choosing something simple like candied ginger for the tops? Kiera's entry looked like it had been made by an expert, but mine looked like a kid had made them. Not a particularly talented kid, either.

"Where's Puffy Fay?" I asked.

"He had to take a phone call," Kiera said importantly. "I'm sure he'll be back to start judging soon. Is your dad here? He must be excited to be in a place with so many *scrumptious* treats." She snickered.

I crossed my arms. "Don't talk about my—"

"Oh, look, there's Francesca. See you later, Mimi." Kiera

dismissed me with a wave of her hand and sauntered off toward the other end of the café.

I took a calming breath, trying to put Kiera and her perfect cake out of my mind, then walked around the table and looked over the other entries. There were beet brownies and carrot bars and some more ambitious items like a pastry topped with potato and persimmon slices, a candied parsnip tart, and a gorgeous icing-topped yellow Bundt cake that I thought was made with turmeric. But nothing could compare with Kiera's carrot cake. Maybe, just maybe, I'd make it to the Bake-Off. But if Kiera was suddenly a master pastry chef, how could I compete?

You won't win, whispered Vik's voice in my head.

The air around me was suddenly stuffy, and I couldn't catch my breath. My siblings chatted with their friends—Cole, Fletcher, and Lily had all showed up—and Mom and Dad talked to our neighbors, but they seemed far away, like I was seeing them through the wrong end of a telescope. I had to get out of the café, even if it was for only a moment.

I pushed my way through the crowded room and reached the back door, which led to a small patio. I stumbled outside, grabbed the metal railing, and took great gulps of air. I gazed at the river making its lazy way toward some distant ocean and wished I could float away on it.

"I said I'll be back as soon as I can," boomed a deep voice behind me.

I turned around in surprise. Puffy Fay sat hunched on a metal stool talking into a cell phone. His chef's jacket was crisp and white and contrasted against his dark jeans and motorcycle boots. He was wearing a dark blue beanie instead of his usual toque, and there were flecks of gray in his black hair and goatee. He had a hoop earring in one ear. He looked like a rock star pirate chef.

"Yeah, I know I've got to be there by eight. Like I said, I'll make it. This shouldn't take more than a couple of hours. . . . Yes. Bye." He brought the phone down from his ear and started tapping on the screen.

I didn't want him to think I'd been spying on him, so I tried to sneak back to the door.

Puffy Fay fixed me with his bright blue gaze. "Did Mrs. T tell you to come out here and check on me? I said I'd be right back in. I had to take a call." His eyes weren't full of fun, like they were on TV.

Puffy Fay's eyes were distinctly annoyed.

"Oh, no, Chef Fay," I said. "I . . . I just came out here to get some air."

"Then have a seat," he said, indicating the stool next to him.

I sat.

I was sitting next to *Puffy Fay*!

I glanced at him out of the corner of my eye, but his attention was focused on his phone, so I watched the river and

246

woods and tried to stop trembling.

"I grew up here in Comity, you know," he said.

"I do know," I said fervently.

"I've always loved Comity Woods. Sometimes I wish I'd never left."

"But . . ." I caught my breath. "You live in New York, and you have your restaurants and your TV show and your cookbook. And I've learned so much from you."

"You have, huh?" He turned to me with an unreadable expression.

"I've read *Mischief and Magic in the Kitchen* so many times, I've pretty much got it memorized. I love all the stories you tell about making food for your family and friends. I try to experiment with herbs and spices in my baking—and it's all thanks to you."

Puffy Fay considered me. "Well then, I guess it's good I moved away after all." He pocketed his phone.

"It's wonderful that you agreed to judge a kids' contest. Is it because you're such good friends with Mrs. T?"

He looked off into the distance. "I only met her last week," he said. "And to tell you the truth, I have no idea why I'm here. She gave me the nastiest bitter chocolate to eat. Once she asked me to come, though, I felt like . . . I had to . . ." His voice trailed off.

"Chef Fay? Are you okay?"

He blinked and shook his head. "You don't just say no to an enchanting woman like that. I've got a new cookbook coming out, and I've got to get back for a book signing event in New York tonight. My publicist wants to kill me. But I told her I needed to stay here this morning. Anyway, it's good to meet a kindred spirit. What's your name?"

"Mimi. I can't wait to read your new book!"

"Well, Mimi—" Puffy Fay shook my hand. "—you might be in luck."

We slid off the stools. Puffy Fay held his arm out, and I took it.

The look on Kiera's face as we went back into the café made me feel like I'd already won.

CHAPTER 22

THE CHEATER

Peaseblossom stood at the table with all the entries. She raised her voice and addressed the whole room. "We humbly thank you all for coming here. A hearty welcome on this lovely day. Midsummer's Eve—it comes but once a year. So please join me to cheer Chef Puffy Fay!"

The café thundered with cheers and applause as Puffy Fay and I made our way to the display table. "Thank you, everyone," said Puffy. "So happy to be back in my hometown meeting the chefs of tomorrow!" He waved and inclined his head as people continued to clap.

Once we got to the table, Puffy Fay was all business.

"Which ones are yours, Mimi?"

"Right here."

"Cream puffs, huh?" He raised an eyebrow.

I swallowed hard. "I loved watching you win the Golden Pastry Tourney with your perfect pumpkin pie cream puffs. And I've made your spiced pâte à choux and pumpkin pastry cream loads of times."

Puffy Fay gave a brisk nod. "You really have memorized my book," he said. "But these don't look like they're pumpkin."

"No. I wanted to give you something original. I was inspired by a favorite dessert of mine. And of course, I had to use a root, so—"

"Don't tell me. Let me taste and guess," said Puffy Fay. He picked up a cream puff, felt its weight, and sniffed it. He placed it on a small white plate and examined it from all angles. He took a fork and cut into the puff, taking a small piece of the pastry only. He chewed, furrowed his brow, and wrote on a small notepad.

I couldn't breathe. *Does he like it? Can he taste the spice I put in the pastry? Is it the right texture? Is it puffy enough?*

Next, he tasted the filling. Smacking his lips, he took another, larger taste. He made another note.

Can he taste the ginger in the cream, or does the pistachio overpower it? And is he familiar with the dessert that inspired me? Will he think there are too many flavors?

Finally, he cut a larger piece containing both pastry and filling. He chewed for quite some time and appeared to swish it around in his mouth. He made more notes.

I had to bite my tongue to keep from asking him what he thought. *Do they go well together? Do the puffs have enough hollow space to hold the filling? Does everything harmonize in the right way?* I thought they were good at home, but now I wasn't so sure.

"Thank you, Mimi," he said. He took a sip of water and blotted his lips with a napkin.

And that was it.

I stepped back from the table and watched Puffy Fay work his way methodically around the two dozen entries. It was hard to tell what he did and didn't like, although he took only a single bite of the potato-persimmon pastry before moving on.

Dad joined me. "How's it going?" he asked.

"Good, I think. I met Puffy Fay!"

"I saw that—you walked into the room with him! What did he think of your food?"

"He made all kinds of notes, but he didn't say anything."

"I'm sure he loved it. Can I try one?"

I nodded. Once the entries had been judged, they were free for anyone to sample.

Dad bit into a puff. "Mimi, this is genius. I don't know how you packed all these flavors into a single bite—ginger, pistachio, and cardamom. And they're so light and airy!" He finished the puff slowly, relishing every bite. "I'm so sorry I wasn't able to help you prepare."

Dad's palate was back! I'd missed being able to talk about food in an in-depth way with the only other person in my family who loved it like I did. "I'm sorry, too—I really could have used your help! But Mom did a great job taste testing. And this morning, I got the bright idea to make this filling, inspired by Mom's kulfi," I said.

"I think you hit it out of the park," said Dad. "And I'm not just saying that because I love you."

We strolled around the table, tasting treats and talking to the kids gathered near their entries. Eventually, we found ourselves goggling at Kiera's professional-looking carrot cake.

Dad took a bite. "Mmm. Pineapple cream cheese frosting—delicious! This is quite light, very difficult to achieve in a carrot cake. Reminds me of the one they serve at Sucre et Sel, the French bakery in Boston. I reviewed them a couple of years ago." He looked across the café. "Mom's waving at me—looks like she wants to introduce me to someone else. I'd better go, honey. Want to come?"

"No, I'll just hang around here, in case Puffy Fay comes back."

Dad walked away.

I looked at Kiera's beautiful cake again and noticed something irregular in the frosting at the bottom.

Subtle but unmistakable, there was a double *S*.

Double *S*. I gasped. *Sucre et Sel!* Had Kiera *bought* this cake from that bakery? No wonder it looked so professional! Disgusted as I was, I was slightly relieved that Kiera hadn't actually made that marvelous cake herself.

I pushed my hair out of my face. I couldn't accuse her without proof, and I couldn't prove she bought it, not unless she'd brought the box from the bakery, or a receipt or something. I looked around quickly. No one seemed to be looking my way, so I ducked and disappeared under the display table. Hidden under the green tablecloth, I crawled the length of the table on my hands and knees. There were a few boxes and paper bags, but none from Sucre et Sel, and definitely nothing with a receipt. I crept out from under the table and straightened up, brushing dust off my knees.

"So thrilled to see you here, my dear, dear Mimi." Mrs. T appeared out of nowhere, looking more ethereal than ever in a delicate layered pink dress. She had tucked a loose-petaled rose behind her ear, and her perfume was so delicious—flowery and pungent in a mysterious way—that I actually caught myself sniffing the air.

"Mrs. T," I said. I angled myself so she couldn't see my red, dusty legs. "Thank you so much for bringing Puffy Fay here. Even if I don't make it into the Bake-Off, this has already been a dream come true."

"Tut-tut, Mimi, dear. Don't be so pessimistic. I know you'll go far." Her emerald eyes glittered.

"I hope so. But even if I don't, it was such a thrill to have Puffy Fay taste my baking."

"Chef Fay has already judged your entry?" Mrs. T seemed flustered. "I've been busy, making . . . the ale, and . . . my chocolates. Where are your treats?"

"Right here—the ginger-pistachio cream puffs," I said. "And I added—"

"What did Chef Fay say?" Mrs. T grasped my arm.

"Not much. He spent a long time tasting them—"

"My dear, you should have brought them to me first!" Mrs. T held up one of my puffs. "It's lovely, Mimi." She took a bite and smiled. "Very tasty, too." She finished it off and elegantly licked her fingers. "Ah, ginger. The most sublime of roots! Promoter of confidence and energy! And cardamom, for joy." She inclined her head gracefully. "And now I must find Chef Fay and tell him . . ." She scanned the room. "Ah! There he is. Chef Fay! Puffy!" She sped away.

I sighed. I wasn't sure my puffs could compete with that carrot cake. But I had no proof that Kiera hadn't made it. And Puffy Fay was an expert, and he spoke to all the contestants. Maybe he'd already recognized what I suspected.

I joined my siblings, eating more treats off rustic wooden platters and drinking more cups of cool golden ginger ale. I tried to avoid looking at the judges' table, where Puffy Fay made more notes and discussed the entries with Mrs. T.

I'd told Mrs. T the truth. Meeting Puffy Fay was a dream come true.

But I had to admit that I wanted something else. I wanted to finally be the best at something—not just anything, but the thing I loved most in the world. I wanted my culinary idol to recognize that I had talent and to help me develop it. I wanted my family to see me excel.

I wanted to win.

Dad came to me at ten minutes to eleven. "They're about to announce the three finalists," he said, squeezing my hand.

"They are?" I could barely get the words out.

Dad nodded. "I had the pleasure of meeting Chef Fay, who, to my surprise, knows and likes my writing. He's a great guy, and as nerdy about baking as we are. He spent a year in India, you know, and loves Indian flavors."

"Attention, please!" called Mrs. T, standing in front of the display table with Puffy Fay. "Dear customers and friends, Chef Fay has made his decision. It was quite difficult to do—there's a lot of talent in this town! A round of applause for all the contestants. Wonderful job, everyone!"

The room erupted in applause and cheers. Mom, Dad,

Henry, Riya, Jules, and even Lily, Fletcher, and Cole beamed at me. Dad whistled through his fingers.

I couldn't help grinning. The cheering felt good, and I felt like I deserved it. I *had* baked something truly special.

But what if I didn't make it to the Bake-Off? *I've met loads of kids who are much better bakers than you,* Vik's voice whispered in my head.

That wiped the grin off my face.

"Now we are ready to announce the names of the three bakers advancing," said Mrs. T.

Puffy Fay glanced at his watch, then addressed the room. "This talented young baker made an exquisite carrot cake that looked and tasted like it could have come from a bakery in Paris."

My stomach did a flip.

"The first contestant advancing to the Bake-Off is: Kiera Jones! Kiera, please join us," said Puffy.

Kiera strutted up to Puffy Fay and shook his hand triumphantly to general applause.

I took a deep breath. A store-bought cake might have gotten Kiera to this point, but how could she fake her way through the Bake-Off?

"The second contestant baked an enchanting turmeric-coconut coffee cake, enhanced with nutmeg and cardamom. It reminds me of a tasty little treat I once had in Goa," said Puffy.

Someone else had used cardamom in their entry? And

it reminded Puffy Fay of an Indian dessert? I broke out in a sweat.

"Guy Smith! Please come up."

A boy wearing sunglasses, a baseball cap, and a hoodie pulled over his head slouched up to Puffy Fay. Instead of shaking his hand, the kid waved vaguely, went to stand on the other side of Kiera, and slumped like he was attempting to blend into the surroundings.

And I thought I had a trouble performing in front of an audience.

Puffy Fay and Mrs. T lowered their voices and talked to each other for a moment.

You won't win. Don't make a fool of yourself.

I looked around at all the people squeezed into the café. It felt like the whole town was here. Maybe it would be a relief if I didn't need to bake in front of everyone.

"I've got it, Mrs. T—I know what I've decided," came Puffy's voice. Then he said more loudly, "Last but certainly not least, our third Bake-Off contestant. This young person had the audacity to make my own signature dessert, but with her own personal spin on it. She baked the most exquisite ginger-pistachio cream puffs, enhanced by the subtle use of carda-mom, which I believe was inspired by the Indian ice cream called kulfi. Mimi Mackson, please come up!"

I couldn't believe it! My family sent up a huge cheer. Mom gave me a swift kiss on the cheek, and Dad ruffled my hair,

259

saying, "I knew it!" Henry give me a high five, Jules jumped up and down, and Riya hugged me tightly and wouldn't let go until Jules made her.

I floated to Puffy Fay and shook his hand. *Puffy Fay thought I had one of the best three desserts! Among dozens of entries!* The embarrassment of the vanilla cookies and Kiera calling me Mimi Mouse faded away. *You were wrong, Vik.*

Mrs. T inclined her head and gave me a triumphant smile.

I was competing in the Bake-Off!

CHAPTER 23

FLOUR AND FLOWERS

"This way, my fine young talents," said Mrs. T, sweeping the three of us to the back of the café.

The dark-haired waitress drew aside the evergreen curtains to reveal three baking stations, each with all the equipment any baker could want. A mixer, food processor, piping bags and pastry tips, a variety of pans, parchment paper, and an oven. There was even a blast chiller, just like on Puffy Fay's TV show.

Kiera sauntered to the station on the left. I took the middle, pulling my hair into a ponytail and hefting my backpack full of baking supplies over my shoulder. Hoodie Boy slunk to the right.

"There is a theme for this, the final Bake-Off," said Mrs. T. She cleared her throat and recited:

"Midsummer's Eve has come again, and so
Our final three must bake and show their powers.
What blooms at last, once sprouts have time to grow?
The last Midsummer's Bake-Off theme is _____!"

Flowers, I thought to myself. I was getting pretty good at these riddles. I snuck a peek at Kiera, who looked terrified.

But Kiera didn't have to sweat for long. Mrs. T nodded to Peaseblossom, who uncovered a table overflowing with bunches of edible flowers—marigolds, dandelions, lavender, hibiscus, roses, chrysanthemums, jasmine, violets, daisies, and some others I didn't recognize. Luckily, I didn't see any honeysuckle.

"Each of you must use at least one type of flower in your baking," said Puffy Fay, seating himself at a small table behind the flower display.

But petals are delicate and could turn to dust in an oven, I thought.

"You have one hour," said Mrs. T, settling in next to Puffy Fay.

"Oh, and one last thing," said Puffy Fay. "After you're done, we'd like to hear your story."

"What story? This is a baking contest." Kiera's voice shook as she tied on an apron. I guessed it was sinking in that she couldn't cheat her way into winning this round.

"Food always tells a story, and the best food tells a memorable one," Puffy Fay said. "I'd like to hear about your inspiration for your dish. You'll find basic ingredients—flour, butter, sugar, spices, and so on—at your stations. The fridge has anything else you might need. On your mark."

"Get set," said Mrs. T.

"GO!" they both said at once.

You won't win, I thought, and shook my head. *Focus, Mimi. Focus on the baking. What are you going to make?*

I considered the flowers on the table, but my mind went blank. My ears started to buzz, and the sides of my vision turned gray.

Desperate, I searched the audience. Mom smiled and nodded, and my siblings looked at me expectantly. If only Emma were here—she would have made a face at Kiera and made me giggle.

I couldn't remember what it felt like to giggle.

Puffy Fay looked at his watch again, then fixed me with a bright blue stare.

Dad stood in the front row behind the judges' table. He caught my eye and mouthed the word *scrumptious* while rubbing his stomach.

I grinned and raced to the flower table.

I was going to make cupcakes, of course! My favorite ones.

I spied a bunch of lavender. I gathered it and a bunch of

purple violets—my favorite shade of my favorite color—and brought them to my station.

I grabbed lemons, buttermilk, butter, eggs, and blackberries. I had to find a way to do everything in an hour. I glanced at the big digital timer. Well, fifty-one minutes.

First, the sugared violets—it would be a challenge to get them ready in time. Vik had hurt me, but I had to admit that his advice was good. These would be the perfect garnish for my cupcakes. I lined a baking sheet with wax paper, added water to meringue powder (less messy than using an egg white) to make a thin solution, and applied it to the violets with a small paintbrush I'd pulled from my backpack. I opened a pack of superfine sugar and sprinkled it on liberally; I gently shook the flowers off and sprinkled again. I put the baking sheet near the already preheated oven, hoping that the warm temperature would help them dry quickly.

Next, the cupcakes. I zested the lemons, scooped sugar from a big bowl, and rubbed the zest in until the mixture was pale yellow and aromatic. I creamed the lemon-flavored sugar with softened butter in the mixer, adding eggs, vanilla, and lemon extract. I measured and sifted together cake flour, baking powder, and salt, then alternated mixing the flour mixture and buttermilk into the butter and sugar mixture. I made sure not to mix too much, since I knew it would make my cakes tough. At the end, I folded in a handful of chopped lavender petals by hand. *Lavender, for luck*, I thought. I scraped the batter into a paper-lined cupcake pan and put it in the oven, hoping the cupcakes would have enough time to cool before I had to frost them.

Finally, the frosting. I mashed the blackberries, strained them into a bowl, then chopped up a handful of lavender and added it to the berries. I whipped the butter until it was fluffy, poured in some of the blackberry-lavender mixture, and then added powdered sugar, beating the whole time, until I had a blackberry-lavender frosting that smelled like summer.

I checked on my cupcakes. They weren't rising the way they should and just lay like little lumps in the wells of the pan. What had gone wrong? I knew my recipe by heart, and in all the times I'd made these cupcakes, this had never happened. Dense balls of batter stared at me accusingly. Horrified, I pulled them out and sniffed them. They didn't even smell sweet! I pinched a piece off the edge of one cupcake, blew on it, and tasted gingerly.

Disgusted, I spit it out.

I dumped the nasty cakes into the trash, returned to my station, and tasted a pinch of sugar from the large bowl.

It wasn't a bowl of sugar. It was salt! What a rookie mistake!

I tasted from the small bowl on my table. That was salt, too!

How did that happen? Was someone trying to sabotage

me? I glowered at Kiera, but she was focused on breaking a bar of white chocolate. Her station was a disaster, with half-used ingredients all over the place.

Thirty minutes to go! I needed to get more cupcakes in the oven, or I wouldn't have anything to show Puffy Fay but a bowl of blackberry frosting.

I raced to Hoodie Boy's station. "Can I take your sugar?" I asked.

He grunted and jerked his head. After tasting to make sure it *was* sugar, I ran back with the bowl.

In a frenzy, I remade the batter, and this time I tasted it before I poured it into the pan. It was good, although I could have used more time to cream the butter and lemon-sugar. I popped the pan into the oven with only twenty-seven minutes to go. I knew these cupcakes needed to bake for fifteen, so I increased the oven temperature a tiny bit and hoped for the best. If I could take them out in thirteen minutes, I might be able to get them cool enough so the frosting wouldn't melt when I piped it onto the cupcakes.

"No, no, no!" Kiera cried. I looked over at her station, and she was poking at a stiff blob of white chocolate she'd pulled from the microwave. "It's the third batch that's ruined!" She had flour on her chin and chocolate in her hair.

I'd let her deal with her disasters by herself, I thought. But then I saw her wipe a tear from her cheek.

I sighed. "Have you tried melting it over a double boiler?" I asked.

"What's a double boiler?"

I grabbed a pot and filled it with an inch of water. "It's gentler than a microwave, and you can stir the whole time," I said.

I stuck the pot on the burner at Kiera's station and put a bowl on top of it so it didn't touch the water. I turned up the flame so the water started to simmer. "Now melt the chocolate in the bowl warmed by the water. That way it won't seize up," I said.

"Okay," mumbled Kiera. She furrowed her brow and stared at me. "Mimi—"

My timer went off. I raced to my station and pulled my cupcakes out—they were barely starting to brown on top. I tested them with a toothpick, and only the slightest bit of crumb stuck to it. But I had to take them out now or I was going to run out of time. I fished them out of the pan, burning several fingers in the process. I set them on the counter to cool and ran to the sink to run cold water over my scorched fingers. I checked on the candied violets, but they were still a little damp, and the sugar wasn't sticking to them completely. Fourteen minutes to go. I turned off the oven and placed the violets inside.

I scooped the frosting into a pastry bag and checked on the cupcakes again—they were cooler, but not cool enough to frost. I had to finish. Suddenly, I got a brainwave: I dropped the cupcakes on a sheet pan and ran them to the blast chiller to cool them quicker. I smiled to myself. It was like being on Puffy Fay's show!

I raced back to the oven to take out the violets. I threw open the oven . . . and cried out in horror.

My beautiful sugared violets had turned into charred husks. Even though I had turned the oven off, it must have still been too hot.

Calm down, Mimi, I thought. I already had lavender flowers in my cupcakes and in the frosting; I didn't need the violets to stick to the theme. I could just use fresh blackberries, like I was planning to before Vik . . .

But Vik had been right. Sugared violets would add a special sparkle to my cupcakes.

Leaving the oven door open, I grabbed more violets. I painted these with the meringue powder solution and dusted them with sugar. Then I put the tray on the open oven door, which was now cool enough to touch. I sent up a prayer to the baking gods that I wouldn't end up with either a soggy mess or another pile of violet-petal jerky.

"Two minutes!" Puffy shouted.

I snatched the cupcakes from the blast chiller, arranged them on a platter, and piped the frosting on. The cupcakes weren't completely cool, but while the ridges on the frosting softened, they didn't turn into a runny mess.

I went back to the violets. I stayed right next to them until there were thirty seconds left, then brought the tray to my waiting platter. Holding my breath, I gingerly laid one shimmering sugared violet on a cupcake.

It looked like a frost-covered flower nestled in a field of purple snow.

"Ten seconds!" said Mrs. T.

"Mimi, hurry!" Jules called.

I quickly placed violets on the rest of the cupcakes.

"Time!" called Puffy Fay. "Hands up, please. That means you, Kiera." Kiera stopped fiddling with her pan and looked up guiltily.

The audience cheered.

"Now please present your creations, one by one," said Mrs. T.

"You first, Kiera," said Puffy Fay.

I wondered what Kiera had managed to make. Her hands shook as she put the platter down; it was piled with swirled brownies decorated with tiny yellow petals.

"And now tell us your story, Kiera, dear," said Mrs. T as she took a brownie off the platter.

Kiera stepped back with terror in her eyes. "Uh . . ." She cleared her throat.

"Pretend you're talking to a friend," said Puffy Fay kindly.

"These are my nana's," said Kiera in an uneven voice. "I mean, my nana made them for me every year on my birthday. Dark chocolate brownies with a white chocolate drizzle, and a different 'surprise' ingredient every year. *Always good to keep things interesting*, she'd say." Kiera smiled, and her voice became stronger. "Nana Grace died last year, and so for the first time ever, she wasn't there to bake brownies for my birthday. Mom and I scrounged around in her notes, and we found this recipe. It wasn't really a recipe, though. It was more like a list of things to put in the brownies, and how to change them depending on how you were feeling. So"—she took a deep breath—"when I saw those marigolds, I knew I needed to make Nana's brownies and sprinkle them on top of the white chocolate frosting. They were her favorite flowers."

The audience applauded, and Kiera wiped away tears again. Though I was almost certain she'd cheated to get this far, it looked like she cared about someone other than herself after all. At least I knew she had actually baked the brownies herself.

"Delicious brownies. Very . . . rustic. Quite a striking contrast to your fancy carrot cake. It's hard to believe they were made by the same person," said Puffy Fay. He gave Kiera a meaningful stare.

Kiera flushed pink and nodded shakily.

I knew it!

"The brownies are very rich, and the white chocolate is a great contrast to the dark."

"Thanks," said Kiera faintly. "I hope I made Nana proud."

Puffy Fay smiled. "You definitely did."

The audience broke out in applause again.

"And next it's Mimi's turn," said Mrs. T, flashing me a smile.

I brought my platter to the judges' table. I closed my eyes for a moment, took a deep breath, and then opened them again.

"I first made these cupcakes for my best friend Emma's birthday last year," I said. "Sunny yellow and mysterious purple—that was us. But she moved away a few weeks ago, and I wondered whether I'd ever find a friend like her again. I was sad for a long time, but then I met someone." My eyes started to sting. "We ate these cupcakes in the woods together. He made me feel like the world was full of adventure and fun again. We spent hours in the woods, talking, sharing food, playing music." My voice became breathy and weak. "But then he left, too." I cleared my throat. "When I saw the ingredients today, I knew I needed to make these cupcakes again. These cupcakes stand for friendship. Because I was lucky to have friends like that, and I believe I'll be lucky enough find it again, and soon."

The audience cheered. Dad whistled piercingly.

"A delectable mix of fruit and flowers," said Puffy Fay.

"Refreshing and sweet. I see you spent quite some time making the sugared violets, even after the first batch went wrong. Why?"

"I wanted to make them extra-special," I said. "I wanted to take them from pretty to . . . lovely."

Puffy Fay nodded and made a note. "Well, you certainly succeeded."

I smiled and gingerly touched the burned skin on my fingers as the crowd cheered again.

"And now, for the final baker," said Puffy Fay. "Guy, please bring up your creation."

Hoodie Boy had made cupcakes, too. They were covered in red and pink rose petals and were so rounded that they looked like mini-bouquets that a flower girl might carry at a wedding.

The boy just stood there for the longest time, and I wondered whether he would refuse to talk. But then he straightened and took a deep breath.

"Once there was a boy who loved his family."

My heart skipped a beat.

I knew that voice.

CHAPTER 24

THE BETRAYAL

He continued: "He watched his father teach. He gathered flowers with his sister—roses most of all, since they were his mother's favorite. He cooked with his mother every day, surrounded by the fragrance of roses. He tasted and laughed and listened to her sing stories of people from faraway lands. The stories wove together like a tapestry and settled in his heart.

"And then, as swiftly as summer turns to winter, the boy's mother died. And then his father died. And his sister died. And all the joy seeped out of teaching, and singing, and cooking. The boy went to live with his mother's dearest friend, one she trusted and admired more than anyone.

"And in her, he found a second mother, one who cared for him and helped him heal. And over time, he was able to find joy in teaching, and singing, and cooking again.

"And so today I present my interpretation of a sweet from my home, one my mother used to make for me. It is decorated with roses, in memory of my mother, and in honor of the one who's been like a mother to me ever since. My heart's work. Red roses and pink, in tribute to them both." The boy tugged off his hood and took off his sunglasses.

The crowd applauded as Vik brought his platter to the judges' table. Puffy Fay beamed in delight, but Mrs. T's smile faded.

"Gulab jamun, am I right?" Puffy Fay asked with his mouth full. "The inspiration for this cupcake?"

Vik nodded. "A friend once told me she loved to take her favorite desserts and make them into something else." He glanced at me briefly.

Gulab jamun. I'd had it plenty of times in India. Creamy fried dumplings soaked in a sugar syrup, flavored with cardamom and—

"Rosewater," said Puffy Fay, "can be a tricky ingredient. But"—he smacked his lips— "you've done an excellent job. And you somehow managed to mimic the flavor of that very sweet dessert without making your cupcake too sweet. Fascinating."

"I coated rose petals in sugar and salt," said Vik. "Sugar for laughter, and salt for tears."

"Now that is profound," said Puffy Fay, scribbling in his notebook.

Mrs. T pursed her lips. "Chef Fay, I—"

"A few minutes, please." Puffy continued writing.

"I have some suggestions," said Mrs. T, trying to peek at the notebook. "Are you sure you wouldn't like a chocolate while you're thinking?"

I could barely breathe. What was Vik doing here? I thought he didn't like contests. And how had he concocted something so beautiful and delicious?

I slapped my forehead. I was so stupid! Vik had lied to me about not liking contests, just like he'd lied about being my friend. That's why he'd told me not to enter—he wanted to win himself! He must have plotted against me from the beginning, trying to steal my baking secrets. Once he saw I had The Book, he read as much of it as he could. And all that time we'd spent reading stories about the stupid Woodland Queen—it was just a distraction.

I stared at the swirls in the marble counter before me.

Vik couldn't win. He couldn't be the champion. He wasn't even from Comity. He was only here for the summer!

He couldn't be the one to spend three days baking with Puffy Fay. He couldn't win the internship of my dreams.

"I need to do some thinking," said Puffy Fay. "Let's take

a ten-minute break." He walked out of the café with his notebook.

"Mimi—" Vik whispered next to me. "I need to talk to you."

I wouldn't look at him. I couldn't.

"Hey, Mimi," said Kiera. "I . . . I just wanted to say thanks."

I looked at her dubiously, but she wasn't smirking. I shrugged.

"I didn't know how I was going to finish. You helped me not fall flat on my face today. I'm—"

"Mimi, come here," Henry called, waving me over.

I gave Kiera one last glance as I joined my family.

"Those cupcakes looked delicious," said Mom.

"And what a story!" said Dad.

Jules raised her eyebrows and play-punched me in the arm. "Can't believe you helped Kiera after all the nasty things she's said to you."

"She's not so bad," I said.

"You stayed so cool, even when things went wrong," said Henry. "Just like the top competitors on TV."

Riya kissed me on the cheek and hovered near me, uncharacteristically quiet.

The room grew silent as Puffy Fay strode back to the judges' table. "I've made my decision," he said. Kiera, Vik, and I lined up. A faint crease appeared between Mrs. T's beautiful eyes.

"This was a difficult decision for me, because these three young people displayed not only extraordinary talent, but also incredibly inspiring stories behind their food. I make food and judge competitions for a living, but I must say there's been something magical about this contest, and about coming back to my roots here in Comity."

Puffy Fay turned to Kiera, Vik, and me. "You should all be proud. No matter what happens today, keep baking."

The crowd thundered.

"In third place: Kiera Jones. Kiera, your nana's brownies were delicious, and your story was heartwarming. But your competitors' efforts were more refined, and you only used the marigolds as a decoration without truly integrating them into your creation. Also, they could have used about five fewer minutes in the oven. Please come up to receive your award—a signed copy of my new cookbook, *The Art of Baking Magically*, and a gift certificate from the While Away."

The audience cheered. Kiera shook hands with Puffy Fay and Mrs. T, then joined her parents. She caught my eye and smiled.

"And now," said Puffy Fay, "for the runner-up and winner. I have to say I honestly didn't know how to make this decision. Both these young people made exquisite cupcakes under incredible time constraints, *and* we asked them to use unusual ingredients, which they both did quite skillfully. And the stories that came with these desserts were also remarkable. Mimi, your cupcakes were delightful, an excellent balance of tart and sweet, a light and fluffy cake topped with a luxurious frosting. Your use of flowers in the cake, in the frosting, and as a decoration was ingenious. The only minor suggestion I have would be to increase the contrast in taste and texture by using something else on the sweet, creamy frosting—say, a fresh, tart blackberry—as your decoration."

The blood drained out of my face.

"And that brings us to Guy. It takes extraordinary talent to take an iconic dessert and translate it into a cupcake that brings something new and fresh. And that story! It was so poignant and spoke of maturity beyond your years. But the most ingenious aspect of your creation was the gorgeous rose petals, not only for the visual pleasure they bring, but for the subtlety of flavor. Sugar and salt. Laughter and tears. And so, it gives me great pleasure to announce the winner of the first annual While Away Café Midsummer Baking Contest."

"Chef Fay, I must insist—" said Mrs. T.

But Puffy Fay hadn't heard her. "The winner is: Guy Smith! I can't wait to work with you in New York."

Peaseblossom and the other waitress gasped, and Mrs. T frowned as the audience roared.

"Mimi, Guy—please come receive your awards," said Puffy Fay.

I barely registered the cheers of the crowd or the smile

on Puffy's face as he handed me his book. Puffy talked to Vik for a few moments, posed for photos, and handed him a card. Then he glanced at his watch, waved to the crowd, and went out to the waiting limo, which whisked him away.

Mrs. T's hand was oddly cold as she shook mine and gave me the gift certificate. "Mimi, would you please come to my office? I'd like to speak with you."

I shook my head numbly. "You've found your apprentice, Mrs. T. His name is Vik. Or Guy, or whatever his real name is."

I'd failed. Not only had I made some stupid mistakes—not tasting my batter, and choosing an overly complicated decoration—but I'd been betrayed by a person I thought was my friend.

My family gathered around me with hugs and words of encouragement, but I pulled away before they could start making excuses or giving sympathetic looks. I returned to my station and packed my equipment. Sure enough, they went back to talking to their friends like nothing terrible had happened. I could disappear into thin air and no one would notice.

Everyone in the café milled around, eating, drinking, laughing, and taking pictures. I abandoned the cookbook and gift certificate on a counter and crept through the empty kitchen and out the back door. I shuffled across the bridge and watched the river flowing below me. I stepped onto the path and disappeared into the woods.

CHAPTER 25

THE BEST CUPCAKES

I wandered on the path, gazing at the packed dirt under my feet as the midday heat rose around me. I breathed in the sharp smells of the woods and tried to make sense of what had just happened.

Vik had been right after all. I *didn't* win. He saw to that. I was such a fool for ever trusting him.

I came to the two hemlocks and stopped. This was where I'd met Vik. Did I want to go back there?

I stomped my foot. I wanted to see the pond and the banyan tree. I wanted to walk in those places and breathe those scents and feel like Vik hadn't ruined everything for me. At least I could still enjoy my woods.

I walked through the hemlocks.

There was no pond or banyan in sight. I shoved my hair out of my face. What was going on?

I headed back through the hemlocks and scratched my head. I stepped through again.

Still no pond, still no banyan.

I held my breath and listened carefully. I hoped the boar showed up. Or the cobra, even. I felt like fighting something.

But the forest stayed silent.

Everyone had forgotten about me. Even the woods.

I walked back on the path, came to my hangout, and went inside. This was the last place I'd seen Vik in the woods, where he'd been so cruel. I hadn't understood why at the time. But now I did, and I wished I could go back to not knowing again. I lay on the cool dirt floor. It would be so nice just to disappear. I closed my eyes, but couldn't sleep; the humiliation of the contest played over and over in my head.

"Mimi?" I opened my eyes to a kid's silhouette in the entrance.

Kiera came in a little awkwardly, clutching a couple of books and a paper bag that rustled.

"Leave me alone." I turned my back on her.

"I'll leave. But first I'll give you your stuff," she said.

I squinted in the dim light. "I don't need any stuff."

"Let me show you, and then you can decide if you want it. By the way, Mrs. T was looking for you. And so was that kid who won."

"Vik?"

"Wasn't his name Guy?" Kiera paused. "Anyway, he was looking for you everywhere. And by then, so were your parents and the rest of your family. You freaked everyone out."

"I didn't mean to—"

"It's okay, I know how you felt. I hate losing. I hate it so much that sometimes I get a little carried away."

I raised my eyebrows. "Carried away, meaning you tried to pass off a carrot cake from a French bakery as your own?"

Kiera flushed and nodded.

I shook my head.

"And don't forget the napoleons," she said. "They were from Sucre et Sel, too."

I rolled my eyes. She was unbelievable!

"Anyway, that weird spiderweb waitress said she'd seen you go out the back door. I told your parents I'd follow you and bring you back. So here I am."

I shrugged.

"You forgot your books." She handed them to me.

It was exhausting just to talk. "The prize was one book."

"Well, Guy or Vik or whatever his name was handed me these two. He said they were yours."

I looked down. The first one was Puffy Fay's new cookbook, *The Art of Baking Magically*, but the second one was mine, too.

It was my copy of Puffy Fay's first cookbook, the one I'd lost in the woods weeks ago.

"*Vik* gave you this?"

Kiera nodded. "He said to tell you he was sorry."

"Yeah, right." So Vik had stolen my book in the first place, before we'd even met. Another lie.

"He also gave me one of these." Kiera reached into the paper bag and held out one of Vik's cupcakes. Even in the dim and musty hangout, it practically glowed with beauty, and the roses smelled intoxicating. *Roses, for love of all types, and longing.*

I scrambled to my feet. "I don't want that! Why did you bring it in here?"

"But don't you want to know?"

"Know what? I *failed*—again!—in front of my family and friends—in front of the whole town! I blew my shot at getting to work with Puffy Fay! I was fooled by a kid who'd pretended to be my friend, then betrayed me. I never want to bake again. I never even want to see a cupcake again!"

Kiera wiggled her eyebrows. "I finished behind you, remember? Even cheating couldn't get me a win." Kiera cradled the cupcake like it was something precious. "But Mimi, it's only humiliating if you make it that way. Emma always said you were the most fantastic baker she'd ever met. And as much as I wanted to win, I have to admit that you deserved to. So how did that kid beat you?"

I shrugged. "How would I know?"

"Well." She looked at me thoughtfully. "Maybe you could try tasting this."

I let out a frustrated sigh and sat down again. "Fine." I took the cupcake and bit into it.

I let all the tastes play in my mouth. The cupcake was light and creamy and subtly infused with aromatic cardamom. It was covered in a luscious rose-cardamom frosting. There were rose petals in the cake and on top, red and pink. They were fragrant and sweet and the tiniest bit salty.

"Joy and sorrow. Laughter and tears," I said. "These cupcakes do taste like love. And love that you wished you still had."

Kiera took the cupcake from me and bit into it. "I'm not sure I can taste *love*," she said, "but it really is *scrumptious*."

I glared at her.

"Too soon? I heard your dad was in the hospital. I hope he's okay." Kiera smiled without a trace of snarkiness. "I'm sorry I've been so mean to you. Emma always said you were cool. But I thought you were stuck-up."

"Stuck-up! *Me*?" I asked.

Kiera shrugged. "You always act like you don't care what

anyone else thinks about you. And your baking . . . you've been a star since we were in first grade, when you brought in that chocolate-peppermint fudge for the fall bake sale."

"I . . . what?" I asked.

"Anyway, you didn't have to go out of your way to help me during the Bake-Off, but you did. And I realized what a jerk I've been," Kiera said.

I stayed silent for a long moment. "You may be a jerk, but at least you have great taste in carrot cake."

Kiera started to laugh. Giggles bubbled inside me until they burst from my mouth and I sprayed cupcake crumbs everywhere, which made us both laugh more. I laughed until tears streamed from my eyes, and I couldn't tell if I was laughing or crying. I laughed until I had to lie down again to stop my head from spinning. When I opened my eyes, Kiera was hunched over clutching her stomach and snickering.

"I have one more thing." She reached into the bag again and brought out two of my lemon-lavender cupcakes; the sugar on the violets sparkled. She handed one to me.

"To friends." She raised her cupcake like a glass for a toast.

"Especially ones you find unexpectedly," I said. I tapped my cupcake to hers, then took a bite. The cupcake was light and sweet, tart and creamy, and the sugared violets gave it a slight crunch. We finished our cakes in silence.

"I'm no expert like Puffy Fay, and I agree they're both

delicious, but I would choose yours, hands down," said Kiera.

We crawled out from under the tarp and blinked in the light of a perfect summer day.

"Want to hang out at my house?"

"Sure," I said. "I'll call my parents from there." I glanced at my watch. "I just need to be back home by six to go to my brother's play." But I didn't need to worry about making something for Henry and his friends.

I knew one thing for sure: I was never baking again.

CHAPTER 26

THE PLAY

The Comity Youth Theater's production of *A Midsummer Night's Dream* opened on a magical summer night. As the sun melted like an enormous sherbet ball, the clear, full moon rose over a small wooden stage at the edge of the woods. The actors played guitars and tambourines, accompanied by the insistent chirruping of cicadas. The air smelled of lilacs and pine trees. It wasn't hard to believe that we had been transported to a different forest, where feuding fairies tangled the fates of regular people in their webs.

My family filled the front row. In the play, Titania and Oberon quarreled over the changeling boy, and Oberon enlisted Puck to help him. Using the love blossom, Puck made Titania fall in love with a donkey-headed man.

The two mortal men, Lysander and Demetrius, both loved Hermia. But Puck made a mistake with the love blossom. Both men were enchanted into loving Helena, who reacted suspiciously and miserably and blamed Hermia for their strange change of heart. The situation was eerily familiar. I glanced over at my sisters, but they seemed to be enjoying themselves, not recognizing the similarities to their own lives this summer.

I enjoyed seeing Lily as petite, confused Hermia and Fletcher as the vain and snarky Demetrius. But no one was better than Henry playing Puck. He delivered his lines like he'd been born knowing them, swung onto the stage on ropes, and jumped and tumbled like an acrobat. He reminded me of Vik and how he could climb up the banyan tree like it was nothing. I shook my head to get rid of the image.

In act three, a fairy fluttered onstage and said her name was Peaseblossom.

Did I hear that right? I flipped to the front of my program, and sure enough, Peaseblossom was listed as one of Titania's fairies. There were also other fairies—named Moth, Mustardseed, and Cobweb. I pushed my hands through my hair and remembered a gigantic spiderweb headband. This was getting way too spooky.

During the intermission, I pulled Jules to a quiet place to talk.

"Did you notice that fairy's name—*Peaseblossom*?" I asked.

"Funny name," Jules said.

"But that waitress at the While Away—she's called Peaseblossom!"

"Huh? Which one? The cranky one, or—"

"The nice one," I said impatiently. "With the pink flowers in her hair."

"So?"

"So? Isn't it weird that this girl with a fairy name has come to our town right when everyone starts acting strange?"

Jules shrugged. "Everyone seems okay now."

"Girls." Mom hurried to us with her purse slung over her shoulder. "Work called. There's an emergency with the go-live, and they need me at the office."

"Now? But the play's not over," Jules said.

"I know." Mom glanced at her watch. "But unfortunately, I don't have a choice. I couldn't find Dad—I guess he's still in line for the bathroom—but I told Riya. You can all go home in Henry's car, or you can get a ride with the Clarks. I might be gone all night. Tell Henry I'm so sorry, and I'll come to another show."

"Okay. Love you," I said.

Mom kissed us and dashed away just as the bell rang, signaling the end of intermission.

As Jules and I went back to our seats, I noticed that Dad's place at the end of the row was still empty.

Act four opened with Titania proclaiming her love to the donkey-headed man. The audience crackled with laughter, but I kept checking Dad's empty chair. I jiggled my leg, and Jules told me to stop.

Puck and Oberon came onstage. After explaining that Titania had given up the Indian changeling boy who'd caused the whole fairy fight, they released Titania from the love spell, resulting in general hilarity when she realized she had fallen in love with a donkey. Dad still hadn't returned. What was taking him so long? He was missing the best parts of Henry's play!

Something flew into the corner of my vision, and I turned away from the stage to look.

The pitta bird landed a few feet in front of me and stared. It hopped a few feet forward and then stared again.

"I'll be back," I whispered to Jules. I slunk away from the audience, away from the stage, to the small shed that contained the bathrooms. As I thought, it was empty. Dad wasn't there.

He'd left. But why? Did it have anything to do with his weird behavior this summer? I thought he'd been cured of that.

I chewed on a strand of hair. *Think, Mimi. Think.*

We thought that Dad had Lyme disease. But Emma had had Lyme last summer, and she didn't eat everything in sight or have purple eyes.

And Fletcher, Cole, and Henry *did* have purple eyes this

summer, when they'd been enchanted by the honeysuckle.

I clapped my hand to my forehead. I'd been a fool!

Dad was under a *spell*.

A *fairy* spell.

And the answer lay in the woods.

I stepped into the trees. The full moon cast everything in sharp shadows. Leaves and branches, fern tops and mushrooms glowed in the silvery light. The path felt as familiar as the hallways in my home. I was searching for a place I knew well, where I knew I would find him. It was just around the bend.

Small creatures scurried in the underbrush, and an owl called to its mate. A breeze set the leaves to whispering. I took deep gulps of night air to steady my whirling mind. I arrived at the two hemlocks leaning against each other.

I stepped through.

There was no pond or banyan tree in sight.

I went back through the hemlock gate. Why couldn't I get to the banyan? There was some fairy magic at work, I was sure of it.

Calm down, Mimi. There had to be something. Some sort of key. What had happened all the other times I had found the banyan tree?

I stood still and listened to the woods. A soft wind rustled through the leaves. Crickets chirped a lullaby. A mockingbird began its song for the night, and it reminded me of the pitta singing and Vik's beautiful, haunting song.

The key.

I knew what it was.

CHAPTER 27

QUESTIONS AND ANSWERS

I began to hum "Come with Me." I couldn't help loving the song and its unearthly beauty—fairy beauty. It was the key to finding the magical parts of the woods, the places I'd never seen before Vik showed up. A secret signal.

I stepped through the gap between the hemlocks. The pond stretched out in front of me, placid and lovely, and along its banks was the banyan, its leaves shining silver in the moonlight.

I ran to the enormous tree. "Come out, Vik! We need to talk." Holding my breath, I circled the trunk. I searched the ground for footprints, but I couldn't see anything in the shadows.

I jumped to the lowest branch and climbed in the dark.

My hands and feet knew what to do, and soon I arrived at the branch where I had first met Vik.

He wasn't there. Neither was Dad.

"Come on!" I pounded the trunk, nearly losing my balance and falling out of the tree. "VIK! COME HERE AND EXPLAIN YOURSELF!"

No answer. I was all alone.

I pulled my hair in frustration. "I need to find Dad! I need help," I whispered.

Something feathery brushed my face. The pitta landed on the branch and regarded me.

"Will you help me? Where's Vik?"

Without a second glance, the bird took off again into the darkness. Had it understood what I'd said? Even if it had, could it get Vik to come here? And if Vik *did* come, how could I convince him to return Dad?

I leaned against the tree trunk, feeling better with something solid behind me. I sat there for what seemed like a very long time. I wondered when Jules had noticed I hadn't returned, and whether she'd alerted Riya and Henry. Was the play over? Were they all searching for me in the woods? I imagined them calling my name and finding the empty hangout. They'd never be able to come here, wherever here actually was. Not without the song.

Then I heard it, moving through the air like an

overwhelming aroma, steadily growing closer.

"Mimi? What are you doing here?" Vik's voice came from the bottom of the tree.

"Vik? Vik, I have to talk to you!"

"I'm coming," he said.

I took a deep breath. I didn't want to see him again. I didn't want to talk to him. But I had to find a way to convince him to return Dad.

A few minutes later, he arrived at the branch. A moonbeam illuminated him, and I forced myself to look. He didn't look like a monster. He looked like a regular kid. But I knew he wasn't.

"Where's my dad?"

"Isn't he at your brother's play?"

I clenched my fists. "You know he's not. You're the one who made Dad's eyes glow purple and made him eat everything in sight. You're the one who made him forget who he is."

Vik shook his head.

"How could you, Vik? I trusted you. I thought you were my friend." My voice cracked on the last word.

"I am your friend."

"I know exactly who you are. And what you are, *Puck*."

"I'm not Puck. If I were, we wouldn't be having this conversation. I'd just be off on my next madcap adventure." Vik smiled.

"Don't smile at me! You've been lying this whole time! What do you want? Just give Dad back!"

Vik sighed. "I don't have your dad."

I glared at him. "Then explain why you've been gathering information all this time, learning everything about my family? I thought it was because of the stupid baking contest," I growled, "but now I see it's because you wanted to get your hands on Dad. Why? Because you miss your own dad? Would having a dad would make you feel more like a 'regular' person? What do you want with him, Puck?"

"Stop calling me Puck."

"Right. Your name is Vik, or Guy, or whatever. And you're just an ordinary boy. Liar."

"I deserve that." He cast his gaze down briefly, but then he looked me in the eye. "It's Vik. For real. I told you the truth."

"You've lied the whole time! You pretended you were a boy, and that you were here visiting your aunt Tanya!"

"I *am* visiting my aunt Tanya. But you're right. I'm not just a boy."

"You're a fairy!"

"Yes," he said slowly. "I guess I am."

"You *guess*? You've been playing that fairy song all summer—"

"Well, to be precise, it wasn't *originally* a fairy song—"

"And you took me to magical parts of the woods, and

showed me all those herbs and flowers—"

"True."

"And you've been pretending to be my friend so you could take Dad and turn him into your fairy dad or whatever!"

Vik shook his head. "Didn't your dad start acting strange before we'd even met?"

"Yeah, but you could have cast a spell on him before that." I snapped my fingers. "He's been running in the woods! That's when you cast your spells!"

"I didn't know there was anything wrong with your dad until you told me. And I listened to you talking about your family because I liked you and I wanted to be your friend. I still do." His eyes glittered gold in the moonlight.

"If you're not Puck, then who are you?"

"I told you my story," Vik said.

My mind raced to remember the details of the play. It had to be connected—there were too many similarities to be a coincidence. "You told me your mom and dad died, and Aunt Tanya took you in." I gasped. "Aunt Tanya—Titania! Otherwise known as . . . Mrs. T?"

Vik nodded.

The shock of recognition rang through me like a bell.

"*A lovely boy, stolen from an Indian king; She never had so sweet a changeling,*" I whispered.

Vik smiled. "I knew you'd figure it out."

"Shakespeare's story? It was *real*?"

"He embellished it, changed some of the details. My father wasn't a king, but he was Indian. I guess it was hard to rhyme *changeling* with *teacher*. And although King Oberon tricked Queen Titania into giving me up temporarily, she got me back pretty fast. She loved my mother too much to give me up forever. If you learn anything about that guy Shakespeare, it should be that he pretty much borrowed every tale he told, but retold it so beautifully that his version's the only one that anyone remembers."

"But that means that . . . you're really *old*!"

Vik snorted. "It's relative. I am the youngest fairy."

I blinked. This was like hearing that Cinderella and Little Red Riding Hood were real.

"This whole thing started because of the Midsummer's Wager." Vik stood and started pacing on the branch like he was on the ground instead of twenty feet in the air.

"Am I supposed to know what that means?" I asked.

"A wager is a bet. Each summer, Aunt Tanya and her husband wager on something. It's usually something ridiculous. They're always arguing."

"And the baking contest was part of it?"

Vik nodded. "It was supposed to help Aunt Tanya win, by making the While Away as successful as possible. All of us were supposed to help, but I was tired of wasting every summer trying to win another idiotic bet. We fairies have plenty of important work to do, guarding the wild places of the world and helping them thrive, in addition to other duties. So I kind of . . . went on strike. I refused to bake anything for the While Away, putting Aunt Tanya at a severe disadvantage since Peaseblossom and the others know nothing about baking."

I raised my eyebrows. "No kidding. The first things I tried there looked delicious but tasted disgusting."

"But then you showed up, Mimi, and I remembered not only how much I love baking, but also that I owe a debt to Aunt Tanya—who, vain and selfish as she can be, has always loved me and treated me like a son. I realized I should help her. So I took your Puffy Fay cookbook and brought it to Peaseblossom and the other fairies. I gave you The Book, to help you succeed. I encouraged you in your baking, hoping you would drum up enthusiasm for the While Away and help Aunt Tanya win the wager. I even relented on my strike and offered to bake for Aunt Tanya, but she was still angry at me, and refused."

"That's why you were so mad that day—the day I ran into the cobra . . . the cobra! Why are there cobras in these woods?"

"Look around you, Mimi. You're in a banyan tree."

"So?" But even as I said it, I realized. I touched the branch gently. "Banyans don't grow in Massachusetts, do they?"

Vik shook his head.

"How is this here, then?"

"This banyan is in India. On the outskirts of my old village, in fact. And so is the pitta, and the boar, and the cobra. So are we."

I held on tight to prevent myself from plummeting to the ground. "You mean—"

"When you hear my song, or sing it, you can go through the gate that divides all parts of The Wild—all the natural places in the world—from each other. You can go anywhere in the world. You got to visit *my* woods."

I couldn't say a word.

"When I saw you had accidentally enchanted your brother and your friends, and then cured them, I realized there was more to you than just a talented young baker. And although I used to find the troubles of humans amusing, you showed me how much the confusion we cause with our fairy interference can hurt people. I wanted to tell you the truth, Mimi. I wanted to reveal what I was. I was going to show you, that last day we saw each other before the contest."

"So why didn't you?"

"You were right," Vik said quietly. "About us being related. I lost my parents and my sister. But my sister had children, and they had children, and *they* had children . . . and my mother's song must have been passed on."

I braced myself against the trunk to stop myself from shaking. It didn't work. I was related to a *fairy*! How could that be?

"Once you told me about the song, how it's been in your family, too—I realized who you were. But then you showed me that fine print on the contest poster, and I knew Aunt Tanya wasn't going to give you a choice. She was going to trick you. So I had to stop you from winning the contest."

"But—"

"Even after I told you not to enter, that you weren't talented enough, I knew you'd try anyway, because you're so smart, and so strong." The words poured out of him. "So I sabotaged you. I switched your sugar for salt, but you figured it out. I had to bake my best, my heart's work, to beat you. You sure didn't make it easy! Your kulfi cream puffs were full of warm energy, and I was so nervous the luck from your friendship cupcakes would make you win."

My mind whirled. Vik did love my baking! But he'd also lied, schemed, and cheated to ruin my chance to work with Puffy Fay . . . because he thought Mrs. T was trying to trick me? None of it made sense. "What does the contest have to do with any of this?"

"I realized Aunt Tanya wasn't just out to win her wager with Oberon. She wanted—"

"My dad. I know." I pulled on my hair and stared into the night. I guess I could forgive Vik for hurting me, since he was trying to save Dad. "Where would Mrs. T be hiding him?" I gasped and looked at Vik. "He's at the While Away, isn't he?"

"He must be," Vik said.

I laughed. "Thanks, my great-great-great-many-times-great-grand-uncle."

Vik gave a barklike laugh. "Why don't you just call me your friend? You're the best one I've found in hundreds of years. I've been lonely, Mimi. But not anymore." His eyes sparkled with more than moonlight.

I stood on the branch and prepared to climb down.

"Mimi, you must understand—one cannot be *forced* to join the Fair Folk. One must choose. And one must give something. Heart's work. Remember the stories we read together."

"Dad's not going to choose to leave us, not unless he's been enchanted into—"

Vik shook his head. "It doesn't work that way. Fairy magic can cause a change of heart—an infatuation, or temporary sleep, forgetfulness—but a human cannot be enchanted into joining the Fair Folk."

"Well, that's good, right?" I said.

"Except tonight."

I shuddered. "Because it's Midsummer's Eve?"

"Yes. The one night a year when fairy enchantments are binding. At midnight, they become permanent."

I shoved my hair out of my eyes. "We'd better get going."

A trumpeting call ripped through the air, followed by a scream.

I looked at Vik in horror.

"This way!" came a faint voice. "Jules, get behind that tree!" Was that Henry?

"Is . . . is that an *elephant*?" I asked Vik.

"We *are* in a forest in India. Your brother and sisters must have slipped through while I played the song."

Another scream.

"We've got to help them!" I cried. I scrambled down the tree with Vik right behind me. "They're looking for *me*! I can't let them get hurt!"

"Time is running out. Go to your father."

"But—"

"Go!" Vik gestured. "It's okay, I'll protect your siblings." He pulled the wooden pipe out of his pocket.

I turned to go, but Vik put his hand on my arm. "You have magic, too, Mimi. Use it. And whatever Aunt Tanya tells you, don't eat or drink *anything*."

I nodded and plunged into the woods.

CHAPTER 28

THE INVITATION

I raced down the path to my hangout.

"Wish me luck, Emma," I called as I hurtled past it.

I ran to the edge of the woods and over the bridge for the second time that day.

How do you fight a fairy? I had no idea.

I took a deep breath, opened the door, and entered the While Away Café.

Moonlight painted every surface in silver, a secret forest hideaway. Dad sat at a table elegantly set for three. He was surrounded by a multitude of baked goods and gold-dusted chocolates. He barely chewed before stuffing more in his mouth. His eyes glowed an unearthly purple.

"Dad!" I rushed to him and grabbed his arm. "Dad, come home with me."

He pulled away and reached for a streusel-topped muffin. "But these are so scrumptious," he said around a crumbly mouthful.

"I see I finally have your attention," came a musical voice.

Mrs. T stepped into a ray of moonlight, and I had to catch my breath. She wore a gossamer gown that looked like it was filled with stars.

"Please return my dad to normal, Mrs. T—I mean, Queen Titania," I said. "You can't just ruin someone's whole life—not over a bet."

Titania's laugh sounded like a running brook. She still had the pink rose tucked behind her ear. "Please, my dear Mimi. Do have a seat. Let's discuss this over refreshments."

"I don't want any."

"As you wish." Titania shrugged and sat next to Dad. She sipped delicately at a goblet full of golden liquid. "Mimi, this is not just any bet. It is the Midsummer's Wager, a most ancient tradition." She paused and lifted a shapely eyebrow. "Drinking morning dew from a flower petal is refreshing—but tasty? Not really. One can only partake of berries, nuts, and herbs for so long before growing tired of them. And I have been tired of them for a long, long time. I do not need eat for sustenance, of course, but it is so delightful to eat for pleasure. And the best food, of course, is always sweet." She picked up a choco-late chip cookie and nibbled on it.

What did this have to do with Dad? "But—"

"Mimi, Mimi. I thought you, of all people, would under-stand. Sweet is infinitely superior to savory. That is what I intend to prove to my *dear* husband this summer."

"*That's* the Midsummer's Wager?"

Titania nodded her lovely head. "Oberon does not agree with me, so we decided to have a competition this summer. I would serve up the most delectable sweets, and he would do the same with savory treats. Humans would choose between them, and the most successful store at the end of the summer would win."

"So the Salt Shaker is Oberon's?" I remembered Darla and her mom standing in line and their strange obsession with potato chips.

"Yes, and I hear it's doing quite well, curse him! Of course, he did not lose his right-hand man this summer, like I did. Vik has caused a great deal of trouble."

"Yeah, he caused me a lot of trouble."

Titania ignored me. "Has it ever occurred to you *why* so many famous, fabulously successful people have come from this little town?"

I looked at her blankly.

"Comity has always been a stronghold of the Fair Folk. We

have blessed this town with our presence, and we have left a lingering magic in the woods for hundreds of years. *This* is why the Midsummer's Wager matters so much!"

"But I don't—"

"What qualities would you like to flourish here, Mimi? Music? Art? *Baking*? This is what my presence brings to this town. Or would you rather have math geniuses, scientific inspirations, and *sports* successes? This is what my husband's presence brings." She flared her nostrils in disdain.

"That doesn't sound so—"

"Understand, Mimi. The loser of the Midsummer's Wager will be banished from this place for two hundred years. Two hundred years without brilliance in art, music, or culinary skills emerging from this town! A blink of the eye for the Fair Folk, but more than two lifetimes for mortals."

I could see her point. But then I glanced at Dad gorging himself. I grabbed two heavily laden platters of baked goods from the table and dumped them in a trash can in the corner of the room before hurrying back. "But what does this have to do with my dad?"

Titania rested her chin on her fingers. "It was never meant for him, you know. It's all your fault."

"*My* fault?" I stopped with my hand hovering over another platter.

"The chocolate, Mimi. The one I gave you when you first

came here. You were the one who was supposed to eat it. It was supposed to make you want to come back here. I wanted your baking talent to make the While Away successful. But you gave the chocolate to your father instead."

"Why would you want to make me unable to tell good food from bad? Why would you want me to eat everything in sight?"

Titania leaned closer. "The chocolate *wouldn't* have done that. But you touched it, and you cast your own spell upon it."

"What? That's ridiculous, I can't cast spells!"

"Can't you?" Titania looked at me coolly. "Are you sure?"

I blinked and tried to remember. "I did take the chocolate out of its box to look at it, and I remember thinking . . . I hoped that Dad wouldn't be too picky about it. I wanted him to like your food so he'd let me enter the contest."

"Aha! I knew it!" Titania cried.

"But . . . *that's* why he ate everything in sight and couldn't identify any flavors?" I was so stunned that I sank into the nearest chair. "It was *me*?"

"And Vik tells me you used honeysuckle cookies to enchant an entire group of young humans, and then put them all back to normal with gotu kola brownies."

I nodded slowly. "It was the magical plants in the forest." I shuddered as Dad attacked a lemon meringue pie.

Titania shook her head. "The plants aren't magical by themselves, Mimi. *You* are."

313

"That's impossible," I said.

I pulled on my hair and tried to think. Mom and I had tasted the honeysuckle, and nothing happened to us. Nothing had happened until I baked with the honeysuckle . . . when I wished that everyone would love each other! I gaped at Mrs. T.

"See? In your heart, you know it is true."

"So you're telling me I can do what *you* do?" I sniffed at the goblet in front of me and then set it aside.

Titania leaned toward me. "The Fair Folk can influence humans through food, but it is imperfect," she said. She let out a short breath. "Possibly because *humans* are imperfect. One never knows exactly how our enchanted food will make a human act."

I regarded her dubiously.

"Oh, Vik is better than most. That is because he is so *young* . . . the youngest of my retinue. He remembers what it is like, to be human. But it is a very inexact science. Take, for example, Chef Fay. I gave him my special chocolate and asked him to come judge the contest."

"Which he did," I said.

Titania raised a finger. "He judged the contest, but he was completely unruly and wouldn't listen to my . . . suggestions. You were supposed to win."

My stomach sank even further. I thought I'd made it to the Bake-Off on my own. "Why would you rig the contest?"

"Never doubt, dear Mimi, that you had the baking skills

to win on your own. But once I understood what you could do, this became much bigger than the Midsummer's Wager. *Methinks this one will save us all from ruin.* That's what I said, when I tasted those genius chocolate-thyme-tangerine cookies. You are exactly what I need," said Titania.

She didn't want Dad. She wanted *me*.

"Why?" I asked.

Titania rose so I had to look up at her. She seemed eight feet tall. "You have the magical ability to bake with plants and herbs and *make humans do exactly what you intend.* You're the best I've ever seen! Better, perhaps, than Vik."

"But . . . but I'm not a fairy!"

Titania continued. "You're not. But once in a very long while, a human is born with . . . the sensitivities, and maybe even some of the powers, of the Fair Folk. It's very rare, but they can affect things in the natural world, like a girl who can grow flowers that no one else could rival."

"Peaseblossom," I whispered.

Mrs. T nodded. "Or a girl who could weave fabrics of unsurpassed beauty and strength . . ."

"Cobweb?" I asked.

She nodded again.

"Or a boy who can make food that tells stories that bring back the past, stories that no one ever wants to stop listening to," I said quietly.

"Yes. You are like us, Mimi. You transform ordinary

ingredients into something extraordinary."

"Even if I believed you, why would I want to turn people into zombies who just do what I say?"

Titania shook her beautiful head. "No, no, not like that. Imagine, Mimi, if we could influence people so they would treat The Wild with respect? What if we could persuade people to listen each other, to open their minds to different ideas? We could create peace in our troubled world."

I'd been ready to argue, but I paused. That *would* be cool.

"You would join our family—with Peaseblossom and Cobweb and others. With Vik. At first, I thought you would be his substitute, his replacement, but he has decided to stay. In us, you have friends, a family who will never leave you. You would do what you love most, every day. You would be honored, celebrated, and treasured among us, not overlooked like you are at home."

I looked at her in confusion.

"Your family can't appreciate you, Mimi, not the way I do. I know you're truly gifted, unique in the whole world." Titania smiled. She was the Woodland Queen, the Queen of The Wild, who knows everyone's deepest desires.

"And I would give you something special," she said. She clapped her hands, and Peaseblossom came out of the kitchen, carrying something heavy.

Peaseblossom set it down, curtsied, and went back to the

kitchen. It was The Book. The ultimate cookbook. I caressed its familiar pages.

"You will have ingredients from all over the world to influence whomever you wish. And of course, I will release your father from this enchantment," said Titania.

I looked at Dad again. He was halfway through a huge pan of bread pudding and didn't look like he was slowing down anytime soon.

"Why didn't my gotu kola brownies work on him?" I wondered aloud.

"An astute question," said Titania fondly. "Remember when you came here with your father, when he was taking notes for his review? He ate more of my chocolates then. And the enchantments of the Queen of The Wild are not easily undone, not even by someone as talented as you. I'm the only one who can return him to normal."

"But he seemed back to normal after the hospital—"

"That's because he ate my 'get-well' chocolate. It had nothing to do with whatever silly treatment the humans gave him. My previous batch of chocolate was a bit . . . potent. I didn't want him to choke to death. That would have ruined everything." Titania's laugh tinkled through the air.

It certainly would have ruined everything for Dad, and my whole family. I didn't see what was so funny.

"It was a simple matter to offer him more of my enchanted

treats at the end of the contest today. Like I said, your father is quite under my spell." Her eyes gleamed. "So what will it be, Mimi? Will you choose immortality and eternal fame? Will you save your father? Vik objected to the way I tried to entice you. *It wasn't fair to trick her,* he said. *You should have asked, not demanded.* Well, now I am asking: Will you join me?"

She offered me everything I'd ever wanted. I wouldn't be last anymore. I wouldn't feel like I was always behind. I would have the best cookbook in the world, be able to bake all the time, and have access to all kinds of incredible ingredients. I could travel anywhere—India, even Australia—anytime I wanted. My friends would never leave me. I could stop people from fighting each other, and do some good in the world. I remembered the pitta's song when it saved me from the cobra. A memory, and an invitation. I belonged in The Wild.

And I'd save Dad. My family would be fine without me, but they needed him.

Titania spread her hands. "Mimi, won't you choose a life that is always sweet? Bake something for me—your heart's work, something only you in all the world can make—and join us."

CHAPTER 29

HEART'S WORK

"You will find everything you need at your station from this morning. I'll remain here with your father."

My mind raced as I stumbled to the baking station. What was I going to make? What could possibly be good enough? I blew a strand of hair out of my face and wandered to a table where spices and herbs were laid out in jewellike bowls. Rosemary, thyme, spearmint, cinnamon, cardamom. Their fragrance beckoned me. My fingers twitched.

A pinch of delicate reddish-orange threads lay in a clear bowl. They smelled of sunshine.

Saffron. For success.

I knew exactly what to make.

I heated milk in a pan and rubbed the bright threads

between my fingers before sprinkling them into the milk. *Let me succeed*, I thought as the warm, floral aroma rose up. I set my intention. I knew the steps. I felt the rhythm of what I wanted.

And then I baked my heart out.

It was fifteen minutes until midnight when I arranged twelve cupcakes on a platter. They were yellow, small but weighty, covered with a swirl of caramel-colored frosting and each topped with a single toasted cashew. I picked up the platter and moved toward Titania and Dad just as Vik entered the café.

"Vik! There you are," said Titania. "See? You were all wrong about our Mimi. You needn't have put on that maudlin display at the contest this morning after all. I have not demanded. I gave her a choice, and she has made it."

Vik glanced at Dad gorging himself on petit fours and raised an eyebrow. "I offered you my heart's work, my queen," Vik said. "I will happily remain your Royal Baker."

"Vik, I've made up my mind," I said.

Vik frowned. "Mimi—"

"I have a story to tell, Queen Titania. Will you listen?" The tray of cupcakes trembled in my hands.

"Of course, my dear girl. I love stories." Titania settled back in her chair next to Dad. He barely looked up as he finished off a piece of spice cake, but his purple eyes gleamed.

I swallowed and shoved my hair out of my eyes. "Once there was a girl who loved to bake." My heart thrummed like a hand mixer on the highest speed. "She baked cookies and pies, cream puffs and brownies, and cupcakes most of all. Baking was what she knew and loved. But the girl felt that no one truly understood her.

"And then she met the Woodland Queen, the Queen of The Wild, who knows everyone's deepest desires.

"The girl made cookies that inspired courage and loyalty. And the Queen was pleased, but still she asked for something more.

"Next, the girl made cupcakes that celebrated friendship, and brought luck and adventure. And the Queen was pleased, but still she asked for something more.

"So one Midsummer's Eve when the moon was full and fairies roamed the woods, the girl brought her heart's work, cakes that were sweet and salty, smooth and gritty, buttery and just the tiniest bit bitter. And she offered it . . ." I set the platter down and selected the best cupcake.

Titania held out her graceful palm and waited as I peeled off the wrapper.

". . . she offered it to one who knew her best."

I handed the cupcake to Dad.

Titania frantically reached out to snatch the cupcake, but Dad, with his insatiable appetite, was too fast for her. He took an enormous bite.

Titania curled her lip.

I held my breath. Would it be good enough? Would it work?

Dad chewed, swallowed, and blinked.

I braced myself for a flash of purple.

Dad shook his head and looked at me with warm brown eyes, the color of good medium-roast coffee. "Hmm, saffron, cardamom, semolina, cashews . . . kesari bhath, huh? What a perfect translation into a cupcake. Has Mom tried one yet?"

I shuddered with relief.

Titania jumped to her feet and gaped at me. "How could you?" Her voice shook with power and rage. "I offered you—I would have given you—I would have treasured you!"

I glanced at Dad. He winked.

I tried to hide my smile. "Queen Titania," I said, "I already have a family that treasures me. And we love each other, even though we argue, and feel jealous, and aren't always as kind as we should be. Besides, as I was trying to tell you, not everything in life can be sweet. Salty and sour, spicy and bitter—it's the combination of tastes that makes food delicious. And that's what makes life worth savoring, too."

Vik grinned. "I should've had more faith in you, Mimi. Your family is amazing, and you'd never let them down."

"And Queen Titania, you already have a family that treasures you," I said.

Peaseblossom and Cobweb poked their heads out from the kitchen and nodded.

"And someone who loves you like a mother. He's not a bad baker, either."

Vik smiled at me, and I gave him a Mimi wink.

"That's all fine and well, but I am still not pleased," said Titania.

"Too bad," came a familiar voice from the door.

A puff of cake and cream burst on Titania's shoulder. Before she could utter a word, she was pelted by two more, then four, then an entire barrage of baked goods.

"Take that!" Jules lobbed a miniature fruit tart. "You can't have our Mimi. Who would bake cookies with me?"

Henry barraged her with blondies. "She's the best acting partner I have!"

Riya launched a cherry pie with both hands. "And we've only just started singing together!"

"I . . . I NEVER!" gasped Titania. "This is not . . . this is not acceptable!" She pushed whipped cream and cake crumbs out of her eyes, and her beautiful dress was covered in sugar and spice.

Peaseblossom and Cobweb giggled in the corner but stopped at Titania's glare.

"Very well, Mimi. You win. You have broken my spell on your father, and you say you will not join me, though I cannot fathom why. But know this: you will never see Vik again. You won't even have the memory of him." She waved her hand. The eyes of the non-fairies in the room closed, like they were sleepwalking. Dad even started to snore.

"B-but—" I stammered. "Dad was the only one who ate anything tonight!"

"Everyone partook of our golden ale this morning," said Titania. "We made sure of it, just in case."

I turned to Vik. First Emma, now Vik. How many best friends could I lose?

"Farewell, Mimi," Vik said. "Our time together was sweet, and all too brief. But I must obey. She is not only my aunt, but also my queen." He bowed.

But then, shielded from Titania's sight, he looked at me and winked.

I heard a footstep at the door. "*Ill met by moonlight, proud Titania,*" said a voice like wind creaking through the trees. "I know you've been cheating." A tall silver-haired man walked into the café.

"As if you've been playing by the rules, Oberon!" cried Titania.

Oberon looked at me, then turned back to Titania. "*Though she be but little, she is fierce. Is she not, my lovely queen?*"

"Oh, enough," said Titania testily. She turned toward me in a huff, raising her arms and chanting,

"If we shadows have offended,
Think but this, and all is mended,
That you have but slumber'd here
While these visions did appear.
And this weak and idle theme,
No more yielding but a dream."

I suddenly felt incredibly sleepy. My eyes closed.

CHAPTER 30

DREAMS AND REALITY

Sunlight woke me on an August morning. I'd had the dream again. It was about the woods. Something about Dad. Yes, and Cole, Henry, Riya, and Jules were all part of it. And there was someone else, too. I reached for the memory, but I couldn't catch it.

Restless, I got out of bed and went to my window. Branches swayed in a gentle breeze. Birds chattered. There was a song, too, something I remembered from somewhere. But I couldn't recall anymore.

In the kitchen, Mom was sipping a cup of tea. "Hi, sweetie," she said with a smile. "Ready for the big party?"

"Yes, but I'm ready for breakfast first." Mom, Dad, and I were leaving the next morning so I could spend three days in

New York baking with my idol, Puffy Fay. I still couldn't believe I had won the While Away baking contest.

I was going to miss the While Away. The last time I'd visited, there was a notice on the door that they'd be closed by Labor Day. Weird, since it was always packed.

Tonight was our big send-off celebration, and no one was letting me bake a thing for it. But they couldn't stop me from baking something for breakfast.

I plucked a sprig of rosemary from the pot in the windowsill, and as I inhaled its fresh scent, something flashed in my mind.

I went to the pantry and took out a jar of wildflower honey. I held it up to make sure I had enough, and the sun lit it up like a jar of gold. There was that flash again—I almost had it, but it slipped away.

I preheated the oven and mixed my ingredients. I sprinkled in the fragrant rosemary. *Remember, Mimi. What have you forgotten?*

By the time I got the pan in the oven, Dad had come downstairs. He sniffed the air. "Rosemary, huh? What are you making?"

"Rosemary–honey–olive oil muffins."

"Did you add white pepper, like we talked about last time?"

I grinned. "A tiny bit. Next time, do you think we should try it with goat's milk?"

"Great idea," said Dad. He kissed the top of my head and went to make coffee.

Mom refilled her mug from the kettle. "I forgot to tell you, Emma's mom emailed me last night," she said. "They want us to visit them in Australia. What do you think? We'd go in December, when Emma has her summer break."

"Are you serious? Can we really? She keeps telling me how much fun she's having. But she misses me. And I miss her."

"Let's see if we can work it out," said Mom.

Henry walked in rubbing his eyes. "Something smells fantastic," he said.

"They'll be ready soon." I laughed.

Jules and Riya came in together, giggling at something on Riya's phone.

"What's so funny?" asked Mom.

"Just ideas for a new dance routine," said Riya. "I think it tells a great story."

"If by 'great,' you mean full of crazy misunderstandings and bizarre coincidences that all turn out right in the end." Jules smiled. "Let's see what Fletcher and Cole think tonight."

Everyone pitched in to finish making breakfast. I took the muffins out of the oven, and we sat down to eat.

"Tonight's going to be so much fun," said Jules. "The whole neighborhood's coming. Can't wait to celebrate you, Mimi!" She raised her glass of orange juice in a toast.

"Here's to baking with Puffy Fay," said Henry, raising his glass.

"Here's to displaying your talent for all the world to see," said Riya.

"Here's to doing what you love," said Mom.

"The greatness was always there," said Dad. "You just needed to see it in yourself. Here's to our Mimi!"

I raised my glass and basked in the warmth of my family.

The rosemary muffins were as delicious as I'd hoped. But I still couldn't shake the nagging feeling that I was forgetting something.

After we finished cleaning up, I went to the back porch. Although the air was warm, I could smell autumn around the corner. What was it I couldn't remember? I'd had a great summer, making friends with Kiera, hanging out in the woods, and inventing all sorts of treats. We had gone to Cape Cod and ridden roller coasters at Six Flags. I'd even enjoyed camp. But there was something else. A movement caught my eye; a brightly colored bird landed on an oak branch.

And then I heard it. Fragments of a song. I walked to the edge of the woods, listening. I peered down the familiar path, held my breath, and stepped into the trees.

And then, I remembered.

ACKNOWLEDGMENTS

A debut novel is like a special meal—carefully planned, lovingly prepared, and beautifully presented for feasting and celebration. I poured my heart into *Midsummer's Mayhem* for years, but there are so many others who have played important roles in bringing it into the world.

Brent Taylor, my brilliant, indefatigable agent, devoured this book in one bite, loved it from the start, and found the perfect home for it. He is the epitome of what an agent should be. Brent has taken my literary dreams and made them all come true.

Charlie Ilgunas has been the loveliest editor possible. His close reading and excellent notes truly brought out the heart of this novel, and made Mimi's story perfectly delectable. Many thanks to the fantastic team at Yellow Jacket, including Bethany Reis, copyeditor; Dave Barrett, managing editor; Lauren Carr and Paul Crichton, publicists; Nadia Almahdi, marketing manager; and Sonali Fry, publisher. David DeWitt, designer, made this book a feast for the eyes. And Rachel Suggs is the supremely talented artist who brought Mimi and her family and friends to life with her exquisite illustrations.

I can't overestimate how much Joy McCullough, Pitch Wars mentor extraordinaire, did for this book and my writing career. Joy gave me excellent suggestions for ways to improve this story, and was my guiding hand and the voice of reason during the frantic two-month editing process that was Pitch Wars. Joy is an outstanding writer, a superb critique partner, and a beautiful human being.

I'm also forever indebted to Brenda Drake, the founder of Pitch Wars, who has paved the way for so many writers' successes. And to my incredible Pitch Wars 2017 class: You are the best! I am so very grateful we went through this journey together. Special shout-outs to Remy Lai, Andrea Contos, Emily Thiede, and Ipuna Black, my incredibly talented Pitch Wars classmates who've shared laughter, tears, and cookies with me.

My marvelous critique partners have helped me from the very beginning, when I was just planning the menu for this story, so to speak. Together, we have read and listened and agonized and celebrated, and this book wouldn't exist without them. Thank you, my fellow chefs: Alison Goldberg, Sharon Abra Hanen, Shannon Falkson, and Hayley Barrett. Thanks also to my dear friend Theresa Milstein, who provided a crucial beta read.

To my teachers, in English and otherwise, from when I first started school to the online and in-person classes I've taken as an adult: Thank you from the bottom of my heart. I've been shaped by all of you.

Just as Mimi's family is the heart of *Midsummer's Mayhem*, my family is my heart. They are the ingredients and the sauce, the main course and dessert to this story and everything I write.

My parents, Chakravarthy and Kasturi Narasimhan, raised me with love, patience, and delicious food, never limited me in scope or imagination, and taught me to set my sights high and strive for what I wanted.

Lou LaRocca, my best friend since the day we met at age eighteen, is the most wonderful husband and father I could ever have imagined. He is also the hilarious, Shakespeare-loving foodie man of my dreams, the one who sings to me (and with me!) in the car and on the dance floor. His support has made all of this possible.

Our son, Joe, a brilliant student and super-talented musician, always motivates me to tackle new challenges. Unfailingly positive and kind, Joe has taught me about determination and perseverance, and his enthusiasm for my writing means more than I can ever say. Somewhat unbelievably, Joe is not a fan of sweets, but he makes up for this with amazing pasta-making (and -eating) skills.

Our daughter, Mira, is a joyful spark that lights up our lives, and the inspiration for my character Mimi. Mira is talented in uncountable ways, with a sharp wit, gentle humor, and incredible inner strength. She's a fellow book lover, my baking BFF, and my rock through the ups and downs of writing and publishing this story. She makes me want to be the best writer—and the best person—I can possibly be.

My final thank-you is to the readers of this book. I hope you found Mimi's story delicious, and I hope it inspires you in your own creations. I hope you dream big, work hard, and reach to make something from your heart, something that in all of the world, only you can do.

Baking Terms

Brioche Dessert-like bread made with lots of butter and eggs.

Buttercream Frosting made by beating butter with confectioners' sugar and other flavorings.

Choux pastry Light pastry dough used to make cream puffs, profiteroles, and éclairs. A mixture of butter, flour, salt, and water is cooked on the stove, then eggs are mixed in one by one.

Clafouti Puffy, pancake-like baked dessert, often flavored with cherries or other fruit.

Cream puff/profiterole Light, hollow pastry filled with whipped cream or pastry cream.

Crème brûlée Dessert of rich custard that is sprinkled with sugar on top, which is then torched to form a thin layer of hard caramel.

Custard Creamy pudding made of milk, sugar, and eggs cooked on the stove.

Macaron Two light cookies made with egg whites, sugar, and ground almonds sandwiching a sweet filling.

Madeleine A small, rich cake, usually baked in a shell-shaped pan.

Meringue Whipped egg whites and sugar, baked until crisp.

Napoleon/mille-feuille Pastry made with three layers of

puff pastry sandwiching two layers of pastry cream. The top layer of pastry is often covered in icing or dusted with confectioners' sugar. In French, mille-feuille literally means "thousand leaves."

Palmier Flaky, crisp puff pastry in a palm leaf or butterfly shape.

Petit four Bite-size cake, usually covered in fancy icing.

Soufflé Sweet or savory dish made with egg yolks, beaten egg whites, and other flavorings and baked until puffed up. From the French verb meaning "to breathe" or "to puff."

HERBS AND SPICES

Cardamom Fragrant seeds of the cardamom plant, from green or black pods, used in sweet and savory cooking.

Cayenne Spicy red powder made from ground dried chili peppers.

Five-spice powder Blend of spices, usually fennel seeds, cinnamon, cloves, star anise, and peppercorns, often used in Chinese cooking.

Gotu kola South Asian herb, used in Ayurveda (the traditional Hindu practice of medicine using diet, herbs, and yoga) for wound healing and improving memory and intelligence.

Lavender Fragrant blue-purple flower often used in perfumes and cooking.

Saffron Red-orange fragrant dried stigmas of the saffron flower, a purple-colored crocus. The most expensive spice in the world!

Tamarind Sticky brown sour pulp of the tamarind tree.

Turmeric Bright yellow powder made from the boiled, dried, and ground root of the turmeric plant.

Wasabi Pungently spicy green paste made from the Japanese horseradish plant.

INDIAN FOODS

Chapati Indian flatbread usually made with whole wheat flour.

Dal Word used to describe many varieties of dried, split legumes (lentils, peas, and beans).

Ghee Also known as "clarified butter." Butter that has been melted and had the milk solids removed.

Gulab jamun Popular Indian dessert of deep-fried dumplings made from milk solids and flour and soaked in a rosewater-cardamom syrup.

Kesari bhath Popular dessert from South India, particularly Karnataka, made as a thick grain pudding with semolina, milk, sugar, ghee, cardamom, and saffron.

Kosumbari South Indian salad made with dal and raw vegetables and seasoned with popped black mustard seeds.

Kulfi Dense, creamy Indian ice cream, often flavored with nuts, cardamom, rosewater, or fruit.

RECIPES FROM
MIDSUMMER'S MAYHEM

Chocolate-Chunk Thyme Cookies with Citrus Zest

Makes approximately 30 cookies

Ingredients

1 cup light brown sugar
¼ cup granulated sugar
2 tablespoons fresh citrus zest: tangerine, orange, or lemon
1 tablespoon finely chopped fresh thyme leaves OR 1 teaspoon dried
    thyme leaves
1½ sticks butter (12 tablespoons), at room temperature
2 teaspoons vanilla extract
2 large eggs, at room temperature
2½ cups all-purpose flour
1 teaspoons baking soda
½ teaspoon salt
1½ cups semisweet chocolate chunks

Directions

1. Combine the sugars, citrus zest, and thyme in the bowl of a stand mixer or another large bowl. Rub them together with your fingers until the sugar is moist and very fragrant. Add the butter, and cream together with the paddle attachment on medium speed until fluffy and pale. If you don't have a stand mixer, you can use a hand mixer or beat really well with a spoon or whisk. Add the vanilla extract and eggs and mix well.

2. In a small bowl, whisk together the flour, baking soda, and salt, then add the dry ingredients to the mixing bowl. Mix on low speed (or with a spoon) until just combined. Add the chocolate chunks and stir in by hand with a rubber spatula, scraping the bottom and sides of the bowl well.

3. Wrap the dough in plastic wrap and chill for at least 2 hours (and up to 24 hours).

4. When you're ready to bake, preheat the oven to 350°F. Line baking sheets with parchment paper. Scoop the dough by the tablespoon and place them 2 inches apart on the baking sheets.

5. Bake the cookies for 8 to 10 minutes, rotating the baking sheets halfway through, until they are light brown on top. Let them cool for 10 minutes on the baking sheets, then transfer to a wire rack to cool completely. Enjoy!

Gulab Jamun Cupcakes

Makes 12 cupcakes

Ingredients

For the Cupcakes

1 cup cake flour
1 teaspoon baking powder
1 cup sugar
½ teaspoon ground cardamom
1 egg
2 tablespoon maple syrup
2 teaspoons rosewater
2 teaspoons fresh lemon juice
5 tablespoons butter, melted and cooled a little
½ cup plain yogurt

For the Frosting

8 ounces Neufchâtel cheese (low-fat cream cheese)
½ stick (4 tablespoons) unsalted butter, softened
¼ tsp salt
4 cups confectioners' sugar
1 teaspoons ground cardamom
2 teaspoons rosewater

Directions

1. Preheat the oven to 325°F. Line a cupcake pan with paper liners.
2. Combine flour, baking powder, sugar, and cardamom in a bowl and whisk together until well blended.
3. In a separate bowl, beat together the egg, maple syrup, rosewater, and lemon juice, then beat in the butter and yogurt.
4. Add the dry ingredients to the wet ingredients and stir until just combined.
5. Spoon the batter into the cupcake pan, filling each liner about ¾ full, and bake for 15 to 20 minutes until golden on top and a cake tester comes out clean. Cool on a wire rack.
6. While cupcakes are baking, combine all frosting ingredients together and beat on medium speed in a mixer with the paddle attachment (or with a hand mixer, or by hand) until fluffy.
7. Once the cupcakes have cooled, frost using a pastry bag with a fancy tip. Garnish with candied rose petals (see below). Enjoy!

CANDIED ROSE PETALS

Ingredients

About 40 edible rose petals, unsprayed (organic)
2 teaspoons meringue powder
2 tablespoons water
1¼ cups superfine sugar

Directions

1. Mix meringue powder and water and stir well until powder is dissolved.

2. With a clean small paintbrush, paint the front and back of the petals with the meringue solution.

3. Sprinkle the petals with superfine sugar. Place on a sheet of waxed paper or parchment paper and allow them to dry overnight. Use as a sparkly topping for cakes or other desserts.

HERE'S A SNEAK PEEK AT THE
COMPANION BOOK!

MUCH ADO
ABOUT
BASEBALL

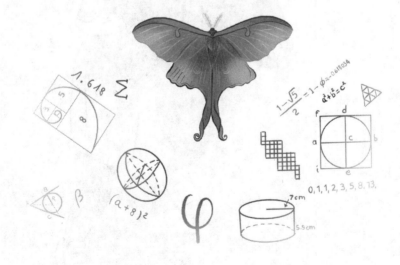

CHAPTER ONE

TRISH

BASEBALL IS MAGIC

Baseball is magic. Time stops between the instant the ball is released and when it makes it over the plate, between the whack of the bat and when the ball finally touches earth again. And this summer, I was holding on to that magic for dear life.

The threads tying me to everything important had snapped, and I was a balloon, floating, flying away on the breeze with nothing to tether me. I was in a new town surrounded by new kids, yanked away from everyone who knew and accepted me.

My brother Sanjay and I were playing catch on a stifling June afternoon in the backyard of our new home. "You'll never be the strongest, so you need to play the smartest," he said as he threw me a scorcher. Sanjay's in high school, and he throws hard, but I got used to hand-stinging catches a long time ago. I'd already run my two miles and finished my push-ups and sit-ups for the day. Physically, I was ready.

"What if no one wants me on the team?" I asked, tossing it back. I'd just left a town where the boys were used to seeing me on a baseball field, but I didn't know what to expect here.

Sanjay caught the ball and laughed. "You're a great teammate, not to mention an amazing ballplayer," he said. "You hit, you run, you deserve a Gold Glove for fielding, and you already throw four-seam and two-seam fastballs. If you can make that circle changeup motion look exactly like your fastball, you'll be a hero." He tossed the ball high in the air, and I moved a few steps to get under it. Sanjay was *my* hero. And he believed in me, no matter what.

The ball smacked into my glove. "I'm just so . . ."

He waited for me to finish, but I didn't want to say the word out loud. *Lost.*

I supposed I could always quit. That might make Mom happy, at least.

"Trish!" Dad called from the garage. "We need to leave now if you want to be early." I tossed the ball back to Sanjay and waved goodbye.

"Ready to meet your new team?" Dad smiled and squeezed my shoulder, but that didn't stop my pulse from pounding in my throat.

"Yeah." I took a deep breath. I had to be the best. That's the only way I'd ever be accepted. So that's what I was going to do this summer.

Mom was at work at the hospital, of course. When she'd landed the chief of cardiology job at Boston General Hospital, it was too good to pass up. Dad could run his graphic design business from anywhere. So we uprooted ourselves from our little town in New Hampshire and moved to Comity, Massachusetts. While Sanjay and I weren't thrilled about changing schools, we didn't have a choice. I knew my brother would be fine. He was so smart, and cute, and hilarious. I was already weird as a girl baseball player and a math kid—well, I *used* to be a math kid—and now I had to make friends with a team full of strangers.

I'd missed travel team tryouts, but I was fine playing in a casual town league. No long trips to games for any of us. And the games were all on weekends, so I hoped that Mom could come to at least a few and not worry about taking too much time off work. Although I knew she'd bring her laptop and would need to keep asking what the score was.

We pulled into the parking lot fifteen minutes before practice was supposed to start.

"Are you sure you don't want me to stay?" Dad asked.

I shook my head. "I'll be fine." I needed to make an impression on my own. "I'll see you in a couple of hours." I smiled in what I hoped was a convincing way as I picked up my bag and climbed out of the car.

I knew it was my last season playing ball. Twelve-year-olds

like me play Little League on a sixty-foot diamond, with forty-six feet between the pitcher's mound and the plate. But in the spring, we move up to the big diamond, which is the size of a Major League infield—ninety feet between bases, and sixty feet six inches from the pitcher's mound to home plate. Lots of boys were already bigger than me. They were growing every second, becoming faster and stronger overnight without even trying. I had serious doubts I'd be able to compete in the spring on the big field. And that was so hard, even harder than moving.

I stopped to survey the baseball fields at Bailey Park. There were two smaller fields and one full-sized diamond where some older players were warming up. The smell of fresh-cut grass and lilacs floated to me. I took a deep breath. There was something in the air. Something that hung like the moment when you take a breath to blow out your birthday candles, and you're not sure what you want to wish for.

I approached the big field where a boy wearing a remarkably sparkly green baseball cap stood at the plate taking practice swings. That hat was incredible. If a baseball cap married a glittery unicorn toy, this would be their baby. As the pitch came in, the boy swung gracefully and was rewarded with the crack of the ball meeting the sweet spot of the bat. The ball sailed over center field, over the fence, and dropped onto the street behind it. If this guy could hit like that—with a wooden bat, no less—he could wear a wizard hat and nobody would care.

An outfielder hopped the fence to retrieve the ball, and everyone else turned back to the boy at the plate, who nodded for another pitch. The pitcher wound up and let go.

Crack. Another perfect swing, and another perfect shot that sailed over left field and bounced off a parked car. It sounded like it left a mammoth dent.

Then the kid switched to a lefty stance and nodded. The pitcher laughed and shook his head, but then wound up and threw again.

This time, the ball sailed over right field and into a dog park, where a golden retriever grabbed it and ran, tail swinging.

How in the world was that boy hitting home runs from both sides of the plate with every single swing? Statistically, that was impossible. If this was the level of talent here in Comity, I was in trouble. I hurried on my way before I lost my nerve completely, and soon arrived at one of the smaller fields, where a coach and a boy were setting up for practice.

"Hello there," said the coach, reaching out and shaking my hand. He was tiny and redheaded, like a slightly oversized elf. "I'm Coach Tom, and this is my son David."

"Nice to meet you, Coach. Hi, David," I said. "I'm Trish."

"Happy to have you on the team this summer," said the coach.

My breathing eased up a little. Apparently, Coach Tom didn't care that I was a girl.

"You two can start warming up while we wait for everyone else," he said.

David, who was already half a foot taller than his dad, nodded and held up a baseball. I ran out onto the field and he started firing throws at me.

After a few minutes, David lobbed a ball way over my head, and it landed on a dead patch and rolled into the woods. I went in after it, and saw a boy there, crouched behind a tree with his eyes squeezed shut. He looked as nervous as I felt.

"Here for practice?" I asked.

The boy opened his eyes and glanced at me, and I couldn't believe it.

I recognized him immediately. Ben. The brilliant math kid who challenged me to do better than ever at the New England Math Puzzler regionals a couple of months ago. He'd been the only sixth grader on his team, just like me. And the best kid on his team, just like me.

I had seen the challenge in Ben's eyes, and I was sure no one could beat him. Neither of our teams won the tournament, but I couldn't believe it when they said I'd gotten the highest individual score. Ben had only missed two points in the final round. But to my surprise, I'd only missed one. Or so I thought.

Standing there in the woods with sunlight filtering through the trees around us and the birds making a riotous racket, I could tell Ben didn't recognize me. No surprise there, since I'd chopped off all my hair since I last saw him. He was dressed for baseball and carried a sports bag big enough to hold a bat. My mind whirled. I didn't think I'd ever have to face him again. I pulled my cap lower over my eyes.

Ben picked up the ball and tossed it to me underhand. It landed a couple feet in front of me.

"Sorry," Ben said, turning red.

"C'mon," I said, scooping the ball and trotting onto the field.

My mouth went dry when Coach Tom called us all in. We stood in a circle while the coach handed out our uniforms. Ben stood next to another kid, and they put their heads together and whispered and laughed easily. I wondered if I'd ever have a friend like that here in Comity.

"A new local business has donated our jerseys to support the league, so our team name is the Comity Salt Shakers," said Coach Tom. I glanced down at the shirt he handed me: green, blue, and white with a salt shaker logo. Lucky number 7. Too bad I didn't believe in luck. Hard work was the only way to success.

Our team had thirteen eleven- and twelve-year-olds in total. Everyone took turns introducing themselves. Ben's friend was named Abhi. The other players included David and the

Mitchell twins, Mike and Garrett. Mike was almost as big as David, with blond hair that reached his shoulders, while Garrett was short, skinny, and dark-haired, with a ratlike nose and a bored expression.

The other two seventh graders on the team were Campbell, a blond kid with braces who never stopped smiling, and Brad, who announced to everyone that he could ride a unicycle, like that had something to do with baseball. There were five tiny soon-to-be sixth graders—this included two boys named Aidan and a freckle-faced kid named George.

And then it was my turn. I swallowed hard. "I'm Trish. I'll be in seventh grade next year."

I looked around, hoping desperately that someone would say something, or smile, or nod. But no one did. Not David, who already knew who I was. Not Ben. He seemed stunned, like a line drive had clocked him in the forehead. Did I look that much like a boy? Or had he finally recognized me from the Math Puzzler tournament?

I crossed my sweaty arms and stared each of them down in turn. "I just moved here from South Ridgefield, New Hampshire. I've been playing ball since I was three. I have three pitches, and I was first in my team's rotation this spring." I'd learned the hard way that you can't show weakness on the field or in the classroom.

Coach Tom smacked his fist into his glove. "Who's ready

to practice? Let's start with grounders. Come with me and I'll explain the first drill." We all followed him onto the field.

By the time practice ended, I'd caught every pop-up that came my way, hit line drives into the outfield, and shown off my two-seamer. When we gathered in the dugout, George the freckle-faced sixth grader tipped his cap at me, the mismatched twins studied me with interest, and Abhi gave me a crooked smirk.

Ben stared at me with his bright blue eyes and I felt exhilarated, like I was back at the Math Puzzler tournament. He'd flubbed some easy catches, though, and most of his throws had been either too short or way too long. I guessed his nerves had gotten the best of him.

As we packed up to leave, Garrett went up to Ben. "Cool shirt."

It was a cool shirt. I'd noticed it right away, and it had made me smile—on the inside, at least. It said, *There are 10 kinds of people: Those who understand binary, and those who don't.*

"Thanks," said Ben.

"Did you bring your calculator?" Garrett asked.

Ben zipped his bag and looked at him. "Why would I—"

"Maybe it'll help you estimate where you need to stand to actually catch something," said Garrett. He and his brother snickered and walked away.

What a jerk!

"*Like the toad; ugly and venomous,*" Abhi said to Ben. "Don't worry about him. You're just rusty because you haven't played in a couple years."

Ben shook his head and mumbled something I couldn't hear.

"You'll be fine," Abhi said. "You just need more practice. Come over and we can throw the ball around after dinner."

"I told my mom I'd eat at home tonight. Maybe tomorrow?"

"Sounds good." They bumped fists. Then to my surprise, Abhi turned to me.

"*I can no other answer make but thanks, and thanks; and ever thanks,*" Abhi said, bowing like I was royalty. Was he making fun of me?

Ben rolled his eyes. "Is this really the right situation for that quote?"

"Of course. If Trish hadn't won the Math Puzzler Championship this spring, you wouldn't be playing ball this summer. She's a good luck charm already. Right, Trish?" Abhi gave me a grin as my face heated up.

What did that mean?

But before I could ask anything, Abhi took off to the parking lot.

Ben finished packing up. Was he as nervous as I felt? Maybe I could help him. I needed to try. Ben and I both loved math and baseball; I hoped we could be friends.

"Is your glove broken in? Maybe that's the problem," I said.

"I don't have a problem." Ben shoved his batting gloves into his bag. "Just because you're a *star pitcher* and *math champion* doesn't mean you know everything." He hoisted his bag and sprinted to the woods as I spluttered word fragments to his retreating back.

I wondered if he resented having a girl on his baseball team, or if he was still upset about the math tournament. Maybe both?

I plodded to the parking lot to wait for Dad. I needed to find a way to feel good in my skin and on the field and, eventually, in the classroom.

And there was Ben. The boy whose brilliance pushed me to be my best. My math motivator.

He hated me. And he didn't even know all of why he should.

I wasn't going to be able to keep my secret for much longer.

Baseball was magic. And this summer, I needed that magic to work for me.

Rajani LaRocca was born in India, raised in Kentucky, and now lives in the Boston area with her wonderful family and impossibly cute dog. She earned a BA and an MD from Harvard, and spends her time writing novels and picture books, practicing medicine, and baking too many sweet treats. She is the author of the middle grade books *Midsummer's Mayhem* and *Red, White, and Whole* and the picture books *Seven Golden Rings, Bracelets for Bina's Brothers,* and *The Secret Code Inside You.* Find her online at RajaniLaRocca.com and on Twitter and Instagram @rajanilarocca.

Photo by Carter Hasegawa